BEGOTTEN

A Cocktail for Murder with a Splash of Romance

By
Sheridan Wray Brett
&
H.M. Brett

A simple vacation shared by two
New memories silenced by old truths
Danger finds a new course, dark corners of fear
Eyes seek to understand and answers to appear

Trips open avenues of surprise
Open eyes to new adventures
Shattered dreams of lost souls
Romance a single venture

Horizons reflect new dawns
Wings of challenge ensure
Death mystifies with answers unknown
Cruelties surface with hearts of stone

Thunder draws lightning into the skies
A history of so many hidden lies
Born again but not as a vision
So many paths; so many divisions

Listen to her broken heart
Step lightly, least you find
Shattered fragments of anguish
False hopes of dreams forgotten

The pages of the broken are closed
Life's chapters concluded too early
So many words unspoken
Too soon for life's stages to end

Soft winds begin to blow, the sun shines
The rivers flow once again with peace
Laughter once again fills the air
As love replaces all the despair

Though it's been days of few
It is time to say goodbye
No mountains, hills nor valleys
Can separate hearts who are now of one

PROLOGUE

A strong hand pushed Jacqueline down as she sunk to her knees, weeping. She felt she was experiencing a terrifying nightmare. Soon, she would wake up, and this horrendous sense of terror and panic would end.

Blinded by floodlights, she felt the cold hard steel of the gun's barrel against her neck. "Please, please," Jacqueline sobbed. "Someone, please help us."

The color drained from her face as she lowered her eyes and stared at her shaking hands. Her thoughts were a jumble of pain and sorrow. She thought she heard her sister scream, but that was not possible. Jeri was dead. Unrelenting remorse washed over her. The death of her sister was Jacqueline's fault, and the burden of that fact weighed heavily on her. She heard Tony's crazed voice shouting as his spittle hit the back of her neck. When she opened her mouth to speak, no words formed on her lips as violent, uncontrollable tremors shook her body.

"You didn't listen to me!" He screamed. His shaking hand held the cold metal revolver against Jacqueline's head. "Are you listening to me now? She's a dead woman!" He shouted. His grip on the gun stiffened. His finger ready to squeeze the trigger.

DAY ONE...

A simple vacation shared by two
New memories silenced by old truths
Danger finds a new course, dark corners of fear
Eyes seek to understand and answers to appear

CHAPTER 1

Jacqueline opened her eyes and stared at the ceiling. She replayed the previous evening's events and wondered, yet again, how and why had she gotten into such a ridiculous situation?

She considered herself a relatively average person, attractive with a decent figure; she had good friends; and good health, so what if she disliked men. Of all the men she had met, most had been jerks. Her natural reaction in meeting any man these days was to build a wall of protection—a result of the lies and the hurt caused in past relationships. She sighed, followed by a tiresome groan. God, she actually gave it one more shot last night, which only reconfirmed her opinion. Men *are* jerks and liars.

She met him on *LoveMatch.com*. After corresponding with him for over a month, they had agreed to meet at an upscale, somewhat trendy restaurant on Murphy Street in Sunnyvale. His profile had been impressive. A master's degree in counseling, established writer for several popular magazines, and trained in martial arts. Jacqueline's vocation in journalism and her classes in martial arts seemed a definite plus. She had earned her brown belt and was looking forward to obtaining her black belt within the next year.

Jacqueline arrived a few minutes early, was seated, and waited for her "Mr. Right." Twenty minutes later, her "match" showed up, sat down, and introduced himself.

"Name's Henry," he said softly. "You must be Jacqueline."

His gaze made her skin crawl, and she was instantly uncomfortable. He was not the person pictured in his profile. Instead of being fifty and attractive, he was overweight, unkempt, and was closer to sixty. A haze of cigarette smoke seemed to enfold his space; the smell drifted across the table and assaulted her. A singed mustache, ten shades darker than his hair, hung just this side of lopsided, giving his face an unbalanced appearance.

At least he had hair, she thought in disgust. She should have bailed right then and there. He ordered two glasses of wine and, for the next half hour, talked non-stop about himself, making sure she understood how impressive he was while dropping super cheesy lines. Bored, Jacqueline decided it was time to leave when, with a wink and while moistening his lips, Henry pulled his chair closer to Jacqueline's. She could smell his putrid breath mingled with the scent of smoke and wine. He checked the neighboring tables on either side and then leaned closer.

"You know why they call me the whisperer?" He breathed in her ear.

Setting her glass of wine down gently while doing a quick survey for a path to an exit, she leaned back to put distance between them.

"No, Henry, I cannot imagine why."

"Because I can whisper what you need."

Jacqueline stared into Henry's inflamed eyes. Speechless, she had no clue how to respond.

"You know, darlin', these lips won't kiss themselves," he said as he belched.

"Ah, excuse me?" Jacqueline murmured feeling nauseated.

"Oh, yeah, I'm all for the ladies who want to express themselves." A drop of sweat trickled down his forehead. "Good God, you are a looker!" He said, putting his nicotine-stained hand on her knee. "Waiter, call me an ambulance. This here looker's beauty is killing me!"

She wanted to smack that twisted look right off his face and crush those meaty fingers. "Really?" While she strained to achieve her most charming smile, she stood slowly, backed away, and excused herself. "I need to use the powder room."

"Take your time, sugar; I'm right here."

She walked toward the restroom sign, passed the ladies' room, and strode through the kitchen. She exited the restaurant and moved quickly towards her car, simultaneously unlocking the car door with her remote. So intent was Jacqueline on leaving for home that she did not notice the figure following her. As she opened the car door, a hand came from behind, slammed it, and grabbed her wrist. She turned and faced a red, blustering Henry.

He pulled her away from the door then pushed her toward the back of the car. "Just where do you think you're going?" He stammered.

"I'm going home, Henry. Let go of my wrist and get out of my way." She screeched, trying to smack his hand away.

A figure appeared at the kitchen door of the restaurant. "Hey, lady. You okay? This guy bothering you?"

"Yes, he is, and no, I am not ok," Jacqueline hollered.

"You leave her alone. I've already called the police."

"Mind your own business." Henry snarled. He stared at the young man a moment longer, then turned his attention back to Jacqueline. "This little lady and I have business to discuss."

"Let go!" Jacqueline cried. She tried to twist her wrist out of Henry's grasp.

Whoop-whoop-whoop. Flashing red and blue lights appeared. A police car approached with a pulsing wail. The cruiser pulled up alongside Jacqueline's car. A depressed-looking police officer emerged. This call interrupted his first break in a ten-hour shift and a mouthwatering T-bone steak dinner. "Damn," he muttered under his breath as he stood. He adjusted his gun belt to a more comfortable position over his protruding midsection.

The officer tipped his hat towards Jacqueline then noted Henry holding Jacqueline's wrist. "Sir, I suggest you let go of the lady's wrist . . . now."

Henry looked down and released his grip as if a hot poker had hit his hand.

"What's the problem here, folks?"

"I'll tell you what the problem is, officer," Henry bellowed. "This woman here just walked out on a bill that she didn't pay. Dine and dash."

The officer turned to Jacqueline. "Miss, is this true?"

"Officer, I walked out on this man to get away from his sexual drivel and unwanted advances. He ordered me one drink that is still untouched on the table. He followed me out here, grabbed my wrist, and pulled me toward the back of my car."

The police officer turned his attention toward Henry and waited for a reply.

"The woman is a troubled soul officer. I pride myself on treating all women with respect. We were having a delightful conversation, and she ups and disappears, leaving me with an unpaid tab."

"That's a lie," Jacqueline said between clenched teeth. She glanced at the officer's name tag. "Officer Braun. This man is a predator. He should be put in jail and the key thrown away."

"Let's decompress, Miss. I need some names here."

"My name's Jonathan Summers, officer, and I am a well-respected businessman in San Francisco. Surely you've heard of me."

"Wait a minute. You told me your name was Henry Cummings."

"Ma'am, your name."

"Jacqueline Renee," she said, glaring at Henry *or Jonathan*. "ID's, please."

While Jonathan took his driver's license out of his wallet, Jacqueline searched her purse for the case holding credit cards and her ID. Both handed their identification to the officer, who walked to his cruiser for confirmation. While doing a preliminary check, a young man dressed in a white chef's uniform stepped up.

"Officer, I saw the whole thing. That guy," he said, pointing to Jonathan, "followed her out here, slammed her car door, grabbed her, and pulled her toward the car. I was the one who called the police."

"I'm sure she appreciates your help; it was the right thing to do," Braun said, walking back to Jonathan and Jacqueline.

"So, Jonathan, do you always give your dates a fake name?" He handed Jonathan his driver's license.

"Officer, it's hard being a successful businessman and meeting honest women. I found this one on *Love.Match.Com.* What kind of a woman do you think gets on these sites? I'll tell you what kind. Ladies who just want a free meal and to fleece you for all you got."

Jacqueline took a step toward the Officer. "I can't believe you are listening to this man and his bullshit."

"Careful how you approach me, Miss," he said, as he held up his hands in a what-did- I-say gesture. He was hungry, tired, and getting agitated.

"What the?" Jacqueline said, flustered as she backed away. "I cannot believe this."

"I'm trying to help you, Miss. A little respect goes a long way when talking to an officer of the law."

"I am merely trying to explain what happened here, and I *am* respectful of the law. Damn it. Not only is this man lying, he accosted me. What are you going to do about it?"

"You can press charges against Mr. Summers."

Jonathan took out his wallet. "Officer, surely we can come to some resolution of this incident,"

The officer looked at the wallet. "Bribery, Mr. Summers?"

"Of course not, officer. I—, ah, need to pay for the drink I ordered. She needs to pay for her part of the bill."

"I certainly will not," Jacqueline said, turning to Officer Braun. "What type of charges?"

"Assault and Battery."

Jacqueline thought for a moment. "I just want this whole thing over. I'm not pressing charges as long as he leaves, now."

Braun turned to Jonathan. "Be a good guy and go in and pay for the total tab."

Jonathan was about to argue until he saw the officer looking at the large bills in his hand. "Yes, I suppose that would be the best thing to do." He turned and started walking back toward the restaurant.

"Miss Renee, I suggest you be a bit more careful in the future. Try not to put yourself in a situation that might do you harm."

"So officer, are you saying this whole situation is my fault?"

Officer Braun sighed. "If there are no charges, we're done here."

"Officer, never underestimate the power of a pissed-off woman. I may be angry and mad, but you know what? I will pull my bootstraps up and move on."

"Evening, Miss Renee." Officer Braun tipped his hat, exhaled, and strode over to his cruiser.

Jacqueline watched him get into his vehicle and drive off. She got in her car, shut the door, and sat staring out the windshield. She started the car, pulled away, and did not try to stop the single tear that slid down her cheek.

CHAPTER 2

No more of this same old song and dance, time to move on. Jacqueline bolted off her bed.

While she dressed, she scanned her open suitcase for last-minute items she might have forgotten. *Like this bathing suit*, she thought, tossing it into her bag.

She stepped to her closet and slid the door open. She flung hangers and clothes to the side, checking several potential outfits for the trip. *No on this one*, she mused. *Too seventies. Where in God's name was my head when I bought that?* She picked out a soft yellow sundress that had always been one of her favorites. She placed the dress on top of her new workout leggings and tops that she had recently splurged on and slammed the suitcase shut.

Jacqueline couldn't wait to see her sister. The last time they had been in South Lake Tahoe together was with their mom and dad. *We were what? Five and four?* It was the last time they all had been together before their father died. Their parents had rented an old house right on the water's edge. There was a two-story boathouse a few feet from the house where she and Jeri spent hours playing pirate games. Closing her eyes, she could visualize those memories as if they were today.

She had dragged Jeri up the stairs of that old boathouse and bellowed. "As brave pirates, we shall jump out this window together!"

"Yes, we will jump together!" Four-year-old Jeri had roared, extending her sword to the sky.

The two young sisters stood ready to jump. Jacqueline had stood back, "You jump first."

"Huh?"

"You're younger and lighter and a simple pirate, whereas; *I am* the ship's captain. You need to show the captain and the crew that you are worthy of being a pirate," Jacqueline had said, prodding her younger sister with her sword.

Jeri looked at Jacqueline with doubt, but with her lower lip trembling, she jumped and screamed with pain when she broke her leg in the fall. Jacqueline, grim, shook her head. *I came close to being sent to an adoption agency on that one.*

Noting the time on her watch, Jacqueline estimated that travel time from Sunnyvale to South Lake Tahoe would be about five and a half hours, barring any unforeseen complications. She picked up Max, her Maltese, grabbed the bag, and struggled with the front door trying not to drop Max or the suitcase. The stubborn door opened a crack as Jacqueline pressed her elbow against the latch. Heaving the door open with her shoulder, Jacqueline stumbled but was able to right herself avoiding a severe fall down the porch steps as she grappled with a shaken pooch, coaxing him into the front seat of the car. "Success," she beamed, and flung her bag into the back seat. Inhaling the soft scent of the summer's breeze, anticipating the excitement of the trip, and feeling carefree, Jacqueline hopped in the car and backed out of the carport. *Another awesome California Day*, she thought, sliding the gear into drive. Spirits high, she hit the gas.

First stop, the Pet Villa, to leave Max off. She strode up to the front desk and watched a tall, striking blond on the telephone. While waiting, Jacqueline looked around the reception area, heard a massive pop, and turned her attention back, just in time to watch the blond peel pink bubblegum off her lower lip. Amused, Jacqueline said, "This is Max. He has a nine-day reservation."

"Have his reservation right here."

Jacqueline pulled out a credit card and moved it across the counter. After processing the payment, the receptionist took Max out of the carrier, hooked his leash, and tried to walk him to the boarding room door. Jacqueline watched Max slide across the reception area floor. "It will be fun, enjoy!" she told him.

Max stubbornly pulled against his leash until he spotted a striking female Maltese. He stopped, sniffed, and then strutted through the door like an irresistible stud muffin. Jacqueline walked back to the car, hit the key to the door, and thought, not for the first time, *why do dogs remind me of men?*

She next stopped at a grocery store to pick up some food and wine, then headed toward Interstate 80. Relaxed, she engaged with the rhythm of the road as the beauty of the California hills flashed by. She thought back to the conversation that she had with her sister Jeri the previous evening.

"Look Jacqueline, this isn't the first time you've gotten yourself into, what I would call, a "situation.""

"A situation?" I was accosted by a deranged sixty-year-old moron who just also happened to be a lying pervert, and I was disrespected by one of Sunnyvale's finest."

"Come on Jacqueline. You are always getting yourself into one quandary after another."

"Excuse me? May I remind you about your own 'situation'? A husband who turned out to be a jerk and left you for another woman."

"Yeah, well, he was a nice guy when we first met. Anyway, nice enough for us to have had two college-aged kids before he morphed into a jerk. We won't discuss your marriage only lasting a few years because, honestly, I don't want to get mired in the weeds. The bottom line here is we women are like an ocean, always moving, swaying, and readjusting with the tide while men are like puddles. We both made the wrong choice and moved on with the tide."

Silence dragged on for several seconds. "Listen, Jacqueline, all I'm saying is that you tend to be impulsive and take risks. Sometimes serious ones."

"I called for a little sympathy here, not a lecture."

Jeri sighed, "I worry about you. Heck, I worry about me. I don't have another sister. It's just you. Don't get cranky with me because I show concern. Look, big sister, we're headed for a great vacation to South Lake Tahoe tomorrow. It's going to be great!

Right now, I am content to be alone. No men in my life. It feels good, and I think I have finally found a lost piece of myself. I think it would be good for you to cool it too. Let's just be two bachelorettes on vacation. No men. No worries."

"I like that," Jacqueline said. She heaved a sigh, "You are pretty terrific, you know."

"Yes, I know, but I'm sure I have some defects somewhere," Jeri said, laughing.

Jacqueline merged onto Interstate 80 and thought of their two attempts at matrimony.

Both had marriages, which ended badly. Jacqueline's brief marriage to her high school sweetheart had lasted barely three years. They married too young and changed too much. Jeri had wed Eric, an English Professor at the University of Colorado. Their union seemed happy for a number of years until Eric took a sabbatical in France. He felt that his wife should stay in the states with the kids so their education would not be interrupted. Jeri thought that a year in a French school would be an enormous educational asset. But Eric stood firm, and she had stayed home. It was hard for Jeri to be away from Eric and even harder to understand his growing impatience and annoyance with her and the kids on his few brief visits home. Two years ago (toward the end of his sabbatical), Eric called from France and said he had accepted a position with the University of Paris, had found someone, and he was in love. He had no intention to return home. Jacqueline had flown to Denver to support Jeri during that difficult time. A week later, Jacqueline had returned to California. Jeri called to tell her that she had donated everything Eric owned to the Salvation Army. "It felt so good," she said. "I just decided Eric didn't need anything that he was unwilling to come home and get himself." Since then, she had put her life back together and recently opened a quilt shop, which was a great success.

Jacqueline had followed her passion for journalism. As a local news reporter, her job was fast-paced and high-pressured. She never knew from one day to the next what type of story she might be assigned or whether her workday would last 8 hours, two days, or more. TV reporting could be a dangerous job, but she loved the work. There had been times when she faced potentially tricky, dangerous, and uncomfortable situations, but she never shied from jumping in to get that story. There were times when she had been scared, felt uncomfortable and extremely nervous, and even worried about her safety. She knew that Jeri worried about her impulsiveness in getting that byline. She had also been shot at when covering a crime scene.

Just missing the Sacramento commuter traffic jams, Jacqueline's thoughts came back to the present as she sailed across the Sacramento county line. She briefly glimpsed the skyline of the city in the distant morning haze. Finally, she merged onto US 50, running east cross country through the foothills toward the Sierra Nevada Mountains. She entered the low-lying foothills range and felt a newfound freedom as the California tension left her body.

The steady rise into the hills brought cooler air. She swerved through several hairpin turns, passed the mountainous town of Pollock Pines and Strawberry Lodge, and headed toward Echo Summit. Although the road demanded her focus, she could not help but glory in the landscape of mountains, lakes, streams, and pine forests.

With the South Fork American River on her right and sporadically placed log cabins passing by on her left, Jacqueline threw in a John Denver "Rocky Mountain High" CD. She started to hum along, tap her left foot, and thump her fingers in rhythm to the music.

She finally headed downward. The landscape quickly changed from mountains covered with pine forests to a fantastic view of the Tahoe Basin and the beautiful lake. She drove down through narrow and somewhat treacherous roadways, at last arriving in South Lake Tahoe. She continued on US 50, drove to Lakeview Lane, and turned left. Following the lake's shore, she passed several seasonal cabins and homes and reached her destination in five hours with time to spare before she needed to pick up Jeri at the airport.

Jacqueline parked in front of the low white picket fence faded with age that stretched across the back of the property. Turning off the engine, she sat back and looked at the cabin and the surrounding area, glad she had talked Jeri into renting this house in this quiet neighborhood on the lake. Jacqueline had vacationed in the old cabin several times with friends in past years. Its walls embraced fond memories. Not for those who looked for a luxurious lakefront rental, the place was rustic yet charmingly simple and provided a more tranquil lake experience, which she loved. The cabin, originally built in 1827 with multiple upgrades and renovations through the years, sat one hundred feet off the lake, protected by tall trees and grassy lawns.

Grabbing her purse and groceries, Jacqueline decided to open the house and unload the rest of the car later. She released the gate in the fence and walked up the footpath to the small porch. Leaning right, she looked toward the front yard, which gave her a narrow view of the lake.

Jacqueline bounded up the three steps onto a small porch, inserted the key, and opened the door to a tight utility room. It housed a stacked washer and dryer on the left, and a trash receptacle, and shelves with cleaning supplies on the right. She walked into the charming but dated kitchen and set her purse and grocery bag on the Formica counter. The kitchen, though small, was well equipped.

She passed through a narrow archway and entered a dining area furnished with a large table with matched benches on both sides. A glass door on the far side of the dining room led to a modest glassed-in porch, where Jacqueline caught her first full glimpse of the lake. It shimmered blue with emerald green and gray hues reflecting the clouded sky. With a smile of satisfaction, she turned left into the living room, which held an old but comfortable couch and two rocking chairs placed in front of a fireplace. Stepping over a grated floor heater, she strode past the fireside and threw back a wall of curtains revealing a panoramic view of the front yard, which led down to the lake. She quietly stood and enjoyed the breathtaking view, with the Sierra Nevada and Carson Mountain Ranges on the far side.

Jacqueline tilted her head and looked around. She thought she heard voices arguing; the sounds so muted she could not distinguish the words. She heard a muffled scream. Perplexed, she remained still and listened intently, but did not hear anything more. Odd, she felt that the voices and cries came from inside the cabin, which did not make sense because she knew she was alone.

Nevertheless, she checked all the rooms but found nothing. She walked to the glassed-in porch, opened the front door, and stepped out into the cool morning sun. She stood in the front yard, cocked her head to the side, but heard only stillness. Strolling down to the water's edge, she saw a large home about fifty yards further down the beach on the right. To her left was an old Victorian mansion that stood by itself, one hundred yards off, with some boarded windows on the upper level ready to stave off winter's hardships, which were no longer a threat in the warmth of summer. Silence. Feeling something or someone behind her, she turned quickly and saw a shadow behind a tree towards the street.

"Hello?" Walking hastily, she reached the tree, but no one was there.

"Hello? Is anyone there?" She slowly turned and surveyed the surrounding area. *I'm just freaking out.* With a sigh, she turned and walked back into the house.

With a glance at her watch, she realized she was now running a bit late. Groceries were quickly put away, and the car unloaded. Afterward, she stood in the kitchen, hesitated, and glanced out the window again, hearing that muted scream in her mind. She shook her head and shrugged. "Imagination…. I'm so good at imagination."

She grabbed her keys, headed for her car, and the Reno Airport to pick up Jeri.

CHAPTER 3

When Jeri's alarm woke her earlier at six o'clock, she had no idea that this day would turn out to be the longest day of her life. A wave of uneasiness had crept over her, which she decided to ignore. Today she was flying to South Lake Tahoe to vacation for a week with her sister. Today she would disregard and not listen to that internal intuition, which, in the past, had served her well and often saved her from making a wrong decision.

The trip to the Denver International Airport took longer than expected due to an accident on I-70, which created a slow-moving ribbon of cars and trucks. Jeri finally made it to long-term parking, boarded the shuttle to airline departures, checked her bag, and passed through security without problems.

So far, so good, she thought as she hopped on the train to Concourse B. Two very handsome men hurried past, deep in conversation. One of them bumped into Jeri before taking a seat at the back of the tramcar.

The men piqued Jeri's interest. The older of the two had a thick head of golden red copper hair with grey streaks. His face reflected maturity and experience. *That man definitely looks like he knows what he's doing,* Jeri thought.

His demeanor showed dominance and masculinity, but not to an extreme. Heavy brows highlighted alluring brown eyes. The younger of the two was about an inch shorter and more attractive in a cute, non-threatening way, with a more boyish quality to his looks and personality. Jeri could see similarities in physique and facial features. She decided they must be brothers.

The train arrived at Concourse B, where passengers filed onto the platform and headed up the escalator to the boarding areas. Jeri trailed behind the two men and picked up bits and pieces of conversation.

"I think that the documents were altered in some way under false pretenses, Alex. It sounds like this guy has attempted to make a claim on our property based on a forged deed. But, at this moment, I am just as baffled as you are."

"We need to talk with Sara."

"I thought she was still in Italy."

"She was, but she's supposed to be home today. I tried to call her, but she's not answering my calls. This land has been in our family for over a century. How could this have possibly happened, Zed? It just doesn't make any sense." They continued their discussion as they hurried forward.

At the gate area, the passengers were ready to board the plane. Once onboard, Jeri hoisted her bag into the overhead, scooted into the window seat, and buckled up. She pulled her book from her purse, a light mystery, and was about to read when she was surprised to see the two men stop next to her seat. The older of the two smiled and shoved his bag next to hers in the overhead compartment. Both he and his companion seated themselves directly behind her.

The plane began to power up for takeoff. Overhead lights flashed off then on. Jeri put her seat back slightly in hopes of hearing more of the brothers' dilemma. But she fell asleep before the wheels retracted and did not wake up until the captain announced the plane was descending. Jeri had missed her soda, her pretzels, and any interesting conversation.

Once the plane reached the terminal, Jeri unbuckled her seatbelt and stood to open the overhead bin. As she struggled with the handle, she felt a hand on her back.

"Here, let me help you with that."

She turned and smiled her appreciation.

"First trip to Reno?" He asked, handing Jeri her suitcase.

"Never been to Reno but vacationed in South Lake Tahoe years ago. This is my first time back. My sister and I rented a place on the lake."

"My family owns a house on Lake Tahoe. Where are you staying?"

"Oh, let me see." Jeri fumbled through her purse and pulled out the address. "My sister made the reservations. I have never seen the place. It's 30 Lakeview Lane. She said it's right on the lake, surrounded by lakeside cabins, homes, and an old Victorian mansion. Do you have any idea where it is?"

Alex laughed, "I do. I live next door, number 28 on Lakeview Lane. It sounds like you and your sister rented our family cottage. Nice coincidence. But then, life can be full of little twists of fate. We will be neighbors. It's a very comfortable bungalow, and I'm sure you will enjoy your stay there. I'm Alex, by the way. This is my brother Zed."

Alex's brother stood and watched the interaction between his brother and the woman. He cleared his throat, "Umm Bro, could you two move it along?"

Jeri looked toward the back of the plane and realized they were holding up the passengers. She turned and smiled at Alex. "I'm Jeri. Thanks for the help," she said, heading off the plane toward the passenger pickup area, where an exuberant Jacqueline stood waiting.

"Hey, Sis, over here!" Jacqueline hollered. She ran over to Jeri and gave her a big kiss and hug. Alex smiled as he and his brother passed by.

Jacqueline looked super. She was taller than Jeri by three inches, and she had that long, lean look people spend big money at fitness centers to achieve. She was a ball of energy.

With bags in tow, the sisters headed for Jacqueline's car. Jacqueline mentioned that she had made a light lunch, and that sounded just fine with Jeri.

They left the Reno Airport, taking in the beauty of Mount Rose and Diamond Peak off highway 431. Turning onto Highway 28, they drove along the lake to the South Shore and the Tahoe Keys area. Jeri briefly filled Jacqueline in on their landlord and new neighbors, Alex and Zed.

"You know," said Jeri after a moment of silence, "for some odd reason, I have this premonition that something is going to happen. Isn't that weird? Where do you think that came from?"

Jacqueline did not answer immediately, but the set of her jaw told Jeri that she did not disagree. "Funny you should say that." she paused. "Earlier today, when I was at the cabin, I swear I heard loud voices arguing, and then I heard what seemed like a muted scream. I searched the cabin but did not find anything; then, I went outside. While I was standing by the lake, I felt someone watching me. I thought I saw a shadow behind some trees by the street. But no one was there when I checked it out. It freaked me out. I thought it just might be my imagination, but now? Well, I'm not so sure."

CHAPTER 4

Tony Russo seethed with anger. He had worked his entire life for this break in his career, and no one was going to take it away from him. Few people could keep pace with Tony when it came to ruthlessness. He was relentless toward competition in business and was not adverse or unwilling to use bribery or coercion toward personal gain. Sitting in his office on the 42nd floor on UN Plaza in Manhattan, he swiveled in a 180-degree turn, and looked out his floor-to-ceiling panoramic view of the Hudson East River to the lighted buildings beyond. The sunset cast flames of orange and red across the evening sky.

First-born child to Italian immigrant parents, Tony grew up in the Bronx, which, back then, was a prime symbol of urban decay. His father was a truck driver, a snake, a drunk and an abuser to both his wife and child. His mother, a seamstress, was helpless to defend herself, and he hated her for her weaknesses.

He learned his life lessons in the streets, defending his turf with other gang members. Fists, knives, and guns were his tools of choice. At fifteen, a gang war erupted in his territory ending with multiple victims of stab and shotgun wounds. Tony found himself arrested, sentenced, and incarcerated in a juvenile facility. Bored, he needed something to keep himself busy, so he enrolled in the GED Program provided by the facility. Once completed, Tony enrolled in an online junior college program, and in the next two years, held a GPA of 4.0.

When released, he immediately enrolled at New York University in the Business Administration program, where he earned his bachelor's in international business, trade, and finance. He then obtained his master's degree at Columbia University in International Economics. He secured a position with the Daniels

Corporation and spent the next years slamming his way to the top. He left his emotions at the door. He never apologized, showed pity, or felt sorry for anyone he had to step on. He showed no tolerance for incompetence, and punished quickly and brutally instilling fear in his peers and those who worked for him. He stayed focused and determined and got the promotion to the Chief Executive Officer of the company.

At forty-one, short, at five feet four inches, his best attribute, according to him, was his sense of presence. He saw himself as charismatic, magnetic, sharp, handsome, charming, and gifted. He loved to love women, but felt most were pathetically weak. Women adored him.

He relied on his keen ability to charm women through his natural personality. He worked out daily at the gym to maintain his solid build. His jet-black hair was his most dominant trait per his assessment. No one loved Tony more than he loved himself.

He answered his ringing cell phone, "Yes."

"I'm sorry for the disruption Mr. Russo, but Mr. Kelly asked that you join him and his colleagues in the conference room."

"Tell him, I'm on my way," Tony said. Still shaken and pissed off by his recent conversation with Nicole, he stood and grabbed a folder for the meeting then swept the rest of his desktop contents to the floor, hearing a loud clunk as his cell phone dropped and cracked. He kicked his chair across the room, slamming it against windows and stared as they flexed from the impact. His face flushed red with anger; he picked up his cracked cell phone and headed toward the conference room.

"Good Evening Mr. Russo."

"Evening Beth."

"They're waiting for you. Go on in."

"Thanks."

A small group of men sat at the far end of a large conference table. All looked up as Tony walked in and took a seat.

"Tony."

"Lex."

"You're late."

"It happens," Tony said with a shrug.

Tony watched as Lex seemed hard-pressed to rein in his impatience and gather his thoughts. "I was talking to the group about Emma," Lex said. He leaned back in his chair and stared at Tony. Turning his attention to the men around the table, he continued. "I spoke with Detective Davies in charge of Emma's case. It has been three weeks since she disappeared, and I do not understand why the police have no clues or leads and no suspects. It's as if she vanished, evaporated into thin air."

Tony stifled a yawn, "Emma is a grown woman, and I'm sure she's fine. She probably took a last-minute vacation or took off with some guy on a trip to God knows where. I mean, this isn't the first time that she has disappeared."

"No, it's not," Lex said with obvious annoyance, "but she has always contacted me and eventually let me, us, know where she is. And it's been three weeks."

"Lex, I know you're worried, and I'm sure the police are doing everything they can do to find her. In the meantime, we need to review these contracts for our newly acquired development company and its subsidiaries. Time is short, and we need to provide them with some answers."

Lex stared at Tony with an edginess of exasperation. He turned his attention to the folder in front of him and the men sitting around the table.

The group began their evaluation of the new company's assets along with its tax and property estimates. Tony's mind drifted back to the telephone call he had twenty minutes ago.

"What was I supposed to do, Tony?"

"You Idiot! You're going to fuck up everything." He had shouted in disgust, disconnecting the call and slamming his cell phone on the desk.

Tony listened to his boss drone on about dollars and cents. He took a deep breath, relaxed his muscles, and worked on cooling his anger.

CHAPTER 5

Her sister turned onto Lakeview Lane. Jeri saw that rustic ski cabins shared the road that ran along the water's edge with multimillion-dollar homes, all with fabulous views of lawns, mountains, and the lake. Houses became more distant from each other as they continued down the lane.

Jacqueline slowed and parked in front of a charming cottage with a short white fence. Tall pine trees framed the peaceful dwelling. The lawn and bushes looked a bit scruffy, which only added to the cabin's magical charm. Jeri could see the roof and upper level of a large house on the right and sensed this must be the home of Alex and his family. Tall trees and some older, well-developed bushes hid the lower portion of the home. Beyond and to the left their cabin, stood an old Victorian mansion, which had seen better days.

"Jacqueline, it's beautiful."

"Just wait." Jacqueline got out of the car and met Jeri around the other side. "Shut your eyes and don't peek," she said.

Jacqueline led her through the gate and along the path to the front porch, both giggling like school girls. "Three steps up," she said, then led Jeri to the cabin's living room window. "Okay, open your eyes."

Jeri stood speechless before the large glass floor to ceiling window, which opened to a long green grassy slope that stretched to the lake's shore. The water was bright blue and sparkled like diamonds caused by the shimmering sun and movement of the waves. Surrounded by green trees and mountains, the view took her breath away.

They marveled at the view for a few moments, then Jacqueline grabbed Jeri's arm, "Come on, let's get you settled, get a bite to eat, and go for a walk. You up for that, Sis?"

"You bet," Jeri responded with enthusiasm.

Jacqueline helped her sister drag her bags into the cabin and set them next to hers. The fun chore of unpacking began. They stored their clothes in closets and drawers, placed toothbrushes and overnight kits in the bathroom, and hurried to take advantage of the beautiful afternoon before evening set in.

Together they made a small salad, sliced fruit and cheese, filled two glasses with Zinfandel, headed for the front lawn, and settled in to eat their light lunch at a small table and chairs.

Jacqueline took in the stunning views of the lake before she turned her attention to her sister.

She felt their similarities were perceptible. Each was attractive in her way. Like her father, Jacqueline was tall and slender, while Jeri, more like their mother, was petite with delicate bone structure. Their most prominent similarities were their hands. Slender expressive fingers often seemed to move as sensitive instruments while each spoke. Jacqueline's straight shoulder-length asymmetrical haircut was bold with warm chestnut hues, the summer sun adding a few streaks of gold. Jeri with salt and pepper hair had a trendy layered cut with eye-grazing bangs, which added a youthful touch.

Jacqueline turned to the lake in silence as she ate and sipped her wine. Looking at her sister, she briefly thought back to their childhood.

Their father died when they were very young. Their mother worked long hours to make ends meet, which left them to their own devices in support of each other. Jeri, filled with worlds of possibilities, was always there with words of encouragement and saw the worst and the best in Jacqueline. She was her soul sister, her rock when she needed that solid ground to stand on, when her earth shifted. Their mutual strength and bond helped keep her vision clear.

"So, all is well with this divorce thing behind you, right? No, heartache?" Jacqueline asked with a warm smile.

Jeri pulled her gaze from the lake, took a sip of her wine, and gently set her glass on the table. "I'm good, Jacqueline. It feels great to get out of that house with its memories and to be here with you. And to be quite honest, I'm enjoying my freedom. I no longer have that dark cloud always hanging over my shoulders. That in and of itself makes it better than good."

"And the kids? They're okay?"

"They're good. At first, I was concerned, especially about Ally. She was always Daddy's little girl, and over the last several years, his absence was hard on her. She was angry and hurt when her father never came back from France. I'm surprised she didn't burn his stuff before I could get it to the Salvation Army. But she's tough and has moved on to her studies and school. Her boyfriend, Harry, has been a huge help in stabilizing her life. I like him a lot. She'll be graduating next year, and I wouldn't be surprised if I saw a ring on her finger."

"I'm glad to hear that."

"Yes, and James has never had a close relationship with his dad, which is sad. He just graduated. Uh, you did get a thank-you note for your gift, right?"

Jacqueline laughed. "Yes, I did, short and sweet, but I did."

"Mmm," Jeri murmured thoughtfully. "I worry about James more than Ally. He keeps it all inside. You never quite know what he is thinking or feeling, but he has a new job with a startup tech company in Silicon Valley, so I'm excited about that. He's a terrific kid."

"I'll look forward to seeing James more often once he comes to California," Jacqueline said. "Sounds like you're all in good shape."

"We are. And talking about good shape, how about we finish up and head out toward the beach and stroll along that beautiful lake?"

"Sounds perfect. Let's do it."

***

A figure stood silent and watched the two sisters eat their lunch. Their being here was truly unfortunate, unfortunately for them. *They are undeniably in the way, and if they start snooping into things that don't concern them, they will become a definite liability. I cannot let that happen.* She watched them chatting and laughing as they walked through the cabin door and disappeared. She stood and stared for several minutes. *I need to get rid of them.*

***

With walking shoes, sunscreen, and sunglasses, the sisters headed for the lake. They paused at the shore to take in the view.

"So, which way to go is the question?" Jeri asked.

"I've always wanted to check out that old mansion. And it looks like a beautiful walk along the lake."

"Okay, sounds like an adventure," Jeri said with a grin.

The two sisters took off to explore the old mansion. They strolled down to the lakeshore. Jeri stooped down, scooped up some sand, and looked up at Jacqueline.

"I think I told you I met two of our next-door neighbors."

"You did in the car. And?" smiled Jacqueline.

"They seemed nice enough. Alex is quite handsome." I overheard a conversation they were having about some problems with their house. Some sort of fraudulent activity. I didn't get the whole story but it sounded serious.

"Uh, don't forget, no men, two bachelorettes on vacation, if you get my drift?"

"You don't have to remind me, if you get *my* drift," Jeri laughed, "but he is nice looking."

"I don't think I've ever seen any of the neighbors when I've been here. Quick," Jacqueline cried, "I'll race you to that dock in front of the mansion."

Jeri dropped the handful of sand, sprinted after her sister, quickly taking the lead. They raced to the front of the old house and stopped, breathless with laughter.

The laughter faded as they squinted in the afternoon sun to get a better look at the old Victorian mansion, which stood alone among tall pine trees. Solitary, its paint peeling, the abandoned mansion had deteriorated with age, disintegrated through weather and lack of care; this once-stately structure cried for its past days of grandeur.

"Let's go and take a peek."

"You think?"

"It's empty! Come on," Jacqueline said as she grabbed Jeri's arm. Together, they ascended decayed wooden steps from the beach to a once-grand gateway entrance then onto a weed-choked slate path that curved toward the crumbling wood-floored wrap around porch. What once was a beautifully landscaped garden with sweeping lawns was now overgrown with brambles and dead shrubs. A patio table with a broken glass tabletop and four broken chairs threatened bodily harm for anyone choosing to rest on them.

They stepped up onto the porch and stopped. The front door was old, with scratches etched along its surface and petrified with green mold. Edges were uneven and cracked. The brass knocker, an intricate gold design with an eagle at its center, lay silent as invitations were no longer extended and visitors no longer welcomed. Overgrown vines hung low on the outside walls obscuring views from windows not yet boarded. Jacqueline tried the door.

CHAPTER 6

"Bummer," said Jacqueline, "it's locked. Let's go to the side and peek into some windows."

With a look back at the lake to see if anyone was watching, Jeri followed her sister along a gravel path to the right side of the mansion. They crept past a large bay window and stopped at a set of French doors that overlooked the gardens. They squinted to see through small French door window-panes. Jacqueline felt the door slowly open.

"Come on, Jeri, let's go inside."

"Do you think we should? I mean, it's not our house."

"It's not a house, it's a mansion, and it's deserted. Get a grip, come on."

Jacqueline opened the door wider and stepped into a living room, followed by a hesitant Jeri. Strips of peeling flocked paper covered the walls, and several old paintings hung askew, yellowed with age. The room let off a hot, fetid odor.

The contents were severely dilapidated, and the once gorgeous fixtures and furniture left behind suggested a sudden flight of the previous residents.

"This place gives me the creeps," Jeri choked back dust as they moved further into the house.

"Are you kidding?" Jacqueline whispered. "This place is awesome! Look, an old staircase. Let's see what's upstairs."

"I broke my leg the last time I followed you upstairs to the second floor in Tahoe. Really, Jacqueline, I think we should leave."

"Come on, Jeri, get into the spirit. Get it?" Jacqueline laughed. "The Spirit!"

"I want to see your spirit when the cops come and arrest us for trespassing."

"Don't be a spoilsport," Jacqueline chided, grabbing Jeri's arm.

She placed her foot on the first step, began the climb, Jeri close behind. The old broken wooden stairs cried out in grief with the unwelcome weight.

"I heard that the old man who owned this place bludgeoned his wife to death with a hammer, threw his daughter down these very stairs to her death, and then committed suicide," Jacqueline whispered as she advanced toward the upper landing. She heard the sound of wood snap and pivoted to see Jeri attempt to retreat down the stairs.

Jeri grabbed the railing and cried out just as the rotted handrail gave way. She tumbled to the living room floor, hit a wood-paneled wall beneath the staircase, and was still.

"Jeri!" Jacqueline yelled. She hurried to the bottom of the stairs. "Are you okay?"

***

"I told you I didn't want to investigate this stupid house, let alone walk up those damn rickety stairs. Look at the tear in my pants; brand new pants, ruined," Jeri said, as she stood massaging her arm.

"What were you doing? I mean, why did you turn around on the stairs?"

"Are you kidding? Some old guy stiffs his wife with a knife, throws his kid down the steps, and offs himself? This place is too creepy."

"I was just kidding. It was a story I made up, for God's sake."

"Yeah? Well, next time, keep your stories to yourself. Lucky for me, we only went up a few steps."

Jeri turned to assess the damage she had inflicted on the banister, wooden-panels, and a door. As she moved away, the door she bumped popped ajar.

She saw what appeared to be a hand.

"What's that disgusting odor?" Jeri asked, perplexed. She gripped the door handle and opened the door wider to reveal an emaciated woman who, on the face of it, looked like she stood tall but was attached to a coat tree rack hook. The sound of material ripping was heard as the body and the coat stand keeled forward. Jeri caught both body and rack the best she could. A trickle of blood dripped from the woman's mouth onto Jeri's arm as she tumbled to the floor, the coat rack missing her head by inches, the body collapsing on top of her. Jeri screamed! Jacqueline joined the chorus.

"Yuk," Jacqueline cried, wrinkling her nose. "It reeks of rotten eggs and rotting garbage."

"Smells more like a loaded diaper," Jeri gagged as she struggled with the body. "I can taste the smell of it! Repulsive! Damn it, can't you help me here," she cried, shoving the deadweight with all her might and scrambled away. She stared at skin and bones covered with dirt, matted red hair, and bruises while trying to rub the blood off her sore arm.

Horrified, Jacqueline stood thunderstruck. "That woman's dead!" Jacqueline whispered as she looked down. "I can't believe I'm seeing this!"

Jeri watched her sister as she stared at the lifeless body. "What should we do now?" Jeri choked.

"Now, we need to get the hell out of this house and call the cops," Jacqueline said, getting some self-control. "Whoever did this may still be hanging around."

The sisters made a speedy exit as Jacqueline grabbed her phone and dialed 911. They hurried to the back of the mansion and stood at the end of the dirt drive. Nervous, they kept a wary eye out for anybody who could do them harm while they waited for the police to arrive.

"Jeri, I," Jacqueline started.

Jeri fixed her sister with a glare. "I told you we shouldn't go in there. Let's just keep quiet while we wait for the police and pray that no one heard us scream."

***

The El Dorado Sheriff's Office (SO) is located at 1360 Johnson Boulevard, South Lake Tahoe, and shares building space with the Public Defender, District Attorney, Civil Court, and the County Jail. Their jurisdiction includes cities from Placerville to Lake Tahoe. The South Lake Tahoe Police Department (PD) is located next door to the SO at 1352 Johnson Boulevard and shares space with the Superior Court. The PD responsible territory includes Stateline to the Center of Town, Ski Run to Al Tahoe Blvd, and Truckee to the end of the city limits. Jacqueline's 911 emergency call was directed to the PD dispatch. Anytime someone dies in El Dorado County, the SO Placerville dispatch (sixty miles away) gets notified. In turn, they inform the SO Detective unit in South Lake Tahoe for coroner's investigative assistance.

***

In less than five minutes, Jacqueline and Jeri heard sirens. *A lifetime when you think a murderer might lurk behind bushes or windows,* Jeri thought.

A Ford Expedition SUV marked "South Lake Tahoe Police" pulled onto a weeded area close to the driveway.

A slim, six-foot-six inch uniformed officer worked his way out of the vehicle without knocking off the cowboy-style police hat that sat just slightly askew on his head. The ruggedly handsome man with sharp features, strong jawline, and broad, well-defined shoulders approached the sisters.

Definitely pleasing to the senses, Jacqueline thought. *But probably a liar and a jerk.*

The officer stopped short. His attention was directed at Jacqueline for several moments. Jacqueline stared at the Officer. Jeri looked from the officer to Jacqueline. "Ah, excuse me?" She mumbled.

The officer cleared his throat, withdrew a notebook, a pen from his breast pocket, and activated his voice-recording device.

"Evening ladies," he said, nodding to both women. "I'm Chief Mac Givens. You called 911 about finding a body?"

"Yes, Officer, we found a dead woman. She fell from a closet located under the stairs," Jacqueline said. "And is it MacGivens, one word, or is your first name Mac and last name Givens? Your name is essential to know, so, if we have a problem here, we can correctly provide information to your Chief of Police."

Amused, the officer smiled, "I am the Chief of Police."

"Oh, then I think we need your superior's name. The person you report to. Two women alone. For our safety or to be sure we're treated in a respectful manner."

"Chief Givens, you need to forgive my sister. She's been through an ordeal. She's upset, she's distressed, my sister needs to shut up," Jeri said, staring at Jacqueline.

"I'm perfectly fine. In fact—"

Their attention shifted as several police vehicles, pulled up and parked behind the Police Chief's SUV. Three Officers walked over and stood next to Givens.

"Officer Jobs. Take your men and make sure the area around this house is controlled and taped off."

"You got it, Chief."

Givens turned his attention back to the sisters. "Are you okay to answer some questions for me?"

"Yes," Both Jacqueline and Jeri said in unison.

"Can you tell me what happened?"

"We decided to explore the house," Jeri spoke up. "When we walked up the stairs to take a look, I stepped on a loose step, the railing broke, and I dropped over the side and fell against a closet door. When I hit the door, it opened slightly, and a hand appeared to reach out. I pulled the door open, and this body collapsed on me. It was a dead woman! The smell was awful. A coat rack also dropped with the body and almost knocked me out." Jeri crossed and hugged her arms around her waist and shuddered. "I'm still in shock."

"Did you get hurt?" Givens asked.

"No, just scared me to death."

"Did you move the body?"

"Yes, I had to move the body off me so I could get up."

"You see, Chief Givens, we just wanted to check out the house." Jacqueline chimed in, "We love old houses, and the door was unlocked."

Chief Givens focused his attention on Jacqueline. "You two entered a home with unlocked doors when you were not invited?

Jacqueline looked at Givens, narrowing her eyes. "How do you know we weren't invited?" She asked.

"Because this house belongs to my family, and I didn't give anyone permission to come in and make themselves at home," Chief Givens said with a frown.

"This is your house?" Jacqueline asked, flabbergasted.

"I'm going to need to see some ID."

"We don't have any ID on us. My sister and I are staying in the cabin over there," Jacqueline said, pointing toward the dwelling about 100 feet away. We left our purses and phones since we were just out for a walk."

He did a quick assessment. "Let's have your names then, please?"

"My name is Jeri Winters, and my sister's name is Jacqueline Renee."

"You both will need to come down to the station for further questioning."

"I don't think you can legally detain me or my sister, Officer."

"Jacqueline," Jeri whispered. "Just shut-up!"

"Because of the circumstances and the ambiguity of the situation, I will have to detain you and your sister."

"Are we suspects?" Jacqueline asked, stunned.

"Again, at this point and based totally on the circumstances and the call to service, we need to have you come down to the station to be interviewed."

"Oh, this is just great! Jeri, they're actually taking us in," Jacqueline choked.

"Look, once we figured this out, you'll be free to go, but for now, yes, we are going to detain you."

"Of course, whatever my sister and I can do to help, right, Jacqueline?"

"I guess," Jacqueline muttered.

CHAPTER 7

Givens escorted the sisters to his vehicle and directed them to sit in the backseat. He shut the car door, took another long look at Jacqueline, and headed toward the house to help the Detective Coroner and other police officers on the scene.

He walked along the side path toward the front of the house, paused, and gazed morosely at the once beautiful Victorian porch, which stretched the full length of the home. The decayed door silently exposing its many past wounds and memories.

Mac set his shoulders straight, stepped onto the porch, and walked through the door. Many years had passed since he had walked through this entrance to the house. Saddened by the state of deterioration, Mac stood still, turned and looked at the lake, the mountains, and pine trees. With a deep sigh, he turned back and continued into the house.

"Chief." Officer Stagg nodded as Mac passed by.

Mac stopped at the staircase. He looked at a body lying face down. "What have we got here?" He asked Detective Mendoza from the SO.

"Mac, it's Sara Kelly."

Givens felt a solid gut punch to his stomach and stopped short. Heart hammering through his chest, he took several mouthfuls of air and tried to catch his breath. He choked down bile and forced himself to get control. Slowly his heart settled, and he felt the fist in his stomach disappear. Related by marriage, the Givens and Kelly family siblings had grown up together. Mac was best friends with Sara's older brother, Alex.

"You okay?" Mendoza asked, concerned.

"Not bad. Shaken to the core, but I'll survive." Mac breathed. Stunned, he listened.

"Looks like a homicide. No blood here. The murder occurred elsewhere. Somebody then moved the decedent to this location. It looks like her assailant hung the body on this coat rack. Strange. When the door opened, both the coat rack and body hit the floor. Decedent is thin, like skin and bone. It doesn't look like she has had a decent meal in weeks. Her clothes, blouse, and skirt are covered in blood and dirt. Doesn't seem to be any sign of sexual assault, at least at this point. We'll have an answer once there's an autopsy. Hair is dirty and matted like she hasn't put a comb or brush through it for some time. And look here," Mendoza said," there are bruises around the wrists and ankles which makes me think she was tied up for a long time."

"Can we determine the approximate time of death?" Mac asked.

"My guess is she expired within the last four to eight hours, based on what I see here. Take a look at the face, neck, arms, and shoulders. Rigor mortis appears typically within the body around two hours after the deceased has passed away. It affects the smaller muscles first. Rigor has begun its work in this area of the face and neck. As we can see here," Mendoza pointed, "the stiffening has also affected some muscle tissue in the arms and shoulders, but the larger muscles are not affected yet. This provides a timeline of death between zero and eight hours. The Sacramento Coroner's facility will have a better time based on the autopsy. The body is cool to the touch."

"Odor is not as bad as some."

"I think that's because the decedent is undernourished. There probably wasn't much food in her system, so fluids expelled would be minimal. Because the body hung on this coat rack, gravity had a larger effect on the decedent's muscles, forcefully pushing a little bit of nasties. Not pleasant but, trust me, I've smelled far worse. It's also pretty warm in that closet. The ambient temperature would have an increased effect on the pace of rigor mortis."

Did you check to see if there was a watch? Might help with our determination relative to the time of death if it stopped.

"No watch. Wouldn't help if we found one. It could have stopped close to the time of death. It could have stopped a day or days before or the day after. We didn't find anything on her, for that matter. No ID, nothing."

"Go ahead and finish up with the photos and your work here. I'll meet you back at the station."

"Sure, Chief. PD might have a few questions for you before you leave."

"Like?"

"Why is the Chief of Police taking this service call?"

"I have a personal interest here, Detective. You know that. My family owns this home."

"That's exactly why they're going to want to ask you some questions. Specifically, your whereabouts in the last eight to ten hours?"

"They would be negligent if they didn't ask."

***

Jeri listened to Jacqueline grumble about their present predicament.

"I feel like a prisoner in this backseat with those windows barred and doors locked. What does he think we are, criminals? I guess our Police Chief isn't too concerned about a killer who lurks around here, or our welfare, or our lives."

"Why do you say that?" Jeri asked, staring at the house to see what was going on.

"Uh, alone, in this police car, by ourselves, need I say more?"

"Oh, I wouldn't worry if I were you, big sister. I think I saw more than you think in those dreamy eyes."

"What do you mean?"

"Jacqueline, seriously?" Jeri smirked. "You are either totally blind or very naive not to see the interest."

"Disgusting! I mean, he's a policeman, he's a jerk, and totally disrespectful. Put us in this police car, by ourselves where we might be murdered at any moment."

"He's the Chief of Police, Jacqueline. I'm just saying," Jeri grinned. She turned her attention back to the house. She could see the police through some un-boarded back windows both downstairs and upstairs as they checked the crime scene for clues and possibly the murderer. Minutes later, the chief and one officer approached Givens' police vehicle.

"Officer Jobs, make sure this crime scene is secure.

"Already taken care of, Chief," replied Jobs.

"Good. Call if you need me for anything."

The police chief got into his vehicle and checked his two passengers. "You two okay back there?"

"Okay? Officer, are you serious! You left my sister and me—"

"—we're just fine, officer," Jeri said, trying to stop Jacqueline by putting her finger on her lips as a gesture to shut up. "My sister is somewhat excitable. The events of this evening have obviously affected her."

"Events have not affected me. I'm just fine. Chief Givens, you left us alone in this car. Someone might have killed us."

"Sweet," Given's uttered under his breath. He turned and started the car. "We need to stop by your cabin for those ID's."

***

A cloud slothfully moved, giving the moon freedom to cast a glow on a silhouette hiding in the woods across the road. Nicole watched the activity surrounding the mansion with growing concern.

"Meddling bitches," she whispered,

She observed two officers walk toward the police vehicle parked with the two women sitting in the back seat. She took a step back into the woods when the car door opened, and a light lit the surrounding area. She tried to pick up their conversation, but the distance was too far. Anger gripped her. She began to shake with rage. *Tony will not like this. They will NOT get in our way; I will make sure of that.*

Fuming, she watched the police vehicle move down the road and gave them the one-finger salute.

***

It took less than two minutes to maneuver his vehicle and park at the cabin.

"We'll be right back." Jacqueline murmured as she tried to open the door. "Ah, the door's locked."

The Police Chief turned and stared at the two women in the back seat through the steel wire mesh. "I'm going to have to come in with you. I'll also unlock that door." He smiled mischievously.

"Jacqueline, don't you say a word," Jeri whispered.

They entered the cabin and quickly found their purses, ID's, and iPhones. Givens immediately checked their identification, and the three headed to the police station. On the way, he called in to ask the dispatcher to contact Alex Kelly. "Have him call me on my cell." A few minutes later, Chief Given's cell phone rang. He told the caller to meet him at the station in five minutes.

Jeri looked at Jacqueline. "That's Alex, our next-door neighbor," Jeri whispered. "What does he have to do with this?"

CHAPTER 8

Once at the station, the Police Chief asked an officer to escort Jeri and Jacqueline to a small twelve-foot square, plain, interview room with Spartan furniture. The room included a little table, a recorder and one real-time camera, and four very basic chairs, not meant for comfort. The walls had been partially soundproofed to eliminate outside noises that might enter the room.

"A typical police station interrogation room," Jeri murmured as she sat down.

"And you know what an interrogation room looks like, how?"

"Criminology course I once took. We did a tour of a police station and a prison." Jeri noticed that the Chief had left the room's one door open. "See these padded walls?" Jeri whispered. "They're to stifle screams of those who get interrogated." Jeri watched with mild amusement as Jacqueline looked at the walls anxiously. Jeri heard some commotion outside the room where they were being held. She turned her attention toward the door to see a few deputies and staff greet Alex Kelly as he walked down the hallway. Jeri immediately perked up. She watched Alex stroll by as he headed toward Chief Givens' office.

Alex spotted Jeri sitting in the room as he passed by. He stopped, smiled, cocked his head as if to question her presence, and started to walk toward her. He shrugged and turned as Chief Givens called him into his office and shut the door.

"Jacqueline, that's the guy I was telling you about. The one I met at the airport," said Jeri.

"So that's our new neighbor, Alex. Very pleasing to the eyes."

Jeri frowned. "I wonder what's up with Alex and the Police Chief. Do you think he could have some connection to the dead woman?"

"I don't have a clue," Jacqueline murmured thoughtfully. "My big question is, why would someone put a dead body in a closet in that old mansion? Which just so happens to belong to the Chief of Police. Coincidence? I have a suspicion that whoever placed that body in that closet did not intend to have it found for a long time. Do you think the killer made the mistake of not locking that door? Oh my God, do you think Chief Givens killed her? That would make sense," she muttered. She stood and began to pace back and forth, chewing on her nail. "How else would that body get into that closet?"

"Shhhhhhhhh, are you crazy? Accusing the Chief of Police?" Jeri said. She checked the hallway to see if anyone heard them.

"If the door had been locked," Jacqueline said thoughtfully, "we would never have gone in. Maybe the murderer just assumed no one would check that old house so soon. Maybe, because the murderer owns that house!"

"Or, maybe our killer is just a simple moron."

"And blood," Jacqueline whispered, lost in thought. "Something that should have been in abundance but wasn't. So that woman was killed somewhere else and dumped after somebody murdered her. When that police Chief comes back, you need to help me look for dried blood on his uniform. Of course," Jacqueline said, taking a deep breath, "he might have changed after killing that woman. He looks like he would be smart enough to think of that."

Jeri gawked at her sister. "You have finally become unhinged. That is just too absurd, silly. Need I mention insane?"

"Why? It is his house, his closet, and if you ask me, Mr. Chief of Police seems just a little too sure of himself. You know, smug, cocky, and he's got this swagger about him."

"Swagger?" Jeri said. "Look, the guy's incredibly fine-looking, gorgeous even. He's entitled to a little swagger."

Jeri's attention refocused on the hallway outside their room. She watched Alex walk by. It was apparent that he was not only upset, but he seemed to have developed a certain steel edge he had not shown before. He stopped, looked toward Jeri, then abruptly turned, continued down the hall, and left the station house without a word.

Chief Givens stood with hands on his hips, and watched Alex leave the station. He walked over to the room where Jacqueline and Jeri waited. He looked as upset as the man who had just left his office.

"So, what was that all about?" Jeri asked, slightly perplexed by Alex's icy demeanor.

"I'll ask the questions," Chief Givens replied. He pulled out a chair and sat across from the sisters.

"Tell me, once again, the circumstances surrounding your visit to the residence and how you found the body."

"As I said before," Jacqueline began, looking briefly at her sister, "we went to the old mansion out of curiosity. When we got there, we found the French doors open. We went in and looked around. We decided to check out the upstairs and—"

"—and that's when I fell over the banister and hit the closet door in my fall," Jeri interrupted. "I saw this hand and opened the door, and the dead body fell on me. We both hit the floor. That poor woman, I can still see the death in her eyes."

"And the rest, you know." Jacqueline murmured, directing her attention to the Police Chief's shirt, sleeves, and pant legs, checking for blood, then lifted her eyes to meet his "We called the police, and here we are."

"Miss Winters, in your previous statement, you said that you hit the floor with the body, and you did move the body, is that correct?"

"Yes, of course," Jeri answered. "I had to move the body off of me to get up. But other than that, neither Jacqueline nor I touched anything."

"There was no murder weapon found on or around the body," Chief Givens noted. "Did either of you see a weapon?"

"No, we didn't see anything, at least I didn't," Jacqueline said, "but then we weren't looking for a murder weapon at the time, were we Jeri."

Jeri watched with curiosity as Jacqueline checked out the Police Chief's shoes, clothes, and hands. *Jacqueline is definitely showing a few fries short of a happy meal.* She thought, somewhat amused. She looked up at the Chief to answer Jacqueline's comment. "No, no, we didn't see a weapon."

Seemingly, not to notice the scrutiny while he digested this piece of information, Chief Givens seemed satisfied with their answers and stood to signal the end of the meeting.

Jeri felt troubled by the Chief's line of questions. Since she was the one who had chanced upon the corpse, she felt she was on the hook for messing with the crime scene—what a predicament.

"Wait, is that a spot on your shirt," Jacqueline blurted. She pointed to a red stain on the Chief's blue shirt.

"Excuse me?" Givens asked. He looked down and saw the red dot where he had spilled sauce earlier. "Ah, spaghetti dinner. I should have changed, but it has been pretty busy. Do we have a problem here?" He asked, puzzled by Jacqueline's outburst.

"No, oh no," said Jeri, catching Jacqueline's eye.

Jacqueline turned back to Chief Givens to avoid the look from her sister. "I just remembered that when I arrived at the cabin earlier today, I thought I heard voices arguing and a scream that sounded muffled."

"And what time was that?"

"It was just after I arrived. It sounded close. I checked the cabin, even though I knew I was alone and then went outside to investigate, but I did not see or hear anything else, so I left to pick up Jeri at the Reno Airport. It must have been around eleven-thirty. I'm not sure of the exact time."

"It's good that you remembered that piece of information, Miss Renee. Can you think of anything else?"

"Not right now, but I'll let you know if I remember anything I've missed."

"I'd like you both back here tomorrow to provide a formal written statement. For now, we are finished. I'll give you a ride back to your cabin."

Both Jacqueline and Jeri got to their feet. "Chief Givens, is it possible for you to tell us why Alex Kelly was here?" Jeri asked.

"You know Alex?"

"We met on the plane today."

The Chief rubbed his chin as he looked from Jacqueline to Jeri.

"Alex, his family, and I are friends. That's all I can share with you at this point." Jeri could not help but show her disappointment.

"It's getting pretty late. I need to get you two ladies home and hit the laundromat," Givens said, with a warm smile directed toward Jacqueline.

"I guess," Jacqueline said with some hesitancy, "since we have no other options, by that I mean no car."

"Fine," the Chief said with amusement, "let's go."

Following the Chief of Police, Jacqueline leaned over and whispered into Jeri's ear. "Spaghetti, my ass."

***

Mac dropped both Jacqueline and Jeri off at their cabin, turned onto highway 50, and headed back to the station. Mac smiled wistfully. He found it hard to believe that just one look at Jacqueline had brought warmth to a heart that had grown cold so long ago. He couldn't imagine and was indeed astounded that anyone could affect him after all these years. She was definitely frisky, spirited, headstrong, and a bit perplexing. What was with the stain on his shirt? Her touch of defiance intrigued him, which made him smile. Beneath that veneer, he sensed a sweet vulnerability. He didn't understand this strong connection he felt but knew he wanted to scratch that external shell and see what lay below the surface. It didn't hurt that she was beautiful as well.

The last woman who stirred his heart was Marcie, the love of his life. Twenty years ago, Mac met Marcie in college. She was everything: beautiful, funny, witty, and intelligent. On the night of their graduation, Mac had taken Marcie to their favorite bistro, where he had asked the chef to write, "Will you marry me?" in chocolate sauce around the rim of her dessert plate.

Marcie said one word, "Yes." Mac had felt like the luckiest guy on the planet. They inherited the old mansion from Mac's grandparents and spent endless hours renovating it with love. They had been married five years when one day Marcie complained of a side ache. She'd ignored the discomfort for several weeks until they finally went to the doctor and found that Marcie had advanced stage four lymphoma. Mac took an extended leave of absence from his job, spent the next seven months with Marcie, and watched her slowly melt away to a mere image of herself. On that last day, she had turned her eyes and met his. "I love you, Mac."

"This is so unfair," he had murmured, stroking her hand, grief etched on his face.

"No," she whispered, "don't let this darkness overshadow your life and happiness. Promise me," she sighed as she drifted away.

Through those following months and years, Mac's friends had tried to support him, and he did have a few dates, but he was never ready or interested in developing a relationship. He'd turned to his job and found solace in his work. He had never set foot in the mansion again until tonight.

The steering wheel vibration and audible hum of a roadside rumble strip jolted Mac back to the present. His thoughts turned to Jacqueline.

CHAPTER 9

Alex sat with his brothers, Zed and Dustin, in the great room of their South Lake Tahoe home. The 7,500 square foot home nestled amid lush landscaped grounds exuded old Tahoe charm. Hardwood floors with natural stone accents, rough-hewn timber mantels, and soaring open beams offered an air of rustic grandeur. Each room provided spectacular views of the lake.

Evening shadows cast touches of shade over the lake and surrounding mountains. Alex sat in silence with his siblings, looking but not seeing the beauty displayed before them.

Though two years younger, Dustin looked like Zed's twin. But that is where similarities ended.

Zed was extroverted chatty, some even saying bossy. He was everyone's friend, all for the girls, and known to be a real party guy. Athletic in his college days, he now worked with his brother in the family business.

Dustin was more introverted, timid, and shy. Quiet, a deep thinker, he dedicated his life to helping others. As a psychotherapist and designer for the Lego Future Laboratory, Dustin customized Lego pieces such as bricks used in play therapy to help children who had been through trauma to tell their stories and help those with autism to develop social and communication skills. Outside the laboratory, he found that interaction with Lego enthusiasts gave him a mental boost, finding Legos a calming and absorbing hobby. It just felt right. He also assisted in the family business when asked.

At an early age, each learned to accept each other and their differences, which ultimately created a strong bond between the brothers and a unique relationship. Each agreed that their brother, Alex, would be the head of the family.

Alex had taken over the seventy-five million dollar Kelly Lumber Company family business upon their father's death. His father's career began in the construction industry, where he ran the enterprise and made a sizable income. It grew over the years and today the company employed 2,500 staff and owned roughly 150,000 acres of SFI certified forestland in Washington and Oregon. The family recently branched off into fine wines. Their first crop of Pinot Noir and Chardonnay grapes established the Kelly Vineyards located in Oregon. The company grew to include forestland and new manufacturing facilities. His dad, and Alex, his brothers, and sister, developed a deep commitment to the community. Those values continued to be at the heart of the organization. And Alex planned on keeping it that way. He was extremely protective of his family, especially Sara, who was his only sister. A fighter. Barely surviving her birth, he had watched her grow into an extraordinary person. It was a gift to be around her. *She could laugh at anything, including herself*, Alex thought warmly. A woman who knew the value of having fun. She never took life too seriously. *Unlike me, at times*, he thought.

Alex felt it was not enough for their parents to have recently passed away and that the estate was in jeopardy, but now this tragedy. Mac Givens had said the body they found in the mansion was Alex's sister, Sara. Mac said they found Sara emaciated, skin and bone, hair dirty and matted. *I just talked to Sara four weeks ago,* he thought, running fingers through his hair. *I can't get my arms around this.*

Sara said she wanted to sink out of sight for a few months and immerse herself into the Italian culture. For the past two months, she stayed with a family that lived on an 18th-century rural farm located twenty-seven km southeast of Florence. His last conversation was four weeks ago. She was excited, having purchased a cookbook specific to her location. She said she had free access to the farm's organic gardens. It was an excellent way to get a sense of the local dishes. Bubbling with enthusiasm, she was thrilled with engaging in the foreign culture with her Homestay family. He mentioned the problems with the family estate. Since she would be arriving in San Francisco, was it possible for her to meet with their attorney? "Not a problem," she had said. She would get a hotel, take a few days in the city and then come home. She was to have been back today.

Staring out the bay windows, he thought back to when he had last spoken with his mother. They had been alone in the dark bedroom. He held her small, frail hand as she lay on her deathbed. Tears of shame and remorse flowed as she released the secrets of the past to her firstborn son. Alex hid the rage that consumed him as his mother spoke. Skeletons of the past bound him to secrecy in the future to protect his sister from the truth. But he had failed. He promised his mother that he would always be there for Sara. To protect her and take care of her. His promise now broken.

***

Zed and Dustin sat quietly, shocked by the news of their sister's death. Each felt the deep personal anguish of this enormous loss. Zed felt nothing could have prepared him for this. His grief came in waves, like an out of control freight train ramming his soul, leaving a void of overwhelming sadness. Dustin sat in disbelief. He felt like someone or something sucked out everything in his guts, his heart, the oxygen needed to breathe. No one spoke. The sorrow was too heavy.

Alex's cell phone rang. The ring brought his thoughts back to the present. Glancing at Zed and Dustin, he picked up his cell.

"Alex, David Mendoza, you have a minute to talk?"

"Sure." *Why is the Detective Coroner's Office calling me?* He wondered. "Alex, something isn't right about the findings with this body. The Sacramento Coroner's Office did some lab tests to be sure we get a positive ID on the murder victim. I don't know, Alex, I—"

The front door opened. A tall, slender, graceful woman who displayed a natural, uncomplicated beauty walked into the room with a purpose. She wore tailored blue pants with a matching long length blouse. Her smile dazzled and delighted all who knew her.

With a quick motion of her hand, she swept her long beautiful lush, radiant red hair behind her ear with exaggerated impatience.

"Guys," she said, "you wouldn't believe the crazy day I've had."

Speechless, Alex, Zed, and Dustin stared at their sister, Sara, in utter silence.

CHAPTER 10

Jacqueline and Jeri drank their tea in silence while they let the events of the day settle in. They looked through the trees toward the lake, watched the sunset and dusk come rushing towards night. To a native of Tahoe, few objects appear more beautiful than a setting sun that disappears behind the splendid mountain range. The clear skies promised the vision of a full moon. The brilliant colors captured and held their gaze.

"Where can you find sunsets equal to this?" Jacqueline sighed. "It's so serene. I love it here. I may never go home. Reminds me of a poem I once read. Let me think if I can remember—"

"Unshackled unbound Beauty is set free
To wield a palette of cerise and rose
Chromatic brush-stroked symphonies disclose
A sensuous foretaste of eternity
As daylight fades and twilight colors dim
The stars awake to sing an evening hymn"[1]

"That's beautiful. Do you know who wrote it?"
"James Tweedie. He's a retired pastor. I love his poetry." Jacqueline sat mesmerized, deep in thought. "The thing is, sometimes I just don't want the sun to set. I want it to stay right there on the horizon. Not below it, not above it, just right there on it, so I can continue to immerse myself in the beauty of it all."
"My sister," Jeri smiled warmly, "the poet *and* the romantic."

---

[1] James Tweedie, Retired Presbyterian Pastor and member of the Society of Classical Poets

Four shadowy figures emerged from the bushes between the Kelly's home and their cabin.

Silhouettes shaded in evening rays of light walked directly towards their front door. Jeri recognized Alex and Zed. She set her tea down and looked at the two people accompanying the brothers, but could not identify them in the waning light. Jeri rose, walked to the front porch and opened the door.

"Alex, what a pleasant surprise."

"I come bearing gifts of wine and a six-pack as a peace offering." Alex grinned.

"I'm sorry, a peace offering?"

"To apologize for my rude behavior at the police station earlier."

Jeri smiled. "No apology is necessary, Alex. Come in. We're in the living room."

The group passed through the glassed-in porch, the dining room, and into the living room. Alex extended a hand and introduced himself.

"You must be Jacqueline. I remember you from the airport when you picked up your sister. It's nice to meet you. Jeri, you know Zed, but neither of you have met my brother Dustin or my sister Sara."

Stunned, Jacqueline dropped her teacup, which shattered in pieces on the floor.

"Oh, my God!" Jeri said. She stood dumbfounded before she jumped back, careful not to step on glass. She looked into the eyes of someone she thought was dead.

Upset, Sara took Jeri's hand in hers and apologized. "I am so sorry to have given you both such a fright."

"But we saw you," Jacqueline said.

"It wasn't me," Sara replied. "I'm thankful to say I'm alive and well. I've been in Italy for two months and San Francisco for the last two days. I just got back."

"Let me say again," Alex grinned, "I've brought a bottle of wine and a six-pack of Blue Moon. We need something to lighten up the moment."

Jeri laughed nervously. "I agree." She maneuvered the group into the dining room while Zed offered to clean up the glass. "I think we just might have an orange to go with that Blue Moon," Jeri said, walking into the kitchen to whip up some simple appetizers, open the beer and uncork the wine.

"Got a church-key, a wine opener, or both?" Alex asked, following her into the kitchen.

"A church-key? What the heck is a church-key?"

"A church-key," Alex eyed Jeri with amusement, "you know, for opening bottles and cans."

"Never heard of it, but if we have such a thing, it will be in that drawer on the left-hand side of the sink."

Alex held up a tool. "That is a bottle opener," Jeri said, laughing.

"This is a church-key," Alex said with a flirtatious wink.

Jeri's cheeks were still flushed when she stepped into the dining room. She set a plate of cheese, liver pâté, crackers, and nuts on the table. Alex, not far behind, placed the opened beer, oranges, and wine.

***

Jacqueline loved friends and family, both old and new, gathered around her table. With a sigh, she felt at home in this old rustic cabin with memories of previous visits.

"How long did you say you've been traveling, Sara?" Jacqueline asked.

"Um, this pâté is delicious," Sara said as she nibbled a cracker with pâté then took a sip of her wine. "I took a two-month vacation in Italy. The idea was to immerse myself in the local culture and work on my Italian. I stayed at this farm, which was an 18th century home in the heart of Tuscany. It was lovely, surrounded by vineyards, hills, and woods. When the sun went down, you could hear the wild boars, crickets singing, and this sense of well-being permeated the senses. I love and miss it already, and I just got back." She laughed and looked at her brother. "Alex asked me to see our attorney since my flight landed in San Francisco Airport, and his office is in San Francisco. Since our parents died, my brothers and I have found ourselves mired in a mortgage dispute."

"That's terrible," Jacqueline said. "But Sara, the woman we found in the mansion? She looked exactly like you! I swear she could be your twin."

"Well, she might have looked like Sara," Alex responded, "but Sara is right here, so it wasn't her. I am sure the dead woman did not look exactly like Sara. You and your sister were upset and frightened, which would have had an impact on your perception of what you did or did not see."

Jacqueline watched Alex as he fidgeted with his beer. She felt he seemed uncomfortable with the discussion. "Maybe," she murmured.

Zed walked into the kitchen with the broken pieces of Jacqueline's cup and tossed them into the trash. He returned to the dining room and sat with the others.

"So, what is the dispute over your property?" Jacqueline asked.

Sara smiled, "It seems my Dad's brother was attached to the syndicate back in the 70s. None of my brothers have seen Uncle Lex for years.

Our uncle became indebted to one of his business partners, according to our attorney. I guess a bad debt was a matter of life and death with these people."

"I always heard Uncle Lex was a real piece of work. Had a mean streak that got him into a lot of trouble. No question, he was the black sheep of our family." Dustin scoffed.

Sara took another sip of wine. "Never met the man, so honestly couldn't say one way or the other. The attorney said Uncle Lex sold his share of our property to Dad for a sizable sum of money. Then he took the money and disappeared. The attorney found that Uncle Lex is now living in New York and the owner of a Daniels Corporation located in Manhattan."

"What's the connection to the house?" Zed asked.

"Because the current casino owner, who at one time mutually owned the Casino with Uncle Lex and his partners, says that our uncle and my Dad deeded our entire property to the Casino to cover my uncle's debts. It's all just crazy."

"Hopefully, this will all be fixed for the positive, and soon," Jeri said.

"Time will tell," sighed Sara. "Our attorney believes that the deed signed by both Uncle Lex and my Dad might be a forgery, and if so, he believes the law is ultimately on our side. But, again, it just takes time to sort these things out."

Everyone sat in silence for a moment with his or her thoughts.

"Any ideas who that woman was we found in the Givens house?" Jacqueline asked.

"Not a clue. All we know is she looked like Sara!" Zed answered.

"That's still conjecture in my book," murmured Alex.

Just then, they heard a knock at the back door. "I'll get that," Jacqueline said as she excused herself.

She opened the door and faced Mac Givens. A flutter of butterflies took a slow roll through her stomach.

"Chief Givens. What a surprise." Jacqueline frowned, ignoring the butterflies, her voice wary. "Is there a problem?"

"No, no problem," Mac said with a warm smile. "I stopped by to see Alex, and no one was home. Saw lights on and thought he might, by chance, be here."

"He is here," Jacqueline said. They stared at each other for several moments in silence.

"Uh, thanks, and please, call me Mac," he smiled warmly. "May I come in?" he asked as he moved up the steps and leaned closer, his focus centered on her eyes.

"Yes, of course," Jacqueline stammered, opening the door wider.

With an entrancing smile, Mac tipped his hat, sidestepped Jacqueline, and walked toward the dining room.

Good grief, get a hold of yourself. You are a grown woman, not a teenager Jacqueline. She thought. Slightly embarrassed, her face flushed, she turned and followed him.

Mac strode into the dining room.

Stunned, he stood silent. "Sara!"

Sara jumped up and quickly moved toward Mac. "I know, Mac. Thinking that the body found was me has been unsettling for everyone."

He took her in his arms, pulling her close. "I swear it was you I saw. Oh, my God." He embraced her for several moments then held her at arm's length taking in the breadth of her.

"You better sit down, Mac, before you fall," Sara said as she pulled the table bench out and sat down. Looking up at him, she patted the seat next to her. He gently sat and continued to stare in disbelief.

"Beer, old friend?" Alex asked. "That's all there is to offer unless you want some wine."

"Beer sounds awesome, Alex, but I have to decline. I'm still on duty."

Jacqueline sat across the table from Mac and could feel the closeness and comfort these two families derived from each other. She watched Mac glance at Sara taking her hand in his. *Was there something going on between them?*

Mac turned. His eyes lingered on Jacqueline for a moment, then slowly looked around the table.

"Mac, we were just talking about that poor dead woman," Dustin said. "How long before you find out information on her identity?"

"At this point, I have no idea," Mac said, shaking his head. "I need to touch base with the Sacramento Coroner's Office."

"Mac, earlier today, I got a call from David Mendoza. He said that something was not right about the findings with this body. The Coroner's Office was doing some additional lab tests to be sure to get a positive ID on the murder victim."

"Interesting Alex. Got a call from Mendoza but haven't gotten back to him yet. Now I know what that call was about."

Mac briefly paused and examined the faces around the table. "It usually takes anywhere from twenty-four to forty-eight hours turnaround time for lab results. We will have to wait and see. Hopefully, we should have some answers soon."

For the next half hour, the conversation turned to a lighter side, the topic of murder put on hold.

"It is getting late," Mac interjected, "I think it would be a good idea for everyone to get a good night's sleep. I would like to see you all at the station in the morning, say around ten o'clock. Does that fit your schedules?"

"Is it necessary for Jeri and me to be there since you've already questioned us?" Jacqueline asked. "We *are* no longer suspects, right?"

"Jacqueline, you are such a boob," Jeri said, bunching her sister's arm. "Of course, we'll come down with the others. We both will try and remember anything we can, in addition to what we've already said. We want to do anything to help."

Sara, amused, watched Jacqueline and Jeri's bantering. She got up to leave with the others.

"Be careful," Mac reminded everyone, "someone killed that woman, and I don't want any of you hurt."

Jacqueline watched Jeri walk the Kellys to the front door.

"Jeri," Alex said, "are you sure you and your sister are okay? Mac told me you both found the body. That had to be a shock."

She nodded, slowly exhaling.

"I don't care what time it is, if you need help or anything, call me. Here's my number at the house and my cell phone."

"I appreciate your concern," Jeri said. She slipped the information into her pocket. The Kelly's exited out the front door and headed home.

Jacqueline turned and watched Mac walk to his vehicle. He turned and smiled with a mischievous sparkle in his eyes. "Evening Ms. Renee," he said once again, tipping his hat as he opened the door to his cruiser.

A brief smile crossed her lips as she nodded and shut the door before joining Jeri in the living room.

"And just what are you grinning about, big sister," Jeri said, pointing and wagging her finger at Jacqueline. "Do I see something going on with you and the police chief?"

Jaqueline's grin quickly vanished with the memory of the murder victim found in his house, in his closet. "Please, you can't be serious," she said. "He seems kind of nice, not bad to look at either, but he could be a murderer."

"Wow, who would have ever thought."

"And just what do you mean by that comment?"

Jeri stared at her sister for a moment. "Just that you might be overdramatizing a bit. I mean, you have overreacted about your observations because of past experiences. Minimal as they were. He's a nice person, Jacqueline. He's the Chief of Police."

"And he owns the home that the murdered woman was found in, Jeri."

"True, but it's an abandoned home. A lot of people around here must know that. Anyone could have put that body in that closet." Jeri murmured in frustration.

"At this point, no one knows anything. An ounce of precaution is not out of the question, no matter how charming the Police Chief is."

"Or good looking." Jeri snickered.

"Okay,...okay. Let's clean up and hit the beds; we have a big day tomorrow."

***

Jeri went to her room while Jacqueline drew a hot bath. Sitting on the tub's edge, Jacqueline checked the temperature and flow of the water and stepped in. She leaned back, eyes closed, submerged herself, felt the water close in around her. With a sigh, Jacqueline relaxed. *There's no better elixir than soaking in a warm bath after a rough day,* she thought. The soothing water eased the day's tensions and stress.

A darkness replaced her peacefulness. She opened her eyes and saw a shadow standing over her. Petrified, she immediately knew it was not Jeri. She closed her eyes and opened them again. The shadow was gone. Heart hammering, she sat up and looked around the bathroom, but no one was there. Badly shaken, she grabbed her robe and hurried to Jeri's room.

Jeri turned to see her sister standing in the doorway. "Jacqueline, you're white as a ghost."

"I—," Jacqueline stumbled to the bed and sat down. "—I thought I saw someone in the bathroom. I was lying down in the tub and…"

Jeri jumped up and ran into the bathroom but found nothing. She hurried to the front door, confirmed it was locked, checked the back door, and found that door unlocked. She opened the door, scanned the backyard, but saw or heard nothing. No movement. She closed the door and made sure it was locked. An uneasiness settled over her as she walked back to her room.

"Can I sleep with you tonight, Jeri?" I'm too upset to be by myself."

"Absolutely. You take the left side, and I'll take the right side." Jeri turned off the night light, and they settled in.

"Could it have been that active imagination of yours?"

"I swear, Jeri, I saw something. Scared me to death."

The night grew silent. Both sisters absorbed in their thoughts. After ten minutes, Jeri whispered. "Are you okay?"

"I'm feeling better."

"So here we are, knee-deep in a mystery," Jeri said, then paused. She turned over to face her sister. Lifting her head slightly, she supported her chin with her hand.

"Listen, Jacqueline, I think you should give the Police Chief a break. He is an okay guy. I feel it. I think I know bad when I see it, and he's not bad. And I get the feeling he kind of likes you."

"I doubt that," Jacqueline mumbled, dozing off. "Besides, he and Sara look pretty close."

"You're so sweet underneath all that bullshit. Sara and Mac? I don't think so. Give him a chance." Jeri laid back and yawned. "Anyway, it's been a pretty exciting day, and I love you."

Feeling heavy-eyed and drowsy, Jacqueline stifled a yawn, turned on her side, and pulled the covers up to her chin. "Love you too, Sis."

DAY TWO....

Trips open avenues of surprise
Open eyes to new adventures
Shattered dreams of lost souls
Romance a single venture

CHAPTER 11

Jacqueline opened her eyes and stared at the alarm clock on the bedside stand. "We're going to be late." She pulled the covers off and jumped out of bed. She immediately remembered last night's scare. *Was it only my imagination*, she thought? In the light of the morning, it seemed nothing more than a bad dream. *I need to lighten up.* Remembering the wild pillow fights they used to have as kids, she picked up her pillow. With a wicked smile, she raised the pillow over her head and dropped it on Jeri with a shout, "Up, sleepyhead, we're late!"

Jeri rolled over, got on her knees, and grabbed her pillow, shouting, "Pillow fight!"

Jacqueline and Jeri batted each other in a fight to the end. Jacqueline heard the loud rip of the pillow. Soft white feathers appearing like snow tumbled through the air. They laughed hysterically and fell on the bed.

"Oh my God, that was a blast from the past," Jeri panted.

As they caught their breath, Jacqueline reached over to check the time on the bedside table. "Mac said we're supposed to be at the police station by 10:00, and it's past 9:00."

"How are you feeling this morning? I mean about last night and all."

"You know it probably was just a figment of my imagination,—a bad dream. Come on! We need to get moving."

Joking, laughing, in lighthearted moods, the two women took showers and dressed. "Since we don't have time for breakfast, let's stop by Starbucks on our way over, pick up lattes and a muffin," Jeri said, zipping up her jeans.

"Good idea, my stomach's growling," Jacqueline muttered with a grin.

They grabbed light jackets, phones, purses and headed out the door. Jacqueline stopped briefly to lock up the cabin.

Jacqueline and her sister embraced Lake Tahoe's timeless beauty, the smell of pine trees, the slight breeze, and the warmth of the sunshine. With all its splendor, the day held a warning of excitement and adventure.

Jacqueline slid into the car seat and started the engine. She entered the police station address into the GPS and pushed 'guide'.

"Please proceed to the highlighted route, then the route guidance will start," a soft feminine voice purred.

"That woman's voice does nothing for me. Why can't they have a sexy Frenchman or Italian macho stud muffin to give the directions?"

"No, Frenchman, please," Jeri said, with a deep frown.

"Sorry, no Frenchman," Jacqueline said. "Just Italians. Sexy Italians with those sexy Italian accents."

Jacqueline disengaged the brakes, backed out of the parking space, and headed for the police station.

***

Mac looked at the clock on the far wall of his office, noting he had only ten minutes before the sisters and the Kellys arrived. He turned his attention to his two top detectives, Ricks and Styker. Both were retired Navy seals, each driven to maintain body and mind.

Deeply dedicated, Ricks' looks were complemented by deep ocean blue eyes, and shoulder-length white-blond hair pulled back into a ponytail. Tall, slender, with well-developed muscles, he would be considered handsome were it not for a horrific scar that began under his chin curved up across his cheek ending at the top of his forehead. A knife wound, which had almost cost him his life. He and Mac were close, like brothers. Mac was a man who walked tall among his peers, superiors, and all who worked with him both inside and outside the department. Fair and just with a strong determination balanced by compassion and a quick wit, he was respected by all who knew him, especially Ricks. Mac had confided his crazy irrational interest in Jacqueline Renee. "One day, I'm going to make that woman my wife." Ricks had laughed and told Mac he had been alone far too long but silently he was pleased that Mac was interested in life again.

No particular single feature defined Styker's characteristics. He was a light African-American with Asian-accented compassionate brown eyes. Eyes that could turn ice cold when provoked or challenged. Tall, medium weight with a solid build, he prided himself on his country's service and now as a cop. His tattoos, reminders of his personal spiritual and cultural traditions. He was tough, had a fierce allegiance to his job and partner. There was a softer side that very few had the opportunity to know or see.

Mac quickly briefed them on the interviews to take place. "I want to separate the sisters. Ricks, you take Jeri Winters, and I will take Jacqueline Renee. Styker, I want you to question Sara. When we have finished with them, we will deal with Zed, Alex, and Dustin. I'll meet you in the conference room in about ten minutes."

"Sure thing," Ricks said.

After they left, Mac concentrated on police reports and paperwork. He was about to leave when his telephone rang.

"Mac here."

"Chief, David Mendoza."

"Morning Detective," Mac said while he quickly cleared his desk, shoved pencils and paper into drawers, and gathered the information needed for the interviews.

"Got some information on your Jane Doe."

"Excellent, let's hear it."

"Name's Emma Kelly. New York address. It turns out she's been missing for about three weeks. Works for a company called the Daniels Corporation located in Manhattan."

"Have you been able to talk with a family member?"

"The Records Division notified Detective Davies, Midtown South Precinct on 35th Street in Manhattan. Davies contacted the next of kin about an hour ago. Says she's the adopted daughter of the owner of the Daniels Corporation. Guy's name is Lex Kelly. Seemed pretty upset. Confirmed that his daughter disappeared three weeks ago."

"Interesting. I wonder if Lex Kelly is the same Lex Kelly, who is the brother of Alex's dad. He disappeared years ago."

"Wouldn't know myself, but that would be pretty coincidental if he's the brother. Said he and two business partners were able to get a flight and should be in Tahoe around three o'clock this afternoon.

"Thanks, David. Appreciate the swift ID."

"We were lucky. Autopsy took an additional few hours. I had to ship the deceased to the Sacramento County Coroner's Office. They ran her prints through the NAMUS system that searches for potential matches between missing and unidentified cases. Got a hit right away."

"Do you, by chance, have the telephone number of the detective handling the case in New York?"

"Yep, have it right here, 212-239-9811."

"Thanks, Detective," Mac said, quickly noting down the information.

"Anytime."

He hung-up, waited a moment, then picked up the phone and dialed the number given to him. A deep baritone voice answered.

"You have reached the 14th Precinct of the New York Police Department. If you need directions to the precinct, press one. If you need to contact the detective unit, press two…" Mac immediately pressed two and waited.

"Detective Davies."

"Detective Davies, this is Mac Givens, South Lake Tahoe PD, Chief of Police."

"What can I do for you?"

"We found a body yesterday, Emma Kelly. She's a missing person, and I understand you are the detective who has worked her case."

"That's correct; she disappeared three weeks ago. You said you found her body in Lake Tahoe?"

"Yes, it's a homicide. We found Emma Kelly's body in a closet. Placed at that location after she was murdered. I'm calling to get information on the decedent and her father, Lex Kelly."

"The dad filed a missing person's report three weeks ago. We have had no leads. The trail ran cold until we were contacted by your records division. We know the daughter was a member of a real estate firm called the Daniels Corporation located in New York City. Her father owns the company. She worked her way up through the firm's organizational structure to the Acquisitions Department. Worked for the firm for about nine years." Her father was grooming her to take over the company, which caused peer conflict and hostility among the rank and file. Mr. Kelly built up a financial empire here in New York. He has friends in high places and is politically connected. Nobody likes the guy; nobody dislikes him. Ballbuster, who works the system and, by the way, has done quite well. He adopted his daughter when she was seventeen, put her through high school and college. Has a BS and MS degree. She had a lot of people who didn't like her in the company, primarily for her lack of work ethics. She was caught several times taking credit for others' work, failing to pass on vital information, sabotaging coworkers, bullying peers, slander, and the list goes on."

"Anyone there capable of murder?"

"We did a lot of interviews and found a lot of folks who had no love lost for the victim, but no, we didn't see anyone who would cross that line."

Mac glanced at the clock, thanked Detective Davies, said he would be in touch, gathered material for his interviews, and headed to the conference room.

***

Jacqueline peeked into the police conference room where the Kellys were already seated.

She smiled at everyone as she walked into the room, followed by Jeri, and sat next to Sara, placing her Starbucks coffee on the conference room table. She noticed Alex smile at Jeri and offer her the seat next to him, which her sister took.

Chapter 12

Mac met Ricks and Styker in the conference room, where the others were waiting. They pulled out the nearest chairs and sat down.

"Thanks for coming down to the station. This is Officer Ricks and Officer Styker. They will assist in taking your statements, which should not take more than a few hours. Any questions?"

"Mac, have you found out who the dead woman is yet?" Asked Alex.

"Her name is Emma Kelly. Her father filed a missing person's report three weeks ago, but there have been no leads. It seems the trail ran cold until Jacqueline and Jeri found her in that closet. We know she was a member of a real estate firm called the Daniels Corporation, located in New York City. Her father owns the company. She worked in the firm's Acquisitions Department for about nine years."

Dustin leaned over. "Sara, isn't that the company the attorney said Uncle Lex was associated with?"

"Yes, I believe it is. Interestingly, that company's name came up in my discussions with the lawyers about the casino group. If it is our uncle and he is connected with the Daniels Corporation, that might be the connection we're looking for with the casino—."

"—Okay, Ms. Winters," Mac interrupted, "I would like you to follow Officer Ricks, Sara, go with Officer Styker and Ms. Renee, you will come with me. The rest of you will stay here in the conference room until we can interview you. If you have any questions or need anything, Officer Jobs is just down the hall. I would also appreciate you not talking with each other about this case until you meet with one of us. After we interview Ms. Winters, Renee, and Kelly, we'll come back to get you."

***

Jeri followed Ricks into the small interview room that she and Jacqueline had been in the evening before.

"Have a seat, Ms. Winters."

"Thank you," Jeri said as she picked out the nearest chair.

Ricks laid his recorder on the table and pushed start.

"Are you going to record me?"

"Yes, I am. Do you have a problem?"

"No... no, I guess not."

"Let's start from the beginning."

For the next forty-five minutes, Jeri reviewed her activities from the previous day until she arrived at the Reno Airport.

"What time did your sister pick you up?"

"I would say around 12:30, not sure of the exact time." Jeri continued with the drive to the cabin, noted a quick lunch, and the decision to take a walk to the lake.

"What made you decide to enter that particular house? It is a private residence."

"It was an adventure. My sister had stayed in this cabin before and always wanted to check out the old mansion, so we did. We found the front door locked, but the French side doors were open, and the house did seem to be empty and abandoned, so we went in. We started to walk up the stairs. Jacqueline was sharing a sick story of a previous owner who murdered his wife and daughter. I turned around to leave, lost my balance, struck the banister, which broke, fell, and hit the door under the stairs in my fall. A door opened just a crack, but enough to see a hand. I opened it all the way and saw this dead woman. Like she just stood there. Creepy. Then she fell on me, and we both slumped to the floor. Let me tell you, Detective Ricks, it was the scariest thing that has ever happened to me."

"You didn't hurt yourself in the fall?" Ricks asked.

"Jacqueline and I had only made it up a few steps when I fell. I guess I was lucky I didn't get injured."

"And what about this murder, your sister said, took place previously?"

"It was a joke. Jacqueline made the story up to frighten me. She did a good job too. "

Ricks and Jeri continued to review her statement. Finished, he escorted her back to the conference room and selected Dustin to question next.

They briefly discussed Dustin's whereabouts the previous day. No, he had no alibi. He was home alone for most of the day, worked on some projects until his brothers arrived with the devastating news of their sister's murder. "Next thing, she just walks through the front door. I can't explain how I felt. I was overwhelmed, shocked. First time since I was a kid that I cried."

"You know of anyone who would want to hurt your sister?"

"No," Dustin said. He shook his head, "absolutely no one."

They wrapped up the interview with Dustin's trip to the cabin next door with his brothers and sister to visit Jeri and Jacqueline.

"Dustin, I'd like you to stick around in case I have any further questions."

"I'm flying to Oregon in the morning, with my brother Zed. We have a stockholders meeting. We'll be gone for two days, but I'm available by phone if you have any questions."

"Can't you postpone the meeting?"

"We tried, but we were unable to cancel. A minimum of two board members from the family have to attend. But again, I will keep my phone on and make myself available for any questions."

"Okay, we'll go with that. Just be sure that the phone is next to you."

***

Mac took Jacqueline to a room down the hall from where her sister and Officer Ricks were meeting. The room was a large common area divided into four cubicles, three with a small desk, chair, and file cabinet. The fourth cubicle accommodated a single round conference table with four chairs, which looked more comfortable than those in the other room. Mac took a seat at the conference table while Jacqueline took the chair across from him. She crossed her arms and stared at her interrogator. Mac was not sure of the meaning of her body language. She was either closed for any discussion, stubborn, or perhaps feeling vulnerable or possibly insecure.

They continued to gaze at each other for a moment.

Mac, sitting back in his seat, turned on his recorder. "Miss Renee, let's go over the events of yesterday beginning with your arrival in South Lake Tahoe."

"I got to the cabin around 11 a.m. and unpacked the car. Just before I left to pick up my sister, I thought I heard voices arguing and then a woman's muted scream."

"Did you report this to the police?"

"No, I didn't."

"Can I ask why?"

"Like I said, it seemed distant and muffled. I was not even sure I heard anything. A call to the police did not enter my mind. In retrospect, I guess I should have."

"Are you sure it was a woman's voice you heard? Could it have been a male?"

"No, I don't think so. The strange thing is that it sounded like it came from the cabin, but I checked all the rooms, and I can say, beyond a doubt, that no one was there but me. When I checked outside, I thought I saw someone near the back of the cabin behind a tree, but when I looked, I didn't see anything or anyone. Frankly, after I checked both inside and outside, I concluded that it was my active imagination."

"Do you still feel it was your imagination?"

Jacqueline thought long and hard. "I'm not so sure about seeing someone. It was more like a shadow, but I am sure I heard arguing, and I am sure I heard a scream. Especially now, with everything that has happened. No, I definitely do not think the voices and muted scream were my imagination."

"Can you give me the time and the duration of the occurrence?"

"It must have been closer to 11:30 a.m. because I had to pick up my sister. The sounds I heard lasted seconds."

"Can you give me a description of the person you saw in the back of the cabin?"

"No, like I said, it was just a shadow, but I felt like someone was watching me. It was unnerving."

Jacqueline repeated the information she had given Mac earlier with no discernible deviation. Picked up her sister, had a quick lunch, took a walk, and found the body.

"What did you do in response to the incident? What were you feeling at the time?"

"Shocked can't begin to describe my feelings. My sister and I were shaken to the core. We were afraid and felt the murderer might still be close by. We wanted to get out of that house quick and call the police." Jacqueline said, looking into the Chief's eyes.

"Interesting that the body found was in your house, isn't it?" Jacqueline said with as much innocence as she could muster.

Slightly taken aback but mildly amused, Mac looked into Jacqueline's eyes. They stared at each other until a knock at the door broke the connection.

"Excuse me, Chief," Officer Jobs said, noting Jacqueline's flushed cheeks, "Ricks wanted to know how much longer you are going to be."

"We've done all we can do here," Mac said. Standing, he thanked Jacqueline for her help.

***

Sara sat across from Officer Styker, tapping her foot. She wasn't sure why she should feel so jumpy. *She was alive, but some poor woman was dead. Moreover, Mac and her brothers had thought she was the victim. I guess that would make anyone edgy.*

Styker perused his notes. He looked up at Sara and briefly assessed her. She was attractive, looked intelligent, but seemed very nervous.

"Miss Kelly, let's begin with your whereabouts for the last couple of months. I understand that you were in Italy for a while?"

"Yes, that's correct. I spent two months with a Homestay family in Italy. Tuscany, to be more specific. About a month ago, Alex, my brother, called and asked that I stop in San Francisco on my way back to meet with our family attorney. Our family is having some issues that need to be resolved, and since my flight from Italy flew non-stop to the San Francisco Airport, it only made sense for me to take the extra time and meet with our attorney. I landed around four o'clock, got a hotel, had an early dinner, and went to bed. I met with our attorney the following morning, then drove home. I arrived late yesterday afternoon."

"Where did you stay in San Francisco?"

"The Fairmont Hotel, on Mason Street."

"Can anyone collaborate your statement?"

"Not physically. I mean, I didn't see anyone until the next morning when I saw my lawyer. But my attorney did telephone me soon after I arrived.

"Can you think of anyone who would want to harm you?"

"I honestly can't think of anyone. I work with great people; my friends are terrific, and my family is very close."

"Any old boyfriends possibly carrying a grudge or jealous over the breakup?"

"No, I live for my job and haven't dated that much in the past several years. I had a relationship that ended some time ago. We were on and off for about four years, but it ended amicably. We eventually just drifted in different directions. I'm not sure why you're asking me these questions. I mean, as far as I know, no one has tried to harm me."

"This woman found, Emma Kelly, did you know her? Know anything about her?"

"No, nothing."

"I understand from the coroner that she's the spitting image of you."

"I heard. It sounds like Emma is a doppelganger."

"Sorry, a what?"

"You know, a doppelganger. It's German, meaning a double walker. A ghost or a shadow of yourself. Someone who looks spookily like you but isn't a twin."

Styker cocked an eye as he looked at her intently. "Because the victim does look like you, Miss Kelly, we want to eliminate any concern there might be for your safety."

"You're scaring me, Officer. Should I be worried?"

"You should be scared. Someone out there, Ms. Kelly, has killed a woman who looks like you, and the victim was found adjacent to your property. Yes, you need to be careful, and yes, you need to keep a close eye on your surroundings until we have more information."

Sara nervously tapped her nails on the table. "I appreciate your concern, and I will be careful. Is there anything else I need to know?"

"Not at this time. But if you can think of anything, don't hesitate to contact me directly," Styker said as he handed her his business card.

Sara looked at the card. "Styker... Officer Styker," Sara smiled. "I will contact you if I have any information to share."

***

Ricks and Styker interviewed Alex and Zed. Both meetings were swift, as both had an alibi. They were together all day on the same flights. They just happened to meet Jeri on the last leg of their trip, who coincidentally just happened to be renting the Kelly family cabin with her sister, Jacqueline. No, neither of them had met either sister before that flight. When they got home, they received news of Sara's death.

"It was devastating," Alex said softly. "I was seized by a mixture of anger and dread. How do people come to terms with losing someone they love? It's crippling. But then to have that person just walk through the door, alive?"

"Man, how crazy is this whole thing," Zed said to Ricks, shaken.

Ricks hesitated. "Do you need some time before we continue?"

"No. Thanks for asking, Detective, but I think we can finish up. An hour later, we walked over to the cabin to visit with Jeri and Jacqueline. We got home around 9:00 p.m."

Zed let Ricks know that he and his brother Dustin would be out of town for two days but available at all times for further questions.

"Thanks, appreciate that," Ricks said, ending the meeting.

Alex and Zed walked into the conference room and joined Dustin, Sara, Jacqueline, and Jeri.

"The officers asked us to wait in here for a bit." "So, I didn't know this Emma Kelly. Did any of you?" Alex asked.

Sara, Dustin, and Zed shook their heads in response.

They heard a knock as the door opened, and Mac stepped in. "You're all free to go, but we may need to ask some additional questions, so stay close to home for the next couple of days. Zed and Dustin, we've got you covered for your trip. Just stay in touch while you're out of town."

The Kellys headed to their car parked in the public parking area.

"Hey guys, I'll be right back," Alex said. He turned from his car and headed back to the police station. Once inside, he approached Jeri as she was about to leave the conference room.

"Jeri, glad I caught you.

"Jacqueline and I were just getting ready to leave."

"Are you available for dinner tonight?"

"Sure, I'd love to."

"Great, if you think Jacqueline would like to join us, I'll ask Mac to come along. We'll make it a double date."

"Well, I can tell you Jacqueline would love to go out to dinner with Mac. She just, last night, told me how nice he is. I'll just say yes for her."

"Awesome, Mac, and I will pick you up at 6:00."

"Sounds perfect."

***

Jeri and Jacqueline hurried to their car. Once in and buckled up, Jeri turned to Jacqueline.

"Hold on to your hat, Sis."

"What's up, Miss Happy?" Jacqueline snickered as she started the car.

"Alex asked me to dinner tonight."

"That's great. Alex seems like a nice guy. Not bad in the looks department, either."

"*And*, you're going out with Mac," Jeri said, holding her breath while waiting for a reaction.

"Ah, what?" Jacqueline said. She turned off the ignition and faced her sister.

"You heard me, sis, you got a date tonight! We both have a date!"

"Ah, no. No way. I'm sorry, Jeri, but most of the men I've met have been heartless and contemptibly obnoxious. Honestly, I've learned my lesson. There has never been a police officer I've ever met that hasn't been a jerk."

"And how many police officers have you met?"

"Alright, one. One lousy experience is all I need to make a sound decision. You can tell the Chief of Police, *no!*"

"I can't. I already told Alex you would love to go. Besides, what is the logic behind your saying no anyway? I know you have an interest."

"Seriously, are you kidding me?"

"You know what your trouble is? No? Well, I'll tell you. You wouldn't know a good time if it fell in your lap, if it popped in your face, if you—"

"—don't go there, Jeri. That's just not fair."

"Come on, Jacqueline, I like Alex. Do it for me. Not for you."

Jacqueline sighed. "What happened to, 'No men in our lives, it feels good to find a piece of yourself, let's be bachelorettes' hello?"

"Jacqueline, I like him. I would like to get to know him better. Please?"

"Let me get this right. You are asking me to date a potential murderer?"

"I'm telling you, get over this murder obsession of yours. Mac is a good person. He has to be if he's a friend of Alex."

"You don't even know, Alex. If I do this, you owe me big time!"

"I'm good with owing you big time."

Jacqueline sighed, started the ignition, and drove out of the police parking lot. Heading back to the cabin, she felt a slight fluttering of anticipation.

CHAPTER 13

North of the "Y" on Highway 89, in South Lake Tahoe, the Lazy S Lodge, sometimes affectionately referred to as the Lazy Ass Lodge, is what someone would look for if they wanted a small, family-friendly place to stay. Cute cottages offered a wealth of charm nestled in the Sierra pines, with beautiful lawns and a pool for guests who wished to spend a lazy afternoon in the sun.

Three men arrived at the Lazy S Lodge in the afternoon. They occupied cottage number ten.

Lex Kelly stared at the floor, trying to come to grips with the murder of his daughter, Emma. "How could this have happened, and why?" Kelly asked as he ran his fingers through thinning gray hair. "How could someone do something so heinous?" He asked, shaking his head while his two companions, Joe Carver and Tony Russo, listened.

Joe, dismayed by this tragic turn of events, watched Lex anxiously.

Tony glanced at the ceiling as he tilted his chair back, balancing on two legs. He took a long drink of his rum and coke.

Lex took a sip of Jack Daniels, struggled to comprehend the murder of his daughter, and became introspective and quiet.

***

His thoughts turned to 1951, South Lake Tahoe, and the home he grew up in.

By the turn of the century, Lake Tahoe had become a haven of the rich. Although many believe a volcanic crater formed the lake, it was actually created by the rise and fall of the landscape due to faulting. The lake held spiritual meaning for those who visited, lived, and roamed its southern shores.

Highway 50 (previously called 'Bonanza Road') was the first West-to-East road across the mountains. The first casino, built in 1944, caused earnest development in road structure enabling permanent residence.

His favorite folklore spoke of the 'The Grave,' located offshore of South Tahoe Casinos. If you were to take a submarine to the bottom, you would find hundreds of bodies wearing clothes from the early to mid-1900s highly preserved due to near-freezing temperatures. The stories of mob activity were endless and aroused his interest in casino ownership and making money. Big money. It was in this atmosphere of beauty, ski slopes, beaches, and sparkling casino lights that Lex and his brother Michael grew up.

When their parents passed away, they inherited the family's lakefront property. From an early age, Michael was always the responsible brother, while Lex, the younger sibling, was the rogue who got into one scrape after another. Hot-headed and fun-seeking, Lex thoroughly enjoyed the lake with its around-the-clock turntable of playing all day and partying all night. Eventually becoming bored, he refocused his attention on the emerging South Shoreline and the potential business opportunities.

In 1968, Lex met Manny Bianchi, a known mobster, at the Cal-Neva Resort and Casino, owned by Frank Sinatra. A haven for Sinatra's celebrity friends and some shady types, it was here Lex felt most at home, rubbing elbows with the elite.

Manny started his career as a hitman for the mob. He also ran floating dice and high-stakes card games until he hooked up with Lex. Strikingly handsome, his piercing eyes often hid the violence that bubbled just below the surface.

In 1969, Lex and Manny purchased a prime corner lot in South Lake Tahoe with a bankrupt casino named The Orbison on it. The Orbison was one of the smaller casinos that operated in Nevada, with $3.00 craps and $1.00 blackjack tables and slot machines.

Lex put his heart and soul into developing a casino start-up investment plan, including projected earnings, growth, and marketing strategies. The inclusion of this feasibility study denoted demand for a casino, and investment justification was provided to potential investors.

Lex and Manny found starting a casino to be very expensive. The cash-on-hand requirements alone would exceed $20 million. They needed to buy new and additional equipment, renovate the casino and purchase the gambling and liquor licenses, not to mention hiring staff.

Lex had a natural sense for business and management, which provided a tremendous asset to The Orbison's success in the first days and months of operation. He hired a local architect to design the casino to meet and comply with all local safety regulations, scouted bankrupt casinos to acquire discounted slot and poker machines, roulette tables, poker tables, blackjack tables, chips, cards, and more. Newly decorated gaming rooms catered to both big and small spenders. Strong drinks, reasonable play, and warm luxury made the Orbison the favorite of Tahoe locals.

Lex and Manny were each twenty-five percent partners in the Orbison. Outside investors owned fifty percent. The first sign of trouble appeared in 1974 when Lex found out that those investors included Manny's East Coast Mafia buddies.

In the 1970s, the New York crime families still maintained control over the hauling and trash industries as well as the pier-related unions. The construction industry aligned with Mafia interests. Though lucrative, investments on the West Coast were inviting. With Manny's encouragement and Lex's investment plan and feasibility study, Manny's buddies eagerly jumped at the chance to invest in The Orbison Casino. These new partners also insisted that an outside entity manage financials for compliance with regulatory bodies and audits of revenue. Unknown to Lex, at the time, Hawthorne and McKinney was an accounting firm employed by the East Coast Mafia families. Over the next few years, the accounting firm manipulated the casino financial records and accounting records to disguise the embezzlement of revenues. A slow but steady process so as not to raise questions. Lex had eventually gotten wind of the theft when reviewing year-end audit reports, which revealed unexpected profit shortfalls.

The second sign of something gone wrong was personnel staff salaries. Lex found that Manny was paid well for his lack of management skills. Payroll records showed payments well above his regular salary.

Lex's expense account was raised as a third sign of looming potential problems. Several large reimbursement requests were denied and put on hold due to a reported shortfall of revenues per the financial department.

And last, various silent partners of the Mafia, through Manny, were moving in to control the casino's operations and assets. Lex was feeling that push to the side. He knew the casino was extremely lucrative, even with the Mafia scamming revenues off the top. He had no doubt; he was out-and-out being lied to.

Furious, Lex implemented a scheme to skim money from the casino by leaving the books open past the end of the month to record additional sales within the prior reporting period. From his point of view, he was being screwed and was due. In time, Hawthorne and McKinney became suspicious and informed their employers who contacted Manny to take care of the problem. Manny confronted Lex and threatened him with exposure unless he made total restitution, including twenty percent interest on the money owed.

Lex knew if he did not pay back the Mafia, he definitely would not see the sun come up the next morning. He figured if he sold his share of the casino to his partner, that would take care of half of what he owed. His only other asset was the house he and Michael owned on the lake, and his share would not be enough to cover the remainder of the debt.

His first step was to draw up a dissolution of partnership for his share of the casino to Manny and his partners. That would take care of a portion of the debt. He contacted Manny and asked to meet with him at the Roadside Inn on Highway 50 the next day. Lex worked the rest of the day, pulling together the paperwork. Since their partnership agreement contained provisions for a dissolution, the process moved along quickly. He also obtained a quitclaim deed for the Tahoe property he and Michael co-owned. He forged Michael's signature for his portion of the property, signed his name for his half, and paid a notary a handsome sum to sign and notarize the fraudulent quitclaim deed.

The next morning Lex walked into the Roadside Inn. Eyeing his soon-to-be ex-partner, he headed to the last booth in the back and slid into the seat opposite Manny. Looking at each other warily, neither spoke. The silence interrupted by a plate crashing to the floor somewhere near.

"What can I get you boys," an old redhead with smoke-stained teeth asked while checking out the mess on the floor.

"Bloody Mary."

"Nothing for me, sweetheart," Manny said, staring at his table mate, waving her off.

The two stared at each other, an underlay of emotions bottled up, ready to explode. Manny was different from Lex in that he did not see that he had ever done anything wrong in this relationship. Whereas Lex did know that what he was doing was criminal, but he kept it hidden.

"You got something for me, friend?" Manny sneered.

Lex moved both documents across the table. "I'm not your friend, you piece of shit."

Manny leaned over to grab Lex by the throat.

"Hey boys, we got a little problem here?" the waitress asked, setting the Bloody Mary on the table.

"Lose it, you old bitch." Manny jeered.

"I've handled the likes of you before, son. Sit down and stop causing trouble, or I'm gonna call the cops."

Manny slowly sat down, his face flushed red with anger.

Lex watched the waitress leave. When she was out of sight, he turned to Manny. "I'm on my way out of town. I'm catching a plane in a few hours. You can take these documents; they've been signed and notarized. All you need to do is file them at the

El Dorado County Records Office. I'm leaving everything. Cash and assets."

"Damn right, you're leaving any hard cash and assets. How do I know there won't be problems here with these documents?"

Lex took a long drink of his Bloody Mary, put out his cigarette, and stood.

"Once filed, the partnership will be dissolved in ninety days. House is yours, once you file the quitclaim deed."

Manny grabbed Lex's arm, hard. "No problem, bro," he sneered, "but just remember, any complications here, *you* are a dead man. Are we on the same page, my friend?"

Lex viciously shook Manny's grip off his arm and walked out the front door.

***

Lex later met with his brother Michael. Over lunch, he discussed his desire to quitclaim deed his portion of the family home to him. Shocked, Michael asked him to rethink this request.

"Are you aware of the potential revenue we will recognize in future years with this property? I mean, why would you do this, Lex?"

"I have to get out of this town; this place isn't good for me anymore. Without money, I can't make this happen. I need cash."

"Cash? You have the casino."

"I paid off a debt with my portion of the casino. Look, Michael, I need the cash, and I need it now."

"You've got to be crazy. How could I get that kind of cash on the spur of the moment to buy you out?"

"You can't get the cash on the house, but you could borrow the money from Dad. He has ten times the amount you need to buy me out. You inherit the company anyway. What's the big deal?"

"Lex, think about this. It's so extreme. I can't let you do this."

"It's not your decision, big brother. It's mine. I've signed the quitclaim deed for my portion of the property. I need the cash by tomorrow afternoon."

By the next afternoon, with cash in hand, Lex left Lake Tahoe. He also left all his problems behind. He figured that he would be long gone before the discrepancy was found, probably when both quitclaim deeds were filed. They could fight it out. It wasn't his problem anymore.

***

Manny celebrated his newfound fortune into the wee hours of the morning. He woke to nurse a debilitating hangover, his head consumed by throbbing pain, his mouth bone dry. He struggled to get out of bed, his stomach lurched, and he stumbled into the bathroom heaving last night's celebration. He leaned his trim physique against the shower stall letting bone-chilling ice-cold water pour over his flesh as he took deep gulps of air. He could feel the rush of blood run through his body, charging him with a new dose of energy. As his mind cleared, he thought of his plan to kick Lex's brother out of Manny's new lakefront property.

He took the quitclaim deed with him, stopped by the county clerk's office, filed the document, and headed for the Tahoe house. He would deal with filing the dissolution of the partnership later when he had more time. He'd also deal with his partners then. Tell the fucking morons they got the casino, but Lex took off with the other half of the dough. Easy. Let them find his ass. He turned left on Highway 50 to Lakeview Lane. He did not see the semi-truck that slammed into his 1955 Porsche 356 Speedster snuffing out all his life's plans.

***

The hotel room was hot, the sound of trees rustled outside in the mid-afternoon sun. The bright rays of the sun created dancing images of color on the far wall formed by a wavy, irregular glass surface. Dust motes seemed to swarm in the sunbeams streaming through the partially open window above a small table on which a single sheet of paper laid when a brief gust of wind lifted the lightweight document. It hovered briefly in a current of air before floating to the floor. Later, one of Manny's partners found the document and filed it, pissed that only half of Kelly's debt was satisfied. Since Manny was the only connection to Lex Kelly and Manny was now gone, they were unable to find Kelly to collect the remaining debt. The trail was cold, a dead end, for now.

***

Several years later, Lex surfaced on the East Coast and created the Daniels Corporation, which dealt primarily with land, development, and acquisitions both nationally and internationally. He was the founder and Chairman of the board, Tony Russo, CEO and Joe Carver, the Co-Chairman. Joe had a spine made of jelly, and was unsuccessful at any task or job put before him. His only qualifications for this job, his father, a state senator. A good friend of Lex's, he paid a large sum of money to keep his idiot son employed.

Recently while researching some property for a client in Lake Tahoe, Lex's daughter Emma, who worked for her father's corporation, found the Kelly house, and the two filed quitclaim deeds. Both filed three days apart.

A Manny Bianchi filed the first deed. The deed gave Bianchi one hundred percent ownership of the Kelly property. Researching further, she found that Manny Bianchi died in an automobile accident the same day the deed was recorded. The second deed was filed by Michael Kelly, three days after the first quitclaim deed was filed. Her research of Michael Kelly found that he had a brother, Lex Kelly, and both parents had been recently deceased. If it was true that Michael and Lex Kelly were brothers, by her calculations, this left a sizable estate to her father as one of those deeds had to be fraudulent. Her father had signed two quitclaim deeds for the same property, and both deeds filed. *"Could this guy be my father's brother?"*

With this information in hand, Emma went straight to her father to confront him. Not because of the crime he had perpetrated but because her father might still own one-half of the lake front property in Tahoe, and she would make sure she received a percentage of the $20,000,000 property value. She confronted her father, and after listening to his denials of any wrongdoing, Emma decided to fly to South Lake Tahoe to further investigate on her own. Emma Kelly never boarded that plane. She disappeared. Vanished without a trace, without a clue as to her whereabouts until today.

Lex Kelly could not let his daughter know of his connection with the Tahoe property, knowing that a door opened, would be his death. The Mafia did not forgive a debt.

***

Thoughts drifting back to the present, Lex stared at his empty glass. He stood and walked over to the table, picked up the Jack Daniels bottle, refilled his glass, gulped it whole, then turned and faced both Joe and Tony.

"What we need to do is find out what the cops know about Emma. Or, more to the point, what they don't know."

Joe leaned over and scratched his side, "and how the hell do we do that boss?"

"We do that by checking out the site where she was murdered. Check out that old mansion. Since we know more than the cops do, we have a better idea of what to look for."

"And just what are we looking for?" asked Joe.

"Clues, you moron. What she was doing here on the West Coast, how she got here. She didn't take a plane or bus."

"Sounds like a start anyway," said Tony.

"Look, let's get some dinner. When it gets dark, we'll drive over to that old mansion and take a look."

"Ok boss, but how do we know where the fucking mansion is?" asked Joe.

"Google it, you moron."

"Oh yeah, why didn't I think of that?"

Sighing, Lex turned. "Let's go."

***

Jet black hair cut short swirled around her pale face as she stood watching in the wind. She possessed a natural beauty, but a hard life showed in the aging of her appearance. Her thin frame was gaunt, almost anorexic. Her past was a series of traumatic, neglectful, and abusive foster homes. Her soul ached with grief and unspeakable hate.

Nicole, seething with anger, watched the three men exit their motel room. The moment she learned of that *one* person, she became his slave. He controlled her dreams, robbing her of her peace of mind. There was no escape. He stole the last moments of consciousness before she slept and invaded her privacy when sleep finally knocked at her door. He was there when she woke. Resentment stifled her life, poisoned her being.

Nicole's childhood, or lack of it was a barrier to forming stable emotional bonds in her early and later years. She couldn't help but be deceitful and coercive, exploiting those around her for instant self-gratification. She was often openly violent and aggressive, showing sociopathic behavior throughout her life. Her life, or lack of it, was *his* fault.

Taking a final drag off her cigarette, she dropped it, grinding it into the asphalt obliterating any trace of its existence as she watched the three men get into their car. She knew Tony. One of the men was Tony's age, so the older man had to be Lex Kelly. Tony had called her in the early hours of the morning to let her know they would arrive in the afternoon. Her thoughts turned briefly to her sisters. They had the breaks, the opportunities, they had the love.

She had nothing, never got a break, opportunities were never an option. She spit in the dirt—*love.*

Her loathing intensified. Fury overcame her when she saw the old man.

She had much to do. She still had to take care of her siblings and those two sisters renting the cabin, but first, she must destroy her father, Lex Kelly, as he had ruined her life.

CHAPTER 14

After a light lunch, Jacqueline and Jeri spent the afternoon strolling through South Lake Tahoe boutiques shopping for outfits for the evening. Once back at the cabin, they chilled by the lake, both reading books.

Mac and Alex were prompt and at the door by 6:00 p.m.

Relaxed, hands in his pockets, with a twinkle in his eye, Alex stood casually dressed in jeans, a sport shirt, and a dark teal blue sweater. Anticipation of a fun evening reflected in his smile.

Wow, thought Jeri.

Mac stood slightly to the side and appeared a bit nervous. Casually dressed as well in double L Jeans, a navy blue shirt with a brownfield jacket, he looked up from the bottom step. His gaze locked onto Jacqueline.

"You look beautiful tonight."

Jacqueline's heart skipped a beat. *No, no, no*, she thought. *I do not want to be attracted to Mac. If he sent me flowers, I would want to throw them on the ground, stomp on them, then pick them up and throw them against the wall. Whack them until they were all broken and torn to shreds, then throw a chair through the window and send those flowers after that chair. Twenty stories below, everything would land in a disgusting mess.*

"Ready?" Mac asked with a sincere smile and a touch of shyness.

"I guess, I mean sure, I mean yes, of course," Jacqueline stammered, stumbling over her words. *That's what my brain says*, she thought, as an unexpected warmth rushed through her.

Mac opened the passenger door of his copper colored Toyota Tundra for Jacqueline.

She slid in and buckled her seat belt. "Big truck."

"Up here, you need big engines and bold style," Mac laughed as he shut the passenger door.

"I'm sure," Jacqueline smiled, leaning toward the passenger door. She glanced behind her and watched Alex help Jeri into her seat.

"Where are we off to?" Jeri asked.

"Café Fiore. It's a great restaurant not too far from here," Mac said. He shifted the truck gear into reverse and backed out of the parking spot onto Lakeview Lane.

They spent the next 30 minutes discussing the beauty of Lake Tahoe, the pluses for those who chose to live there year-round, and issues with people moving to the region.

"The only problem with increased population and growth is pollution which threatens the lake," Mac said. "I love living here. Lake Tahoe is my home, has been for years, and I want to protect the environment. A group of residents formed a team. We call ourselves the Tahoe Forest Volunteers. We plant trees and restore trails. Alex is also a part of the group."

"Our goal is to preserve the beauty of Lake Tahoe for our kids and their kids." Alex chimed in. "If you, Jeri, or your sister, ever decide to make a move to the lake, you should check us out. We'd love to have you join us."

"I don't think a move is in the stars," Jeri said. "But then, again, never say never."

"Here we are," Mac beamed.

They pulled into the Café Fiore parking lot. Tucked away on one of South Lake Tahoe's back lanes, the restaurant itself was a tiny alpine gingerbread house.

"It's adorable," said Jeri.

This restaurant is just amazing, thought Jacqueline. They walked through the front door into a cozy room with only seven dining tables. Aromas of authentic Italian cuisine filled the air. The décor included wine bottles tastefully displayed around the perimeter of the restaurant, half curtains on large bay windows overlooked the pine woods and outdoor gardens. White tablecloths accented with burgundy napkins adorned each table as soft candlelight at each table set the mood for a quiet, intimate, and relaxing dinner. In Jacqueline's opinion, the image of perfection.

Nick, Café Fiore's owner, waved Mac and his guests over. He slapped Mac on the back while shaking his friend's hand; a warm smile lit up his face.

"Good to see you again, Mac. It's been far, far too long."

"Good to see you too, Nick. You know, Alex."

"Sure. Good to see you again, Alex." "And this is Jacqueline and Jeri."

"It's always a pleasure to meet friends of Mac's," said Nick, with a short bow to both women. He turned and escorted the group to their table. "I suggest a bottle of Dunstan Pinot Noir Durell with the Bruschetta Siciliana for your appetizer? A gift from me to my good friend. Mac, let's talk and catch up for a few minutes before you leave."

"Thanks, Nick. That's very thoughtful. Why don't you join us for an after-dinner drink?"

"Good, good, enjoy." Nick nodded as he left.

The wine and appetizer came. They ordered four spinach salads with two Scaloppini di Vitello's and two Arista Dijon pork tenderloin entrees and toasted the evening.

"To new friendships," Alex said, raising his wine glass.

"To new friendships," Jeri smiled warmly, looking at Alex, then at Jacqueline. "Jacqueline?"

"Yes, to friends," Jacqueline said as she raised her wine glass. Mac raised his glass to toast and gazed into Jacqueline's eyes,

The foursome slid into a relaxed atmosphere of chatter, exchanging various points of view on everything from best movies to the best teams in sports.

In a moment of silence, Jacqueline spoke up. "Alex, how did your family wind up here in Lake Tahoe?"

"Wasn't easy from what I've read. I picked up most of the information about our family from old journals kept throughout the years. My great-great-grandmother, Isabel, wrote a favorite journal of mine. She was something. Wrote about the challenges they all went through back then. The settlers and my great-great-grandfather, Thomas, who she loved dearly. Said when she met and married Thomas, she knew she had come home."

"That's so touching, Alex," Jeri said, smiling.

"I've always thought of Isabel as somewhat of a contradiction though. On the one hand, she described herself in such a sweet, soft, feminine way. But, on the other hand, she believed in rugged individualism."

"I guess you had to if you were going to survive," Jacqueline said thoughtfully.

"I agree," Alex continued. "According to her journal, women had to be pretty resourceful to cope with the harsh conditions surrounding them. She was not a modest woman, either. When it came to riding and hunting, she wrote she was as good, if not better, than any of her male counterparts. I suspect that included my great-great-grandfather," Alex mused. "A good shot and a fearless rider were the words she used."

"Those journals are fascinating reads," Mac said. "I read where she said she donned male clothes to ride as a scout to fight the Indians."

"I love it," Jeri laughed and held up her wine glass in salute.

Alex smiled. "She was something, no doubt about that. Through her, I've gotten a good sense of what it must have been like back in the 1800s.

"She boasted that Grandpa Thomas was the greatest trailblazer there ever was. Led a group of men through the Sierras, and according to Grandma Isabel, found a new route that eventually led to the Tahoe Basin. After that, people just started coming to Lake Tahoe in staggering numbers. Folks were encouraged to colonize."

"You are so lucky to have that family history in your grandparents own words," Jacqueline said

Thoughtful, Mac interjected. "My understanding is that the government encouraged that colonization through an 'encroachment' process."

"You're right, Mac," Alex said. "Our family laid claim to the four acres our houses stand on today. They built the cabin you and Jeri are staying in back in 1827. They had two sons, Thomas Jr. and Geoffrey."

"If the land belonged to your Great-Great-Grandfather Thomas, Alex, when did the property get divided between your family and Mac's?" Jacqueline asked.

"My family bought the mansion in 1894," Mac said.

"Do you know why your family sold the property, Alex?" Jacqueline asked.

"My Aunt Abigail found out my Uncle Geoffrey was having an affair. She shot them both and threw herself down the stairs to her death."

"Oh my God, Alex. How horrible," Jeri said, in astonishment.

"According to my Aunt Abigail's journals, Uncle Geoffrey was a real son of a bitch. Their marriage was childless, and he blamed her. She loved my Uncle, but could not deal with not having an heir. They built a small cabin near where the mansion now sits. In 1860, construction began on the mansion, which they finished in 1890. They then tore down the cabin. Aunt Abigail detailed the sadness and abuse of their relationship during that time."

"Why didn't they get a divorce?" Jacqueline asked.

"In those days, the subject of divorce never came up," Mac said. You played the cards dealt. A heartbreaking journey for poor Abigail, that's for sure."

"Was her failure to get a divorce the reason she threw herself down those steps?" Jeri asked.

"No, not according to the journals I have read," Alex said. "Aunt Abigail noted that when they built the mansion, Uncle Geoffrey also built an underground cellar. She raged about his being down in the cellar for days and weeks. He said he hated the sight of her. He began to have men; he called friends down there with him. She heard noises day and night. Said it sounded like hammering and loud thumping. After many months it stopped.

Abigail had no idea why. She ranted for pages and pages in her journals about a hypothetical tunnel.

Uncle Geoffrey's parents lived in the cabin you're renting now into their senior years. After they passed away, the place sat empty for some time. A woman by the name of Mamie moved in. She and Uncle Geoffrey would meet in this supposed tunnel. Abigail found out and shot them both before throwing herself down the stairs. The mansion sat empty for two years until it was sold to Mac's family along with 1.2 acres."

"What about that tunnel? That does sound intriguing." Jacqueline said.

"Although Abigail mentioned a tunnel in her journal, no one has ever found one. I think Abigail found Geoffrey and Mamie in the mansion, shot them, and threw herself down the stairs. The tunnel is no more than a notation of a deranged, jealous woman who simply lost it."

"My family lived in the mansion from 1894 to 1955. They never mentioned a cellar or a tunnel." Mac said. When my great-grandmother died of pneumonia, my great-grandfather was devastated. He just upped and walked away. The mansion sat for the next forty years until my wife and I moved in. That was in 1995, and we never saw or found a cellar or tunnel either."

"Mac, I didn't know you were married," Jacqueline said, surprised.

"She died five years after we moved into the house. After her death, I moved out. It's been standing vacant since."

"I'm so sorry, Mac."

Jacqueline's fingertip accidentally touched Mac's hand as she set her wine glass on the table. Their eyes briefly met. A spark, an unspoken special connection passed between them.

CHAPTER 15

The two couples left the restaurant and headed for the cabin.

"Mac, going back to our conversation at the restaurant about your home," Jacqueline said, "just where is that underground tunnel you were talking about?"

"Oh, that, it's more gossip than fact," Mac answered. "More of a myth."

"How do you know for sure?" Jeri interjected. "Has anyone ever checked it out?"

"No, because it is what it is, just gossip. Trust me. If it were true, we would have found the tunnel years ago," said Mac.

"And not to change the subject, but this has been a great night," Alex broke in. "I can't remember when I have enjoyed a date as much. Are you ladies up for an after-dinner drink?"

Laughing and in high spirits, Jeri responded, "Alex, any other evening that would sound like fun, but to be honest, I feel like I need some rest. It has been a super long day, and a lot has happened. Sleep sounds so good right now. I don't think I could stay awake."

"I can't disagree that it's been a ball-buster the last couple of days."

"Okay with you, Jacqueline?"

"Sure, I'm tired myself," she said, stifling a yawn. Mac pulled off the road and parked by the fence.

Mac grabbed a flashlight. "Jacqueline, can you show me where you saw that shadow?"

"Sure, it was over there," she said, getting out of the truck. "I thought I saw someone behind that tree."

Jeri ran over to the porch and opened the door. "I'll turn the porch light on. Hopefully, that will give you more light." Jeri said.

She joined the others as they walked over to where Jacqueline pointed. Mac knelt to check the ground surrounding the tree. Moving some leaves carefully around, he stopped, focused the flashlight on a particular spot, and took a closer look.

"See here?" he pointed. "Shoe impressions on mud can produce a three-dimensional footprint. There is more grass than dirt here, though. Footprints will rebound and regain a flat surface within a short time on grass. But, there are still some stains and minor residue, leaving a two-dimensional mark." Mac stood up.

"I need to get a camera from my truck and take a picture of this print."

Coming back, Mac photographed the footprint with a ruler to show scale. He positioned the camera parallel to the plane of the print and took another shot.

"Need to send these to forensic podiatry to have them analyze these prints."

"Mac, do you mean someone was watching me?"

"There definitely was someone by this tree. You and your sister need to watch yourselves. Keep an eye on your surroundings. In the meantime, I'll have forensics run out here and see if they can create a better visual image of this impression."

"Mac, should we be scared?"

"Alex and his family are next door, and I'm a phone call away. Try not to worry, but keep those doors locked."

"I'll let Sara know to keep an eye open for anything that doesn't look right," Alex said.

"Look, if it makes you feel better, I'll have a patrol car swing by the cabin to keep an eye on things."

"That would make us feel better for sure, thanks," Jacqueline said as they all walked to the cabin steps.

"We, and I know I'm speaking for Mac as well, had a great time tonight," Alex said.

Jeri and Jacqueline agreed. Mac gave Jacqueline's hand a quick squeeze. Mildly surprised, she looked into his eyes, glimpsing sweet tenderness in his smile. Her heart skipped a beat before she turned and walked up the steps to the door. Alex gave Jeri a hug then followed Mac to the car.

"Whew," murmured Mac as he got behind the wheel of the Tundra. "Jacqueline is incredible. I'm feeling a bit thunderstruck."

"My friend, I hate to be the bearer of bad news, but she doesn't exactly seem to be your number one fan."

"She's crazy about me Alex, trust me on this one. Besides, women are meant to be loved, not understood."

"Yeah, and a woman's apathy is far more devastating than her wrath," Alex laughed.

Mac started the truck. "I'm just wondering. Why would someone be interested in spying on those two? It doesn't make sense to me."

***

Mac left Alex off at Alex's home and checked his watch. It was only nine o'clock, and the night was still young. He decided to pay a visit to the scene of the crime. Check it out. See if he could find some answers to a few questions he still had on his mind. Questions like, how did the body wind up in that closet? Why his home? What was the connection between the corpse and that particular location? He wanted to do this before he met with Ricks and Styker.

He parked his vehicle across the street from the mansion, stepped over the yellow barrier police tape that surrounded the house, and walked to the door that Jeri and Jacqueline had used to gain entrance the day before. He unlocked the French doors and walked into the dark living room. Mac flipped the light switch and was not surprised it did not work. As he snapped on his flashlight and slowly walked toward the staircase, he could see the damage done to the stairs and railing where Jeri fell. He walked around the stairs to the staircase door and stepped over debris, focusing his flashlight on the floor that surrounded the entrance. He saw nothing new.

Opening the staircase door, Mac tried the light switch. No dice. He ducked his head as he walked into the two-foot by three-and-a-half-foot wide closet. Aiming his flashlight, he searched for something that the police failed to catch on their previous searches. Noticeably very little blood, but other than this fact, he saw nothing more.

Mac's shoulder hit an object as he turned to leave. Swiveling around, Mac stared at the electrical box door standing slightly ajar. Lifting his hand to shut the door, he stopped short. Squinting to get a better look, he got up close to examine what appeared to be a strand of black hair.

"Interesting," Mac said to no one. "Emma Kelly had red hair." Taking surgical gloves and an evidence bag from his pocket, he carefully withdrew the strand and slid it into the plastic bag.

Moving his flashlight slowly across the back wall, he noticed a slight crack in the wall in the upper left-hand closet corner. Reaching up, he gingerly touched the fracture. A small trickle of dust floated down. Kneeling, Mac scraped up some of the dust and deposited it into a separate bag. Standing as he sealed the bag, Mac felt the wall but found no further cracks in the wall or ceiling. Putting both bags in his breast pocket, he turned, walked out of the closet, and headed for the French doors.

***

Jacqueline could not sleep. Her mind pictured floating dead bodies dressed in black, instead of jumping sheep, which kept her tossing and turning for fifteen minutes. Sliding out of bed and walking across the hall to Jeri's room, she sat on Jeri's bed. She put her hand on her sisters back, ready to shake her.

"YEOOOOOOOO!" Jeri screamed. She bolted up and over the bed tossing Jacqueline hard onto the floor.

Jacqueline got up, rubbing her side, dazed but laughing.

"You scared me to death. What the heck are you doing, waking me up in the middle of the night?"

"First of all," Jacqueline said, still laughing, "it's not the middle of the night, and second, I was only trying to see if you were asleep."

"Well, I was, and now I'm not," Jeri said. She tried valiantly to hide the laugh bubbling up inside her but was not able to.

"I can't sleep," Jacqueline said. "I keep thinking about that poor girl. Let's get dressed and sit by the lake. It's a beautiful night, and there's no way I can go back to sleep now."

"So, I gave up an extended evening with the potential man of my dreams to sit on the beach at, let's see, what time is it? With my sister?"

"It's 9:30, and I can't sleep, Jeri," Jacqueline said. She bent down and pulled her sister's arm. "Come on, get up."

Stifling another yawn, Jeri muttered. "All right, since I obviously have no choice."

Both sisters got dressed and headed for the lake. A short time later, they sat on the beach, sharing the tranquility and the hush of the night while watching the stars overhead and the reflection of the moon on the lake.

Glancing to the left, Jacqueline saw a light in the old mansion.

"Jeri!" Jacqueline said as she grabbed her sister's arm. "Look, there's a light flickering in the old mansion."

Turning, Jeri saw it too.

"Come on," Jacqueline said, pulling her sister's arm. "Let's investigate."

"Are you crazy? We should call the police," Jeri said, yanking her arm away.

"The police will take forever; we're right here. We'll just peek in the window. No one will see us. Come on!" Jacqueline got to her feet and brushed the sand off her jeans.

"It's too dangerous," Jeri said. "We should call the police. We don't have any idea what that light is. It could be the murderer. Stop being an investigative reporter and use your brain. It's not safe. Let's wait for the police."

"Look, I've never shied away from possibilities, and the keyword here is, *could*. It could be dangerous. I'll just have to go by myself," said Jacqueline, heading toward the mansion.

"Pigheaded and too stubborn to admit it," Jeri snarled. She punched in 911 on her iPhone, listened to the ringing on the other end, and watched her sister disappear.

"911, what's the nature of your emergency?"

My name is Jeri Winters, and I am at 30 Lakeview Lane. There was a murder at 32 Lakeview Lane yesterday, and right now, I see a light in that window."

"Okay, I'm sending a police car to the address. Stay on the line with me until they get there."

"There shouldn't be a light because no one lives there. My sister has taken off to check it out, and I'm afraid the murderer might be back."

"Did you say that your sister is in the house?"

"No, she's not in the house. She's headed over there. You need to get ahold of Police Chief Givens; it's his house. You need to send a police car right away."

"Please stay on the line. An officer has been dispatched to your location."

"Okay, but you need to get a hold of Chief Givens, too."

"We are contacting the Chief as well. Do not hang up; stay on the line with me."

"I won't hang up, but please hurry!"

***

Jacqueline drew closer to the old mansion. Tense, her steps a series of rhythmic movements, she crept through the dark, briefly paused, and listened, hearing only the wind whistling through the trees and continued to retrace steps she and Jeri had taken earlier. She slipped by the large bay window and slowly approached the French doors. Turning to look back at the window, Jacqueline saw the beam of light slowly moving through the living room toward her. Drawing in a sharp breath, she quickly squatted down between the window and the doors.

"Someone *is still* roaming around in the living room," she murmured to herself. She looked over her shoulder for Jeri, but there was no sign of her sister. "Where is she?" she whispered, flattening herself against the wall. *It's okay,* she thought. *Jeri called the police. They'll be here any second."*

A shadow emerged and stood above her. Thinking she might be sick, Jacqueline put her head between her knees. Waiting for that final blow, she raised her arms in hopes of defending herself.

.

CHAPTER 16

Mac stood over Jacqueline, surprised as well as angry. "Would it be too much to ask what you are doing here in the middle of the night?"

Sheepishly, Jacqueline looked up, realizing that Mac was on the other end of the flashlight and that she had been caught red-handed. She ignored his hand, his question and tried to get to her feet without falling on her ass and embarrassing herself further.

Jeri hurried around the corner and stopped short, staring at her sister and Chief Givens. Mac turned and motioned her forward. She hesitantly walked over and joined them.

"What the hell are you doing here?" He said angrily, addressing Jacqueline. "Don't you know you put yourself in a dangerous situation?"

"How did you know I was here?"

"I got a text from dispatch that your sister called 911 informing them that you came here to check out a possible intruder. That was so damn irresponsible."

"I'm sorry, Mac," Jacqueline said with sincerity. "We were sitting out by the lake, saw the light, and came to check it out. We didn't mean any harm."

"You mean, you checked it out, not me. You should know that Jacqueline tried to drag me over here after seeing your light and—"

Jacqueline stared at her sister; her brows furrowed as she bit her lip.

Mac shook his head. "The thing is, you didn't know who was in the house, and you may have unknowingly interrupted the murderer, putting both you and your sister in imminent danger. Why didn't you call me before you came here, Jacqueline?

Thankfully, Jeri did the right thing by not following you. Instead, she called 911."

"Thanks, Mac. I told you, Jacqueline," Jeri fumed.

"Mac, honestly, I'm sorry for causing so much trouble," Jacqueline said, giving her sister the evil eye.

They heard car doors slam shut in the distance, followed by footsteps on the east side of the mansion. The three turned their attention towards the commotion. They stood still and listened to the intruders stumble on worn, cracked cement and jagged rocks. Moments later, a disturbance narrowed the location of the prowlers to the locked front door. Muted mutterings and shuffling sounds disclosed a change in direction.

Mac gripped both Jacqueline and Jeri by the arm. "There's a gazebo over there, hidden in the trees." He pulled both sisters toward the darkened structure. "Follow me."

Three figures turned the corner of the mansion and entered through the French doors. "I want you both to stay put."

"Where are you going?" Jacqueline asked, panicked.

"Wait… Look!" Jeri whispered as she grabbed Mac and Jacqueline. She turned them in the direction of yet another set of car headlights parked further up the road. The light from inside the car illuminated the silhouette of a person in dark clothing and a cap. A dark shadow got out of the vehicle. The figure silently shut the car door, and blackness returned.

They heard the intruder walk to the east side of the mansion, then to the front porch, and climb the steps. Unable to enter the front door, the intruder walked toward the west side of the house to the French doors. The person stopped, checked the surroundings, stepped through the door, and was instantly swallowed by the darkness.

The sisters and Mac froze at the sound of three loud pops, like a car backfiring. Shots!

"You bastard," a female voice yelled. A figure ran out the French doors and disappeared around the back corner of the house toward the street. A car engine started. Headlights seemed to ignite a ring of light into the surrounding trees while wheels screamed, and dirt flew through the air. The automobile shot into the night and disappeared.

"Do not leave this gazebo," Mac ordered. He removed his gun from his holster. Crouching low, he ran toward the house and entered through the French doors.

Jacqueline watched him cross the lawn and disappear. "Come on, let's follow Mac."

"Excuse me, but did the Chief of Police just ask us to stay put?"

"Honestly, Jeri, do you want to stay hidden here while we could be helping."

"But he told us to stay," Jeri urgently whispered.

"Dogs stay," Jacqueline said over her shoulder, chomping at the bit to go.

"Dogs listen," Jeri snapped as she held Jacqueline back with all her might.

More shots rang out, echoing in the dark. Jacqueline shook off Jeri's hold on her and ran toward the house. Simultaneously two men crashed through the French doors, one running directly into Jacqueline, causing both to fall and roll on the grass. She felt a foot slam into her side and a punch to her stomach while frantically trying to disentangle herself from her assailant. She cried out in pain.

Hands roughly pushed her to the side. The breath knocked out of her; she curled up into a fetal position and laid still. She heard someone run toward the back of the house. A car started in the distance and drove off.

Jeri ran over to her sister. "Are you hurt?" Damn it, Jacqueline, will you ever listen."

"Got kicked in the side and punched in my stomach. Hurts, but I think I'm ok. I was worried about Mac and all the shots fired."

"What the hell? You don't even like him."

With a grimace, Jacqueline slowly got to her feet and rushed to the French doors. Jeri followed close behind.

Jacqueline stepped into the darkened living room, stumbled over something, but regained her balance. She looked down at a body. "Mac!" She screamed. "Mac!"

CHAPTER 17

Jacqueline heard a groan from the other side of the room, ran over, and found Mac lying on his back. Kneeling, she yelled, "Jeri, call 911. Tell them the Chief of Police is wounded. Someone shot him, and we need an ambulance." Moving closer to Mac, she took his hand in hers. "Mac," she whispered.

Jeri called 911 while she ran to the street to direct the police when they arrived.

For the second time in two days, the Givens' mansion was surrounded by harsh red and blue strobe lights, turning the night into a bright swirl of motion. Police vehicles spanned the driveway and street along with an ambulance and paramedic vehicle.

Weapons drawn, Officer Jobs and his backup ran to the west side of the house toward the French doors while he directed other officers to run to the east side of the home to surround the dwelling. Jobs and his backup cautiously approached the French doors, simultaneously scanning the entire outside garden area to assess and ensure no secondary crime scene.

"Unit 21, clear here." Jobs radioed.

"Unit 22, we're clear in the front of the house."

"10-4."

Once they determined there was no threat to their safety, they entered the mansion and secured the crime scene. Inside the door, Jobs found a body with multiple gunshot wounds. He squatted down, checked for a pulse, found none. He contacted dispatch.

"Unit 21."

"Go ahead, Unit 21."

"Got a 1141."

"Confirm 1141."

"Contact SO Coroner, Detective Mendoza, respond to the scene."

"10-4."

Jobs moved forward. He saw Mac, lying on the floor with a gunshot wound to the shoulder and the head. Jacqueline was leaning over him, holding his hand.

"Let's get those paramedics in here, stat." Jobs shouted, then turned to his backup. "Bates, escort Ms. Renee outside."

"I don't want to leave Mac," Jacqueline whispered.

"We need this area secured to minimize contamination and disturbance of physical evidence. Bates, question both sisters on what they witnessed and get back to me."

"Yes, sir. Ma'am, please follow me."

Jacqueline followed Officer Bates. She turned for one last look at Mac before stepping through the door.

The paramedics arrived and immediately ascertained that the first victim was indeed deceased. They turned their full attention to Mac, who was losing a significant amount of blood. They removed clothing to enable a visual inspection of his wounds. They did a quick assessment of his injuries, noting that one gunshot entry wound penetrated the left front shoulder, the exit wound more substantial, leaving ragged edges. They checked the head injury and found it was a flesh wound, the force of a bullet not causing significant damage to the skull. The paramedic's assessment included airways, breathing, circulation, and neurological status.

"What's your name?"

"You know my name, Hank."

"Mac, cooperate."

"Mac, my name is Mac. Damn, my shoulder hurts like hell."

"What year is it?"

"2018."

"It's 2019."

"One good answer out of two isn't bad, in my book."

"Mac, follow my finger with your eyes. To the left, to the right. How's your head feel?"

"Tylenol would help."

"Squeeze my hand with both of your hands and move your legs. Can you do that, Mac?"

"Can't squeeze with my left hand, Hank. In case you haven't noticed, I caught a bullet in my left shoulder."

"Hands, legs, and mobility is good. Victim's sense of humor needs a definite adjustment."

Hank assessed Mac's vital signs as well as blood loss, then addressed and controlled the external bleeding to both the shoulder and the head wound. A medical team member placed a warm blanket over Mac, while another team member administered IV intravenous fluids.

"You're damn lucky, Mac," Hank murmured. "Looks like that bullet went clean through the shoulder, and you now have a keen sexy buzz cut above your left ear. In short, you are one lucky son of a bitch."

"You know it, and I know it," Mac whispered as he winced in pain. "Thanks, Hank."

"Okay, let's move the Chief onto the stretcher and get him to emergency."

As the paramedics settled Mac onto the stretcher, Jobs strolled over after a brief conversation with Officer Ricks.

"Chief, I hope you're feeling better than you look."

"Had better days, Jobs," Mac softly mumbled. He grimaced as Hank and his assistant lifted him onto the stretcher.

"You know anything about the deceased?"

"Not a clue. Saw three people enter through those French doors; a few seconds later, a fourth person entered. I heard shots fired and heard footsteps as someone ran out and disappeared. When I came into the living room, I got shot twice. Heard two people run through the same doors."

"Need to get him on his way, Jobs," Hank said.

"Right, sorry, Hank. Chief, I'll handle this and report to you later."

The paramedics rolled the stretcher through the door and headed toward the ambulance.

Passing Jacqueline and Jeri, Mac asked the paramedics to stop. Bates, with recorder in hand, was wrapping up their statements.

Mac looked at Jacqueline with a weak smile as he pointed his finger at her.

"I know you were concerned. I heard it in your voice; I felt it. I think you like me."

"You think too much."

"I think we should start over."

"Over?"

"Yeah," he grinned as he extended his hand. "My name's Mac Givens."

Taking his hand, she asked, "Is that Mac Givens, one name or Mac Givens, two names?"

"You're beautiful."

Squeezing his hand gently, she whispered, "Get some rest."

"Only if I can see you in the morning."

"You're pushing it."

"I've been shot. Not once but twice. That deserves a visit, don't you think?" He frowned.

The paramedics continued to the ambulance, slid Mac in, and took off toward the South Lake Tahoe Hospital with lights flashing and sirens blaring. Watching the vehicle disappear, Jacqueline smiled, feeling a warm tug at her heart. She turned and walked over to Jeri.

Inside the mansion, cameras flashed as officers detailed the crime scene, and the SO coroner prepared the body for transport to the morgue.

Jobs strode over. "You two should get some sleep. We'll want to talk with you further tomorrow, but it's late, and you need some rest after what you have been through." Jobs tipped his hat and walked over to assist fellow officers.

Jacqueline turned away. "Come on, Jeri, we need to get some sleep. I need to be at the hospital in the morning."

Returning to their cabin, a very weary Jacqueline and Jeri headed back to bed.

CHAPTER 18

Marian Procini walked out of the front door of Café Madeline with her friends. They chatted and laughed while saying their goodbyes. She had driven into San Francisco to meet her friends for lunch in Union Square. A monthly event. Stepping back, Marian felt unseen eyes on her. An uneasiness settled on her as it had earlier in the day. Marian was the adopted daughter of Jerome Procini, CEO of the Procisions Financial Empire. Stunning, tall, and slender with lush red hair, Marian was a strong woman who recognized her strengths and used them to maintain her goals. Despite her confidence and capabilities, she never felt that she was better than anyone else. Marian knew she was blessed and was thankful for the opportunities her adoptive family provided her.

"Marian, what's wrong?"

"Honestly, I'm not sure. All-day, I've had this feeling that someone is watching me."

"I don't see anyone looking our way. Cheer up, girl, it's been a great afternoon, and I'm going to miss you. Don't let that mind of yours run amok."

Marian kissed her friend on her cheek, smiled, and gave her a warm hug. "You're probably right. Still?" she said, looking around. "See you all next month?"

"It's a date," her three friends said in unison.

Marian turned and walked to her car, unable to shake the apprehension that continued to overwhelm her. She checked her watch and guessed she should be home in about an hour and a half with the flow of traffic. She caught a red light and checked to see if she was being followed. The light turned green. With a sigh, she merged toward I80E, heading to her home in Sacramento.

Taking the Norwood Avenue exit, she felt a car bash the rear end of her car. Marian was so startled by the loud cracking noise that she was unsure of what was happening. The vehicle crashed into the back of her car again, pushing her vehicle off the road. She heard the groans of metal being twisted beyond its limit as she tried to get control of her Lexus. She finally was able to bring the car to a stop and watched as a damaged SUV flew past. Marian sat in a state of shock. Shaken and feeling numb, she continued to be afraid even though the incident was over.

***

The night was cold and damp. Nicole turned up the heat in the car, put the car in drive, and drove to the motel to pick up Tony. She checked her watch. It was 1:00 a.m. Right on time. A shadow crossed the motel lawn, opened the car door, and slid into the passenger's seat.

"Where's the SUV?" Tony asked, looking around.

"Turned it in for a used Chevy."

"What the hell for?"

"Got in a minor fender bender. Piece of crap wasn't worth fixing."

Tony shrugged. "Got everything?"

"In the back seat."

Tony turned and did inventory. Duct tape, rope, knife, cotton, a rag, a bottle of chloroform, and tools to disconnect an alarm. "Where's the flashlights?"

"On the floor, next to your feet."

Tony grabbed the flashlights and tossed them into the back seat.

They headed for Sacramento. Passing few vehicles, they arrived in two hours.

"What's that address?"

"7240 Fifth Street. Big fuckin' mansion, like over sixty-two hundred square feet. Her bedroom is in the back of the house overlooking the swimming pool, upper right-hand corner."

Turning off the lights, Nicole drove up to the side of the house and parked the car.

They crept to the side yard gate. Tony opened the alarm box and easily disconnected the wires.

Tony silently opened the gate. An old flagstone walkway with grass growing between the stones led to the back yard. They saw a pair of French doors in the back of the house that overlooked the swimming pool. Tony stepped onto a veranda and checked the door, which he anticipated would be locked. He folded the rag he had brought along around his hand and gently hit the window. Nicole held her breath, waiting for sirens and alarms to go off as Tony reached in through the jagged broken glass and unlocked the door from the inside. They walked into a den, stopped, and turned left. They saw the stairway leading to the upper level of the house, slowly tiptoed up the stairs, then stopped and listened when they reached the landing. Tony pointed to the right, and they went into the master bedroom. Marian was lying on her back, a slight snore echoing in the room. Tony took out the cotton soaked with chloroform and covered her face. She violently struggled, but the chloroform quickly sedated her.

"Jesus, Tony, how are we going to get her out of here and to the car?"

"We'll put her in some sheets and drag her."

Descending the staircase, Nicole was delighted to see the sheeted form hit the steps, one at a time. Thump! Thump! Thump!

They pulled her out onto the veranda, down some brick steps, and headed for the car.

Looking around to make sure no one was in sight, they dragged the body to the trunk.

Car lights glared in the distance. "Forget tying her up. We need to get out of here and fast." Tony said, slamming the trunk shut.

Two hours later, they were at the Givens' mansion. Nicole stopped and parked the car.

"What the fuck, Nicole. There's yellow tape strung all around this frigging mansion."

"Of course, there is, you idiot! They found Emma's body in that damn closet yesterday and your pal Joe's dead body tonight. What do you think the cops are going to do? Leave a note on the front door? Jesus Tony, for a guy with a master's degree, you are one dumb—"

"—Can it, Nicole. Get out of the car and get the girl. And don't turn any flashlight on. We don't want anyone to see us."

Nicole grunted with frustration as she got out of the car, walked back to the trunk, and opened the lid. Her prisoner bounded up, knocking Nicole to the ground, as she attempted to run.

"Not going to happen, sister," Nicole whispered. She caught her hostage's foot, causing her to fall, giving Nicole the perfect opportunity to slam her fist into her captive's jaw.

Running over to help, Tony used more chloroform to ensure their prisoner was out cold.

"Damn, that was close. Listen, Nicole, we need to get rid of these footprints and tire tracks. Cops for sure will know something is up. But first, we need to get this bitch stashed away."

Together they dragged Marian's dead weight into the mansion.

DAY THREE...

Horizons reflect new dawns
Wings of challenge ensure
Death mystifies with answers unknown
Cruelties surface with hearts of stone

CHAPTER 19

As Jacqueline slumbered in a deep exhaustive sleep, dawn broke, the visible sign of a new day. In an instant, the upper limb of the sun appeared. Red and orange hues streamed across the horizon and sky.

A large, heavy-set hawk with broad wings slowly soared in full circles above the cabin. It appeared to enjoy the view, but hunger is what drove the hawk forward, while below, a lone kayaker paddled silently alongside a flock of Canada Geese at the lake edge. Noiselessly the kayaker glided past the cabin in the tranquil quiet waters.

Heavy eyelids opened. Jacqueline turned with a groan onto her back and stared at the ceiling, her mind still blank with the haze from a deep sleep. She rolled over onto her right side, sat up, leaning on one elbow, stared out the cabin window, and watched a hawk swoop down to catch its prey. Her mind and body now fully awake, Jacqueline sat up, grimaced, and stretched her arms wide above her head. She snuggled back under the blankets, stared at the ceiling and listened to the morning silence. Thoughts of Mac brought a slow smile to her lips and fluttering sensations of excitement.

"Are you awake?"

"Hmmm, just woke," she said.

Jeri sat on the edge of Jacqueline's bed. "How's that wound on your side?"

"The wound is still black and blue and hurts when I breathe, but it feels a lot better than it did last night."

"Should you see a doctor?"

"No broken ribs, but it will take time to heal." Jacqueline smiled. "What I need is a strong cup of coffee and something to eat." She threw the covers off, slid out of bed, headed to the kitchen, followed by Jeri, poured water into the coffee maker, measured six scoops of coffee, and flipped the switch.

"You know, the family history related to these three houses is quite the story. I wonder if that history has any significance to the murders."

Jeri gathered napkins and silverware to set the table. "I don't see how."

"Well, think about it," Jacqueline said. "This Emma Kelly disappeared three weeks before her body surfaced. Where could she have been before the police found her body in the mansion closet? Mac said that there was minimal blood and no murder weapon found at the scene. She had to have been murdered somewhere else and her body placed in the closet after her death. And, how did she get in that closet, and why that particular location?"

"Yeah," Jeri murmured thoughtfully, "and who was this guy who got shot last night?

Two murders in as many days in the same place. I can't believe there isn't some connection."

Jacqueline selected two cups from the cupboard and poured the coffee while Jeri made some toast and soft-boiled eggs. They carried the coffee and eggs into the dining room table. Jeri sat with her legs crossed underneath her, while Jacqueline pulled out the bench and sat across from her.

"All I'm saying is it's just too coincidental," Jacqueline said as they ate their breakfast. "Also, I wonder about that underground tunnel. What if there is a tunnel? Could it possibly be a missing piece of the puzzle?"

"You heard Mac and Alex; it's all gossip, a myth, family rumors."

"I know, I know, but remember, I did think I heard voices and a muffled scream that came from this cabin. And Mac did find a footprint by the tree in the backyard. So, I don't think it would hurt for us to investigate on our own."

"Like?"

"Like driving over to the library and using their computer to check it out."

"But what would we look for?"

"Land deeds, construction requests, transfers of property, something that might give us a clue."

"Hmm," Jeri hesitated in thought. "It can't hurt."

"I think we should check out this cabin first. Imagination or not, I swear I heard voices and a scream. And, I felt it did come from this cabin, or someplace near. So, I think we should start here."

"It would seem to me that if a tunnel did exist, someone would know about it," Jeri said. "I'm getting a feeling that something just isn't adding up. I guess it makes sense to check things out. Let's get dressed. Search the cabin, and then head for the library."

"I'll take the first shower while you clean up the breakfast dishes," Jacqueline said, heading for the bathroom.

"Sure, make me do all the work," Jeri sighed as she took the dirty dishes to the kitchen.

***

A half-hour later, they stood in the living room. "Where do we start?" Jeri asked. "And what specifically do we look for?"

"Well, I would think there would be telltale signs, like disturbed dust, pry marks by an opened area, or scratches on the wall or floor. We might even find something behind a picture or mirror. Tap the floors and walls, and listen for a hollow sound. There might be a locked device or something with a code. You take the front of the cabin, and I'll take the bedrooms and bathroom."

The sisters checked their assigned areas for the next hour. Jacqueline tapped walls but heard no hollow sounds. She knocked on closet walls and floors, checked the bedrooms and under beds, and hallway walls and floors but found no cracks or hidden devices. Jeri searched cupboards, rapped on walls, inspected the back panel of a bookcase, and examined the fireplace but found no suspicious areas of concern.

Jacqueline walked into the living room and found Jeri. "Didn't find anything in the back," she said, "and there aren't any crawl spaces below or above the cabin to check, at least not that I can see."

"I didn't find anything in the front here. So, what now?" Jeri asked.

"I say, we stop by and see Mac. Then run over to the library and see if we can find out any information there."

***

Mac sat on the edge of the hospital bed, dressed and ready to go when Jacqueline and Jeri arrived. Alex and Sara were already there.

"Mac," said Jacqueline, "what on earth are you doing up? You've been shot not once but twice, and you think you can honestly get up and walk out of the hospital?"

"You tell him," Sara said, "We've talked until we're blue in the face trying to get him back into that bed for the last half hour."

"Love the concern," Mac grinned, "but turns out both shots were superficial. Bullets didn't hit any bones, just flesh. Shoulder shot sailed in and out with no damage but an ugly scar. I'm pretty damn lucky. I understand everyone's concern, but we've had two people murdered, and I need to get on the case. I feel okay, maybe a bit stiff, but trust me, I would not be leaving if I thought I would pass out or die. I'm good, guys. Besides, I got a call from Lex Kelly."

"Uncle Lex?" said Sara bewildered.

"If that's the Lex Kelly that called, then that's the man. He is Emma Kelly's father.

"He has a daughter?" Sara asked, surprised.

"Yes, he does. I have an appointment to meet with him down at the Police Station in an hour." Mac looked at Jacqueline. "Can I talk to you for a moment—," he asked, "alone?"

"Yes, of course," she said, briefly looking at the others.

Mac took her hand and looked for a quiet place to talk. He led her to a patient waiting room, which was vacant, stopped, and turned to her. He looked into her eyes for what seemed like an eternity. Jacqueline's heart fluttered.

"I've known heartbreak that shattered me, left me like dust in the wind. At one point in my life, I wasn't sure I wanted to live." Jacqueline started to speak. Mac held up his hand. "Please let me finish. I'm not sure this is even understandable. There is something amazing here between us. I see it. I feel it. I know it. And I feel you know it too." He stopped, looked into her eyes, and grinned.

She smiled. A rush of warmth began to shake her world.

"How I feel is not wrong, but the time is not right. This investigation—it's a barrier, and I can't cross that barrier. I need you to know that, to wait for that. If there is a chance, a place for us, it will happen when this is over."

"I'll be here when this investigation is over." She reached up and impulsively hugged Mac. Mac groaned and winced with pain.

"Oh my God, I'm so sorry I did that to your shoulder." She blushed, backing away.

"Officer Jobs said you were hurt in the skirmish last night."

"Just some bruises. I'm okay." When this is over, you have a date."

"Yes?"

"Yes," she smiled warmly.

CHAPTER 20

Mac parked his cruiser in the designated space for the Chief of Police. His shoulder felt sore, but overall he felt good. Glad he was alive! An unexpected sense of contentment suddenly filled his world after so many years of darkness.

He strolled into the police station and headed directly to the Public Service Office. "Have an appointment with Lex Kelly. Has he come in yet?"

"Gentleman's in the interview room, Sir." The Public Service Officer angled her chin toward the hallway leading to the room.

An elegantly dressed man was seated at the table. Mac reached out his hand, which was ignored. With a brief look at his snubbed hand and a bemused look at the person seated in front of him, he asked his visitor to follow him. He opened his office door and threw his keys on his desk.

"So you are the Kelly's long lost Uncle. I'll be damned. It's been a long time. You left in, let me see, 1975."

"My past life is of no concern to you, Chief Givens. I'm here to answer questions about my daughter's disappearance and murder."

"Can I get you anything before we begin?" Mac asked. He took a seat behind his desk and nodded to a chair across from him.

Kelly looked at the chair offered and sat, "No, I would just like to get on with this."

"Okay, Mr. Kelly. Can I call you, Lex?"

"Suppose I can't stop you."

"I'm sure this has been a difficult time for you. My sympathies for the loss of your daughter."

"Your condolences are appreciated."

Mac leaned back in his chair, picked up a pencil, and slowly flipped it through his fingers, while observing Lex. "Can you give me some details regarding your daughter's disappearance?"

"Like?"

"Any idea how she wound up in South Lake Tahoe?"

"I have no idea. My daughter did mention that she had a client who wanted some research done on some property in Lake Tahoe, but she didn't expand upon it."

"Did she tell you who this client was?"

"Emma said that she contacted them directly. She did not share the name of her client or any of the documentation with me.

"Is that normal?"

"Staff at Emma's level often bring in their clients and maintain the paperwork on prospective customers. They don't need to share all their sources with me. They have the autonomy to make decisions. I don't have the time to review everything everyone is doing.

"Any idea why she disappeared?"

"No, none. Emma just disappeared with no trace. No trace until now, that is."

"Did she have any enemies?"

"The police talked to her friends and staff in our Acquisition Department with no results. And no, I can't believe Emma would have had any enemies. Although she had a tough time in her youth, she turned her life completely around, and her career took on a positive track. Emma is my adopted daughter. When very young, she was abandoned by her foster family, wandered the streets huddling under bridges, slept in woods, beaches, or abandoned buildings, and forced into panhandling, theft, and prostitution to survive. My daughter felt being on the street was far better than the abuse she received from her foster parents. It was a tough life, but she was a survivor." Lex sat silent for a moment in thought. "I saw her sneak through a shopping mall with some clothes and shoes she had just stolen. I was shocked that she looked so much like someone else I knew."

"That would be Sara Kelly?"

Lex looked at Mac in momentary silence. "I wouldn't know. I've never met Sara Kelly."

"But she's your niece. Are you telling me you never met your niece?"

"I do not know Sara Kelly," he said with annoyance. Incensed, he continued. "Emma was young, dirty, tired, and hungry, so I offered to buy her a meal in a nearby coffee shop. I took her into my home and gave her the life she never knew. I eventually adopted her as my daughter. She flourished into a beautiful, intelligent, talented woman. After she finished school and worked a few jobs, she asked to work in my corporation. I gave her a job and over time she worked her way up into our Real Estate Acquisition Department. She excelled, and I'm proud to say that she gave much more than she received."

"That would be the Daniels Corporation?" Mac asked.

"Yes, that's right."

Mac tapped his pencil on the desk and watched Lex with curiosity. "I'm sorry, but I'm a bit confused. In an earlier conversation I had with Detective Davies of the NYPD, he said that Emma was not well-liked due to her lack of work ethics. He also noted that she was caught several times taking credit for work that others had done, and she often failed to pass on vital information. She sabotaged coworkers and bullied her peers. A description that doesn't jibe with what I'm hearing from you."

"Jealous people." Lex snapped. "Staff were resentful of her stature in the company. Jealous that she was my daughter, that one day she would take over the company. Pettiness. That's all that is," he said with resentment and bitterness.

Mac wondered if this man was holding something back. *Call it a hunch.* He thought as he continued. "There was another murder at the Givens Mansion last night. Can you tell me where you were at about 9:30 p.m.?"

"I was in bed at the motel, turned in early. Tony Russo can confirm that."

"You came to Tahoe with two gentlemen."

"I did. Joe Carver left early to get some dinner and gamble a bit. He must have had a good time because I haven't seen him since."

"And that doesn't bother you that your friend didn't show up this morning at the motel? Still hasn't shown up?"

"He's an adult," Lex said in an unfriendly tone.

"Do you have any more information you can provide that might help us?"

"I have no further information."

"Since you are the next of kin, we'll need you to go over to MacFarlane's Mortuary to make a positive ID. Here is the telephone number, if you need to contact them. We moved your daughter after the completion of the autopsy performed at the Sacramento Coroner's Office. Just go out to Highway 50, turn left and follow 50 to Emerald Bay Road. Street number 887. Have all this information written out for you." Mac said, handing Lex the piece of paper. "I expect you'll want to take your daughter back to New York?"

"As soon as we're finished here, my next stop is the morgue." Lex sat very still. "Emma has no family other than myself, and she's all I had. This whole situation, with my daughter, is devastating," he whispered.

"I'm truly sorry."

"I am going to have her cremated immediately," Lex said, composing himself as he sat up straight. "She'll be laid to rest at the Gates of Heaven Cemetery outside of New York. I'll let you know once I've finished making the arrangements."

"Sure thing,"

"I have a question," Lex said. Leaning his elbows on the desk, his hands forming a steeple as if ready to pray.

"OK."

"The Givens Mansion. That's your property."

"Yes, it is."

"My daughter was found in your closet. How did my daughter end up in your home, dead? Can you answer that question, for me, Chief Givens?"

"No, I can't, Lex, but I can assure you that I have asked myself the same question. This investigation is ongoing. But, let me reassure you, we will get to the bottom of this, and we will find the person who murdered your daughter."

Lex nodded, stood, and opened the door. He turned and faced Mac. "You have questions that need answers yourself. I hope *you* have reasonable answers, Chief Givens." Kelly quietly shut the door with no further comment.

Mac stared at the closed door. Understanding Kelly's comments, he still felt Lex was not straightforward with information. There was something, but Mac could not put his finger on it.

He also felt Lex was damn cold, but there was no doubt he was at a loss over his daughter's death.

***

After he wrapped up some minor police business, Mac leaned back in his worn brown office chair and grimaced from the movement of his injured shoulder. His thoughts settled on Jacqueline and their brief hospital visit. A tender smile formed at the corners of his lips. His thoughts then took a 180-degree turn to Lex. Mac's lips compressed, a deep furrow formed down the middle of his forehead.

After he reexamined the interview with Lex, Mac, once again, felt he was not telling everything he knew. The guy came across as just a little too slick. Without question, he had a chip on his shoulders. Mac looked up at the ceiling fan, which slowly circulated air around an otherwise stuffy office. What the hell had he missed?

He leaned back further and again flinched in discomfort. A puzzled look remained on Mac's face. Looking up at the spinning ceiling fan, he continued to ponder Lex's responses. Mac began to methodically focus on what he knew to be true regarding Lex's part of this case.

The Givens and Kelly families had always been close, sharing a set of great-great-grandparents and a common ancestor. Mac's mother had told him that Annie Kelly, Michael Kelly's wife, and the mother to Alex, Zed, Dustin, and Sara, had quadruplets, but three died in childbirth. Sara was the only surviving quadruplet. The doctor had told Annie and Michael that the three babies were stillborn and horribly malformed, so he felt it best for the parents not to see the babies for their peace of mind. Unlike today's closure concepts, those many years ago, it seemed to be a different story. Michael and Annie buried the three deceased infants in three small closed caskets. Mac could still remember in later years the worry his mother and father had for the grieved parents. Michael and Annie were devastated by the loss of the three babies, but with time, they were able to focus on their beautiful baby girl, Sara.

Lex had not been heard from since he sold his portion of the property to his brother, Michael, in 1975. He left no trace of his whereabouts until now.

There was no doubt that Emma Kelly was a carbon copy of Sara. What were the odds of two people, unrelated, being so similar? Lex's order, of what seemed like a quick cremation, did not make sense. Why would he hurry that process along unless he was trying to hide something? Would it be to bury information that pertained to Sara and Emma Kelly? Could the girls be identical twins? Unlikely, but how could Mac know if there was any truth to this theory?

Mac dialed Detective Mendoza. "David, do me a favor."

"Sure, Mac."

"Lex Kelly is going to have his daughter cremated. We need to get a DNA sample from her before this happens."

"Not a problem.

"I'm also going to ask Sara Kelly to see you. I need a DNA test, and I needed the results yesterday."

"You'll have to send her over to the Health Street Lab facilities. They provide the DNA lab tests for South Lake Tahoe."

"Fine, but can you have them rush it? It's urgent."

"It's always urgent, Mac," David said, chuckling. "I'll call and see if I can get you a time frame for the results. I'll ask them to rush it."

"One more thing." "Sure."

"I need to exhume the bodies of the three Kelly children who died at birth."

"Ah… okay, but you'll need a court order for issuing a special license that authorizes the exhumation. Also, you will need the consent of the family. Since the parents are no longer alive, it will need to be one of the Kelly kids, probably Alex, since he is the oldest."

"Okay. I will get that request to the courts today. I'll try and get Alex to consent this afternoon. How long do you think it will take?"

"Once we get the authorization, we can exhume the bodies the same day." "Good, I need the exhumations by tomorrow morning,"

"Got it."

"Thanks, David." Mac hit line two and punched in Alex's number. It took four rings for him to answer.

"Hey, Mac, how are you, bro?"

"Good, thanks. Alex, I need to talk with you. Can you come down to the station and meet me in about, say—," Mac checked his watch, "one hour?"

"Sure, but what's this about?"

"I would prefer to talk to you in person. See you in an hour." Mac disconnected and settled in his chair. He thought about Lex Kelly and the exhumation of three small caskets.

***

An hour later, Alex walked into the police station. He strolled up to the Public Services Office. "Have an appointment with the Chief. He's waiting for me."

"Sure thing Alex, he already let us know," Mable said as she buzzed Alex in.

He stuck his head through the Chief's open door and greeted Mac with a broad smile. "You have a bit more color in those cheeks."

Mac looked up from his desk, smiling, he motioned Alex in. "I'm much better."

"So, what's up?" he asked. He turned the chair, straddled his legs on each side, and focused his attention on Mac.

"Alex, I need to get your permission." "No problem, bro, you got it."

"I need your permission to open your three sisters' caskets." Alex stared at Mac. "Why?"

"I have a theory. Just a theory, mind you, but I need to get some confirmation. Sara and Emma Kelly are identical in their appearance. What are the odds?"

"It happens. You read about stuff like that all the time."

"I need to ask Sara to see the Health Street Lab facilities to get a DNA test. I've also requested Detective David Mendoza to get a DNA sample from Emma Kelly before she's cremated.

"God damn it! You can't do this." Alex whispered. "I will not permit you to exhume any casket. That would kill Sara."

"Alex, I have two dead bodies here. I have to follow all suspicions, and this is one of them."

"And just what the hell is this theory of yours, Mac?"

"I believe that Sara and Emma are twins. I also think that all of the quadruplets survived and that those three caskets are empty. Sara and Emma have two sisters, and I think one of them is out to kill the other two."

"The answer is NO!" Alex kicked the chair, opened the door, and slammed it on his way out.

CHAPTER 21

Jacqueline and Jeri spent the morning in the Tahoe library pouring over property records dating back to the 1800s. Jacqueline brought up Google. She searched government websites, then selected main.edcgov.us. From the directory listed, she chose 'Recorded Document Look-up', which presented a pop-up window. Though the internet was slow, like watching a badly dubbed foreign film, it was free, so she was not about to complain.

She typed in 'Thomas Kelly 1848' when asked for a record name and pressed submit. A simple list appeared. Thomas Kelly, Grantee: U.S. Government (a survey of the property noted those acres that were part of the U.S. encroachment project). The survey also indicated property lines that equaled four acres of prime land located on Lake Tahoe.

"Hmmm, that makes sense," murmured Jacqueline as she typed in the date 1860, which then listed Thomas Kelly, Jr, and Geoffrey Kelly, Grantee: Thomas Kelly.

"When did Alex say the mansion was built?"

"I think he said they started building in 1860 and finished in 1890."

I do not see anything here about building requirements or codes back then. It looks like you're right. They finished the mansion in 1890, so a tunnel could have easily been added without notations on the property records. But there is a notation here that describes four structures on the property. One built in 1827, that's the cabin we're staying in, two built in 1850, that's the first house they built before they finished the mansion, and one built in 1890, that's the mansion. It looks like a fourth structure was built where the Kellys' house now stands."

"Type in 1894," said Jeri.

"It notes the change of 1.2 acres here. George Givens, Grantee Thomas Kelly Jr. Then the rest of the property passes on to Michael and Lex, Alex's dad and uncle."

"Put in 1900 to the present date."

Jacqueline punched in the new dates. "Under new construction and improvements, the Kelly house was noted as being built in 1946. It looks like that fourth cabin built on that same portion of land in 1850 was demolished to build the new house. That would be Alex's house. There are no notations recorded by the planning commission for an underground extension or tunnel. Here are two records that show Lex Kelly granting the same two portions of the property to two different owners. One quitclaim deed gives full ownership to Michael, his brother. It looks like he signed over his half of the property. Then there is another quitclaim deed that grants the entire property to a Manny Bianchi/The Orbison Casino. That must be the issue that the Kellys' attorneys are trying to sort out."

"They look legit to me," Jeri said.

"Look up Manny Bianchi. What's his story?"

Jacqueline entered Manny's name. Immediately ten results appeared. Jacqueline selected obituaries from the list. An obituary page from the old Tahoe Sentinel appeared.

The sisters gazed at a large grainy black-and-white photo of an old semi-truck straddled over what appeared to be a twisted metal ball. The article stated it had once been a Porsche and that the owner, Manny Bianchi, was still incarcerated within the metal prison.

"Is that a finger? UGH!! I think that black stuff is blood. WOW!! Is that the top of his head?"

"Jesus, Jeri! Enough!" Jacqueline said, her face pale.

"Jacqueline?" Jeri said excitedly. "Look at the date of the accident." Jacqueline and Jeri stared at the screen.

"This guy Manny died on June 2, 1975, and the deed filed the same day." But this other deed was filed three days later by Michael Kelly. Lex Kelly and his brother signed both deeds. But

144

one deed gives 100% to Manny Bianchi, and the other gives 100% to Michael Kelly."

"I'm sure the attorneys are dealing with the same issues and these same questions. At least, for the sake of the Kellys, I hope they are." Jeri sat back and looked up at her sister. Now what?"

"Well, we didn't find anything about a tunnel, which leaves me very disappointed. I say we get our bathing suits on, grab our books, and relax by the lake. In short, let's start working on our vacation."

***

The dark tunnel felt like a labyrinth of an abandoned concrete passageway with decayed walls and unknown dangers. Nine feet high and eight feet wide, the tunnel was included in the original construction plans in 1860. Within the mansion was a closet located under the stairwell.

A hidden door located in the back of the closet could only open with a secret mechanism concealed in the back wall's upper left-hand side. When released, the passageway led to a stone staircase and down to a tunnel. The original purpose was to provide a hidden shelter, storage, and a wine cellar. It also offered a discreet way for lovers to meet and hastily exit, if necessary. Those lovers were Uncle Geoffrey and Mamie, who met often. The tunnel allowed them the opportunity to rendezvous in secret over the years.

Within the tunnel was a hidden room concealed by an invisible door, structured so that it appeared to be part of the tunnel wall. The naked eye could not detect the door.

The iron door was only large enough for one person to enter at a time. Once inside, the air was cold with a chill that seeped into one's bones. The walls shimmered with drops of moisture condensed on cool walls.

The foul smell of mildew and rat droppings permeated the air. No windows shed light into the room, which left a dark heavy feel interrupted by a small candle casting shadows against the walls.

Old wooden wine crates lined the far wall. A soiled mattress covered by dirty blankets lay near the crates on the floor. A single figure sat on the mattress, legs crossed, humming a tune while swaying back and forth. A lighted cigarette burned in an ashtray at her feet. A roll of duct tape, a pair of handcuffs, a large kitchen knife, and a gun laid next to the ashtray. A bottle of scotch with a small sip of the brown liquid left sat on the dirt floor.

The melody suddenly stopped. Silence.

"Goddamn it!" She shouted as she stood and threw the ashtray across the room. "Me, why didn't they keep me?" She wailed in frustration. "Why didn't he help me?" Nicole began to walk back and forth, beating her fists to her thighs. "I need to kill them, kill them all!" She suddenly stopped and stood very still. A single tear rolled down her cheek. "I need to kill them so that I can find peace… I need peace," she whispered. Silence.

Nicole sluggishly sat back down on the mattress and crossed her legs. She again began to hum the tune, which played in her head while she swayed back and forth. "I need to find peace. I need peace, peace…" She murmured as she shook her head.

A figure huddled in the opposite corner of the room. Duct tape, wrapped too tight, hurt her wrists while she felt her legs slowly grow numb from the tape wrapped around her ankles. It was becoming increasingly difficult to breathe with even more tape pressed tightly across her mouth, causing more swelling to her jaw. She watched the figure seated on the mattress from the shadows, eyes reflecting her revulsion. Hot tears flowed down her cheeks. Her name, Marian Procini. Her father, owner and CEO of the Procisions Empire.

CHAPTER 22

Jacqueline sat at the table in the front yard playing a card game of Golf with Jeri. The sun felt warm on her skin. She picked up a card and threw it on the discarded pile, and turned over one of the cards placed in front of her. "Damn, it's a queen. I'm going to lose this game for sure. Your skin is pink, just this side of red. You need some sunscreen on your shoulders and back."

Jeri moved the lotion across the table while she thought about the card she picked up from the deck. "Can you do me, Sis?"

"Sure." Jacqueline picked up the tube and walked behind Jeri. She squeezed the right amount of cream and began to rub the ointment into Jeri's shoulders and back. "You know, I've been thinking about that tunnel."

"Hmm—"

"I've heard about underground tunnels that were built. Some guy in Rossendale, Lancashire, built a tunnel under his house, and it developed into a huge sinkhole. His neighbors were majorly pissed."

"Yeah! I got a Joker! Ten points for me. I'm good. I'm so good."

"I read somewhere that people in the Hamptons build caves under their houses all the time. It's like the big thing if you have big bucks."

"It's your turn. What's your point?"

"My point is," Jacqueline said as she sat down and picked up a card, "why couldn't there be a tunnel. They are, like, all over the place, if you look up tunnels on Google. We need to find the answers. We already know the location if there is a passage. So, instead of sitting here getting burned, we should get dressed and check out the area. That road that turns towards the wooded area just west of the Kelly house is intriguing. Let's check out the people that live around here. Someone might know something."

Jeri picked up her last card and turned it over. "I won." She threw her cards on the table.

"Sure, okay, let's check it out."

Dressed, with windbreakers in hand, they walked out to the street, turned right, and strolled past the mansion. They glimpsed a small park just beyond where people meandered as they took in the lake, its beauty, and played Frisbee with their dogs. Kids laughed with delight as parents pushed them on swings while other children played on the jungle gym bars. The sky was blue with scattered clouds that covered treetops, creating a canopy of illusion over the girl's heads. A gentle breeze created the sound of rustling leaves. In the distance, they saw the road Jacqueline mentioned to their left. They turned and followed the path. Pine needles and other flora formed a springy carpet to walk on. Jacqueline watched a single sparrow flutter high above the trees while a few feet away, an eager chipmunk darted from tree to tree. They admired the beauty of the woods surrounding them, the smell pure and clean, in a forest that appeared to be undisturbed.

The sun dimmed as the woods thickened. They hiked about a mile before they saw a house. It was evident that the structure was well cared for. A light blue picket fence surrounded a lovely yard. Flowers and flower pots filled with colorful dream red petunias, geraniums, and penny blue pansies accented the path that led to the front porch.

They walked along the fence and noticed a figure bent over tending marigolds that bordered the fence line. An older woman, who appeared to be in her early eighties, stood and looked at the girls.

"Well, hello," she said. Her smile was warm, her eyes pure and honest, a kind soul shining through them.

Jacqueline stopped. "Hi!" she said, looking around. The area looked like a wilderness. Trees grew thick and tall. Some trees large enough to shade some afternoon sun. "You have a lovely garden."

"Why, thank you, dear. I work out here every day. It's my exercise and mental therapy all rolled into one. I do love my garden."

Jacqueline glanced up at the sky. A medley of cumulus clouds that looked like cotton-balls gave the sky the appearance of a light blue fabric "Little bit cloudy."

"Best time to garden," the old woman quipped. "Watch the fruits of our efforts unfold."

"What's that, Edna?" A taller yet younger version of Edna stood up. "You want me to dig up the marigolds? Why would I want to do such a foolish thing?"

Edna sighed. "My sister. She's as confused as a fart in a fan factory." "I said we like to watch our efforts unfold." She yelled.

"Well, love, you don't have to shout. I am right here. Oh, how nice, visitors, I'm Gracie, don't mind my sister," she said as she removed her garden gloves and joined the group by the fence.

Jeri nearly choked, trying to stifle a giggle while Jacqueline gave her a knock-it-off look.

Jeri reached out to shake hands. "Pleased to meet you. I'm Jeri Winters, and this is my sister Jacqueline Renee."

"Edna Banks and Gracie Clairborn. Nice to meet you both. I don't recognize either of you. You just up here for a vacation?"

"Yes," Jacqueline said. "We're staying at the Kelly cabin on Lakeview Lane."

"Well, yes, of course. We heard two young ladies were staying there. Aren't you two just as pretty as a bucket of peaches."

"You know the Kellys?"

"Cousins, my dear—"

"— first cousins twice removed with the Kellys and third cousins twice removed with the Givens clan," Edna said. "We moved here seventy-five years ago. We came up from Mississippi to be close to our family. Only family we got."

"I had no idea that Mac, Alex, and their families were related," Jeri said.

"Close as two coats of paint. Ancestor lines go back to the 1800s. Oh!" Edna said as she remembered something important and elbowed Gracie. "Gracie, this is Jacqueline Renee."

"What's gotten into you? Why do I need to pray, for heaven's sake?"

"Not pray," Edna shouted. "Renee, you know 'the' Jacqueline Renee."

Gracie's face lit up as if she finally understood a difficult math problem. "Oh—!"

"—Yes!" Edna replied, shaking her head up and down. Both sisters turned, stood arm and arm, and looked at the other sisters with a mischievous smile.

Confused Jacqueline, and Jeri gazed at each other.

"Edna, don't just stand there, invite these girls in for a cup of tea," Gracie said, as she took Jacqueline's arm and Edna took Jeri's. Together they walked up the path to the cabin, chatting and admiring the gardens. Inside, the bungalow was small but cozy. They settled in a sunroom just off the kitchen.

"This is our keeping room," Gracie said.

"What's a keeping room?" Jacqueline said with a laugh.

"It's the place where I 'keep' my sister out of the way while I cook," Gracie said as she put a tea kettle on the stove.

"So, how do you know my sister and me?" Jacqueline asked.

"My daughter, Mabel. Mabel Clairborn. She works at the Police Department. She's the Public Service Officer." Gracie said with pride. You see her when you first walk into the station. Everyone knows who you are. You and your sister found that body in the Givens mansion. That poor girl. How awful that you had to go through such a harrowing experience. And that poor man they found shot in the same place the very next day."

"It was difficult, that is for sure." Thoughtful for a moment, Jacqueline asked, "Edna, may I ask you a question?"

"Certainly, dear."

"Have you ever heard of a secret passage under the Givens or Kelly homes, or a possible tunnel connected to the cabin we're staying in?" She watched Gracie place the teapot and four beautiful English teacups on the table then pour steaming hot lavender tea in each cup.

"What was the question?" Gracie asked.

"They want to know if there is a secret passage connecting Mac's and Alex's houses or a tunnel under the cabin. You know, there have always been rumors, but I can't say there is any truth to the stories," Edna said.

"I remember when Lex Kelly was about eight years old, he began to have nightmares about a tunnel. It had his mother, Mary, quite worried." Gracie said thoughtfully, sipping her tea then placing her cup gently on the saucer. "She was such a pretty thing. Wild as a June bug on a string. She was our father's first cousin. The reason why we moved here was her. But that son of hers. Well, all I can say is if brains were dynamite, he couldn't blow his nose."

"Do you think he might have found the tunnel?" Jeri asked.

"Don't know, Honey. There was something that scared that child. That's for sure."

"Have you seen anything suspicious? Cars or people roaming around here you haven't seen before?" Jeri asked.

"Other than you two, I haven't noticed anyone around here lately. Of course, we do have the occasional tourists, like yourselves, who walk by but no one who has set off alarms." Edna said.

"Not to change the subject," Gracie said as she leaned toward Jacqueline, "but my Mabel says there is one Police Chief in this town who happens to be smitten by you, although he did hint that you're a bit high spirited and somewhat excitable. Even so, she says he is always worried about your whereabouts. What with these murders and you girls all by yourselves in that cabin."

Jacqueline couldn't help smiling as she listened and gave Jeri a questionable look.

"Yes, our Mac has been sad for all these years after losing his wife. They were as happy as clams at high tide. Her passing hit him hard, but it's been too many years. It's time for him to start livin' again."

Jacqueline blushed as she glanced at her watch and stood. "It's getting late. We need to get back. I'm sure Mac will find the right person someday. It's wonderful that he has you two."

"This has been such a wonderful visit," Jeri said. "I hope that we see you again and soon. And thank you so much for the tea."

"Our pleasure. Now, don't you forget us. Our home is always open to you." Gracie said as she kissed both sisters on the cheek and walked them to the door.

"They are wonderful," Jacqueline said, walking with Jeri back to the cabin. "Are we looking at wedding bells and happily ever after?" Jeri chided.

"He thinks I'm high spirited and excitable. Interesting."

CHAPTER 23

At 3:00 p.m., Mac drove his squad car into the police station parking lot and headed for the front door. A group of newspaper reporters were waiting and quickly surrounded him.

"Chief, can you give us any information on the murders?"

"Sorry, it's an open investigation."

"Got any suspects?"

"No suspects."

"What about the names of the two murder victims. Know anything about them? Come on, Chief, give us something."

"Once families of all the victims have been notified, we will release the names. Until then, we have to respect their privacy. Trust me when I say, we're working hard on breaking these cases."

"Chief, both murders occurred in that old mansion on the lake. That old mansion happens to be owned by your family. Fluke? Twist of fate? Care to comment?"

Mac ignored the question and entered the station. "Officer Clairborn, there are some reporters outside. Do me a favor and give the gentlemen the information sheets we prepared for the news media."

"Sure thing, Chief."

He headed to Ricks' Office, knocked on the door, and stepped in. Ricks tossed a basketball into a hoop located above the door across from his desk, just missing Mac.

"You need to move that damn hoop," Mac said, as he ducked, placed his hat on the desk, and eased himself into the nearest chair.

Styker strolled in, closing the door behind him. "Afternoon, Chief."

"Styker."

"Hey Chief, still on that road to matrimony?" Ricks teased as he threw and aced another basket.

"If I could interrupt you for just one moment, Ricks?"

"Just wondering about that tux I need to save for if I'm going to be the best man." He said, tossing the basketball to Mac. "And I am assuming I will be that best man."

Mac caught the ball. "Not to change the subject, but we do have two dead bodies and some issues needing attention here. Focus Ricks," Mac said, tossing the ball back to him. "And you will be the best man."

Ricks threw another ringer, smiled, sighed, and turned his attention to Mac and Styker.

"We do not know how or if these murders are connected," Mac began. "Because both bodies were found in the mansion; we must assume a connection in some way. We have Emma Kelly, who was abducted three weeks ago and showed up dead. What we do know is that she is a lookalike of Sara. She was adopted by Lex Kelly, who found her wandering at the young age of seventeen. Quite a coincidence, I would say. What we don't know is how she got from New York to Lake Tahoe. We've checked the airlines, trains, buses, and car rentals. Nothing found, but we're still checking. We don't know who killed her or where the murder weapon is. We also know she was murdered somewhere else and brought to that closet. We've found hair fibers from both an unknown person, probably the murderer, and the victim. One hair fiber red and the second fiber black. Tests show the darker hair fibers were due to hair dye and that the original hair color was red. I also found some fine dust from a crack in the closet wall."

"Any significance with that dust?" asked Ricks.

"Not that I can see. Could mean nothing, but the dirt is still being analyzed," said Mac. "How about the autopsy reports from Detective Mendoza?"

Styker opened his folder. "The wound on Ms. Kelly was located in the back. She had multiple stab wounds. Doc says the murder weapon was a kitchen knife. The depth of penetration was four and five inches. The knife wounds were fatal. The time of death was around 11:30 a.m. give or take a half-hour. She had black dirt under her fingernails. We found a strand of black hair in her fist, which matched the strand found in the closet. The decedent had a purple birthmark on the upper left thigh, scar tissue, possibly an old incision across the stomach cavity, and two small tattoos on the left heel. That's it." he said, closing the folder.

"We have an ID on our John Doe." Ricks broke in. "Names Joe Carver. He worked for the Daniels Corporation back in New York. Found some interesting stuff here." Ricks said as he continued to check his notes. "Turns out he worked for Lex Kelly, so he probably knew Emma Kelly. Joe Carver, as well as a Tony Rosso, accompanied Lex Kelly to Lake Tahoe yesterday, and they are staying at the Lazy S Lodge out on Highway 89."

"So, it's a pretty safe conclusion that our three visitors at the murder scene last night were Carver, Russo, and Kelly."

"I would not say that's a safe conclusion," Mac said thoughtfully. "I interviewed Lex this morning and asked where he and his friends were last night. Said he turned in early and that Tony Russo can confirm his alibi."

"What about this, Joe Carver?" Styker asked.

"Said that Carver went out on the town. To gamble a little, get a bite to eat, but he never returned to the motel. When Carver didn't show up, he figured he was out having an extended night of fun."

"You believe his story?" asked Ricks.

"There were three people in that room. Carver got shot, so who were the other two?" "No, our Mr. Kelly is not telling us the truth. But why?"

Styker spoke up. "We know that Emma Kelly was stabbed and that Carver was shot. Neither murder weapon has surfaced. We know one of the intruders was a woman and that she was the alleged murderer of Joe Carver. But we have no idea who she is, nor do we have a motive."

"Jacqueline Renee said she heard voices arguing and a muted scream that seemed to come from the cabin the morning she arrived. About 11:30. She also said she thought she saw someone, a shadow behind a tree in the backyard. I took a look, and there is a footprint."

"Anything from forensics?" asked Ricks.

"Shoe size six and a half, female, weight probably between 100 to 110 pounds based on the print depth. I heard a woman's voice before the shooting last night. Could that female intruder and the owner of that footprint be the same? That's all we have so far." Mac hesitated. "I see no connection between the murders, kidnappings, and Jeri and Jacqueline? So why are Jeri and Jacqueline being stalked and by whom?"

"We have another possible piece of this puzzle which just occurred," Ricks continued. "A recent APB crossed the wire. A woman was abducted this morning in Sacramento. The reason the regular 24-hour wait was waived is that the woman is the daughter of billionaire Jerome Procini, the owner and CEO of the Procisions Financial Empire. She too is a spot-on identical to both Sara and Emma Kelly."

"Find out what you can on this missing woman out of Sacramento. What was her name?"

Checking his notes Ricks, spoke up. "Marian Procini."

"Right, keep on that one," Mac said thoughtfully tapping his chin. "Had a meeting with Alex this morning. I told him I had a theory and wanted to have Sara do a DNA test. Let him know we obtained DNA from Emma Kelly before her father had her cremated. My theory is they might be twins. Which opens up a whole new can of worms."

"Like?" asked Styker.

"Like, if she is Sara's twin, who is buried in those three Kelly baby caskets in the cemetery? I asked his permission to exhume the bodies. His reply was an emphatic, No!"

"Why would he say no?" Styker asked, confused.

"Have no idea."

"What do we do now?"

"I'm going to go directly to Sara and ask her to take that DNA test. I'll take this form along, just in case, but I feel we'll need to put a hold on the exhumations, for the moment."

***

Mac parked in the Kelly driveway, walked up the steps to the front door, and rang the bell.

Sara answered. "Hey buddy, come on in. Alex is out back."

"I didn't come here to see Alex, Sara. I came here to ask you a question."

"Oh? Well, come in and ask away," she said as she pulled Mac into the living room. Sara snuggled into a large Lazy-boy chair, while Mac settled on the edge of the couch.

He twisted his hat in his hands as he stared at the floor. He flexed the fingers of his left hand, then twirled his hat a few more times. He finally looked up at Sara with his question.

"I'm working a hunch, Sara. I came here to ask you to take a DNA test. I've already asked Detective Mendoza to get a DNA sample from Emma Kelly."

"Why? What's this all about, Mac?"

"I believe that Emma Kelly might be your sister."

"That's not possible. My sisters are buried in the cemetery."

"I understand, but you and Emma are identical, and it wouldn't hurt to rule out that possibility. I have a murder here and need to check out all possible theories."

Sara sat, looking into Mac's eyes. "Hypothetically, and I do mean hypothetically, what if this Emma Kelly were my sister. What does that say about my buried sisters?"

"Enough," Alex interrupted. "What the hell are you doing here, Mac? I told you, No!"

"You told him no to what question, Alex?"

"To the exhumation of our sisters' caskets."

Sara turned from her brother to Mac. "You need to tell me what's going on, and Alex, you are not to interrupt. This situation isn't about you now, Alex. It's about me. Mac?"

"I think that there is a strong possibility that you may be the killer's next victim, Sara. I believe there is a strong possibility that Emma Kelly, maybe your sister. There is another woman who has been kidnapped, but we have no idea where she is at this time. She also could be your sister. I asked Alex to give me permission to exhume the caskets. That's the only way we can be sure."

"Sure of what, Mac?"

"That your sisters were alive and not buried in those three caskets.

"And I said, no!"

"This isn't your decision Alex," Sara said softly, taking her brother's hand. "If there is a chance that my sisters are alive and not buried in that cemetery, I have the right to know."

"There is one more piece of information I need, Sara."

"And that is?"

"I need to ask one of your brothers to take a DNA test."

"Whatever for?"

"If these two women are your sisters, I need to confirm your biological mother and father."

"Good God," Sara said as she massaged her forehead, trying to calm the beginning of a headache. She stood in the middle of the living room, which was silent but for the tick-tock-tick of the grandfather clock. Turning to Mac, she said, "Tell me what I need to do. Alex, will you take the test?"

"Absolutely not, this is ridiculous."

"I'll ask Dustin. I know he'll do it for me."

"And Alex, sign that permission to exhume the caskets. If you don't, then I will."

Mac took the permission form from his breast pocket and gave it to a very shaken and pale Alex.

CHAPTER 24

Nicole couldn't sleep. The dank underground room was beginning to depress her. She was having trouble thinking. *How can anyone think in this shit hole?* Her mind raced over options to get rid of those snoopy sisters. *Run them down in a car? No . . . someone might recognize her. Besides, she tried that with Marian, and the bitch is still here. Shoot them.* Nicole sighed, *too many cops hanging around. Burn the cabin down?* She lifted the bottle of vodka and took a healthy swallow. *Hmmm . . . that's a thought.* She looked at her watch. *Two-thirty. Well? Why not. It's late. No one's around. I can get in and out without being seen. By morning those sisters will be charred. Gone!*

A little shaky, she stood, steadied herself, walked to the door, and slipped out. She stopped. "Where's my friggin' mind?" She crept back into the room and grabbed matches, a newspaper, and a flashlight, then once again entered the tunnel.

"Damn, can't believe I keep leaving stuff!" She re-entered the room for a second time, scooped up the half-empty bottle of vodka, took a sip, put the cap on the bottle then walked back to the tunnel heading toward the stairs.

Breathing in the fresh night air, Nicole stooped and gathered brushwood and several more substantial pieces of wood as she moved toward the cabin. She hurried through the pine trees. It was shady, dark, and cool, almost cold. Coming to the end of the trees, she saw the lake. The air felt warmer; the sound of insects was almost too loud. The lake seemed a black void without the sun dancing off the surface. She approached the cabin, stopped at the front door, looked around, and saw a pair of raccoon eyes examine her before it darted off. She tried the door but knew it would be locked. Unloading her burden, she pulled her driver's license from her pocket. She inserted the plastic card parallel to the doorknob, hit it hard, thrust it down, and pushed the door open. She stood still. No sound. She stepped down the steps and picked up the twigs, wood, paper, and matches.

Balled up paper was placed on the floor. Damp kindling, from the chilly night air, laid on top. A match burned, and the paper caught fire. More sticks of wood were added. The fire briefly flared, then smoldered.

"Damn."

Nicole lit a second match and again held it to the paper. The flame flickered, then caught and burned. After watching the fire catch-hold for a moment, Nicole laid a larger piece of wood on the flames; and then stuffed more paper into the fire. Smoke began to fill the glassed-in porch. She reached over and opened the door leading into the cabin. Smoke drifted into the dining room.

Finished, Nicole ran down the porch stairs, picked up her bottle of vodka, and headed to the lake. She stepped into the lake and shivered; the water was cold. She ran toward the mansion, tripped, fell, and looked back. The fire had caught the curtains on the porch and flared. Wet but elated and electrified, Nicole laughed, slipped into the house, bounced up the stairs, two at a time, to the second floor. She opened the window and stooped down to watch the show. She opened the vodka and took a mouthful, feeling the heat travel down to her stomach.

The relaxing rhythm of gentle rolling waves from the lakeshore and the sound of crackling firewood could be heard. Bright orange flames lit the night.

***

Jacqueline dreamed she was reading a good novel sitting next to a crackling fire. Lamps lit, as it was dark outside. Suddenly loud popping, snapping sounds occurred that scared her.

The cozy fire became a threat; the fireplace exploded. She woke alarmed that something wasn't right. Dream fading, she smelled smoke and jumped out of bed. She grabbed her cell phone and dialed 911 while running to Jeri's room.

"Jeri, Jeri, get up. There's a fire. We need to get out of the cabin!" Jacqueline shook Jeri hard.

Jeri mumbled. "What's up? What's the problem? Leave me alone, go back to bed."

"Jeri, the cabin's on fire! We need to get out of here, now!"

Jeri turned, smelled smoke, and immediately understood. She leaped out of bed and, with her sister, ran into the dining room.

Jacqueline saw the fire first, ran back into her bedroom, grabbed a blanket, and darted back to the front porch as the burned curtains fell to the floor. Jacqueline threw the blanket over the smoldering curtains and fire suffocating the flames.

Jeri came from behind and poured liquid on top of the blanket.

"Seriously, Jeri, milk?"

"That's all I could find. What? It's wet."

They went out the back door to meet the firemen after hearing fire engines with their sirens blaring.

***

The fire was out; the firemen were pulling in their hoses. Mac and Ricks were standing on the glassed-in porch examining the ashes with the Fire Chief.

"Women did a good job putting this fire out." The Fire Chief said to Mac. "They stopped the fire from entering through the ceiling, which minimized smoke damage and loss. Porch will need a new floor, those damaged walls will need to be replaced, and new curtains will be needed, but quick thinking saved the day. My question is, who would set a fire in this glassed porch?"

"Who would set a fire on this glassed porch at 3:00 in the morning?" Mac asked. "This was no accident. It was a blatant attempt to destroy the cabin and do harm to Jeri and Jacqueline. But why? Why would someone want to hurt these two? I don't get it."

"Whoever it was, ran down to the lake. The footprints disappeared in the water." Ricks said.

Mac and Ricks walked down to the lake.

Mac knelt and examined a footprint that was not washed away by the waves. He looked left and right. "No way of knowing which way the intruder went. This footprint is small—, the same size as our shadow friend behind the tree. Will have a definite confirmation on that once forensics gets finished with their analysis." He stood up.

"Ricks . . . Jacqueline and Jeri are either a target or the unluckiest two I've ever met." Mac stared at Ricks for a moment, then turned and walked back to the house. Alex and Sara joined him.

"Mac, what on earth is going on? We smelled the smoke and heard the fire engines."

"Someone set fire to the cabin."

"Oh my God, are Jeri and Jacqueline okay?" Sara cried.

"Yes, they're fine. The cabin has a small amount of damage here on the porch."

"Do you know how the fire started?"

"Looks like someone set the fire with paper and wood. Burned the curtains, and the floor and walls will have to be replaced." Mac said. He directed both Alex and Sara into the cabin and joined Jeri and Jacqueline in the living room.

"Mac, why would anyone want to harm Jacqueline and Jeri?" Sara asked. She turned to Jacqueline. "Do you have any idea who would want to hurt you?"

"No . . . none." Jacqueline murmured. "None."

"Me either," Jeri whispered as Alex took her hand.

"Mac, I'm terrified. First, someone is watching us, and now this fire. Could this have something to do with the murders?" Jacqueline asked.

"I can't see how. Tell you the truth; I don't know at this point, Jacqueline. But I will have a squad car assigned to watch the cabin for the next twenty-four hours."

***

Nicole watched her show with great remorse. Remorse that these two somehow avoided death.

DAY FOUR...

Thunder draws lightning into the skies
A history of so many hidden lies
Born again but not as a vision
So many paths; so many divisions

CHAPTER 25

After a fitful sleep, Jeri woke to threatening dark skies, the roll of distant thunder, and the smell of rain. She threw on PrAna yoga pants, flip-flops, and a cream-colored tank top and headed for Starbucks.

After she ordered two Venti Americanos and two cheese Danish, she returned to the cabin. She walked into the kitchen, trying to ignore the burnt aroma coming from the front porch, just as Jacqueline was coming to life in her bedroom.

"Coffee's on," Jeri yelled loud enough for Jacqueline to hear.

Jacqueline strolled into the kitchen, looked at Jeri's outfit, and laughed. Both sisters wore PrAna yoga pants, flip-flops, and cream-colored tank tops.

"Brilliant minds!" Jacqueline said with a thumbs-up sign. She wrinkled her nose. "Whew, that smell. Let's go sit in the gazebo. Maybe returning to the scene of the murder or, in this case, 'murders' will get our thoughts and juices flowing. Possibly provide us a clue about last night?"

"Not sure Mac would appreciate our being on his property uninvited."

"I honestly don't think Mac will mind. He doesn't seem quite the jerk I thought, given past experiences with other jerks." Jacqueline said with a wink. "Anyway, we're merely having a cup of coffee, and it's so nice and quiet there. We should open some windows and let the cabin air out while we're gone. Come on."

"Okay," Jeri said, opening the kitchen window.

They took a shortcut along a dirt path between the mansion and the cabin to the gazebo. Jeri noticed a police car parked in the street.

The gazebo looked much different in the morning light, a beautiful memory of its former life. What once, in past years, were lush gardens were now overgrown with weeds. The grounds still showed a touch of their former beauty with a combination of pink and purple flowers surrounding the amber wood structure. Old lighting fixtures livened up evening hours with flickering candles in past times. Surrounded by tall trees, the gazebo seemed more like a sanctuary, still a hidden gem. Monarch butterflies fluttered about, giving the garden an enchanting feel.

They settled in two old wicker chairs.

"Yum, *this* is good," Jacqueline sighed with the first bite of her Danish. The sisters settled back to enjoy the gazebo and its quiet gardens. A good nights sleep had helped to dim the events of the previous evening. They chatted about the recent unsettling incidents while they watched dark clouds gather.

***

Sitting across from Ricks and Styker in his office, Mac stifled a yawn. He wasn't able to get a lot of sleep. The fire was troubling him, and he worried about Jacqueline and Jeri and their safety. He tasted his hot, very strong coffee and thought of the old adage, "There is no such thing as coffee that is too strong, only people that are too weak." His thoughts briefly took a turn to Lex Kelly. Mac refocused on the two men seated across from him.

"Anything from forensics on the footprint we found last night?" Ricks asked.

"Said it was a match to the footprint we found earlier behind the tree. We know that someone is behind stalking Jacqueline and Jeri. What we don't know is why?"

Mac leaned back in his chair. "I got a call from the Sheriff's office. Detective Mendoza."

"And?" Ricks and Stryker said in unison.

"They exhumed the caskets this morning, and they *are* empty."

"Jesus, so what does this mean for us?" asked Styker shifting in his seat.

Mac stared at the two Officers. "It means," he said in frustration, "a lot of heartache for some folks. I asked Detective Mendoza to coordinate securing DNA tests for both Sara and Dustin. It turns out that Dustin is directly related to his Dad, Michael, but Sara's DNA does not match. I want to do a DNA test on Lex, but we have not been able to contact him at this point. Have an APB out on him."

"Why on Lex?"

"Just a hunch," Mac said thoughtfully. "Lex sees a seventeen-year-old wandering the streets, takes her in, and provides parental care because she looks like someone he knows. Could be innocent, but—? I'm just trying to eliminate possibilities with validation."

"Mac, since Sara's father is deceased, how can we know, for sure, if she's a match or not to Michael Kelly's DNA?" Ricks asked.

"We were able to secure the biological remains of Michael Kelly, which were obtained from the hospital where there were still both biopsy and blood donation samples available. Through this approach, we were able to establish Dustin's paternity, but this same approach denied Sara's paternity. Once we locate Lex Kelly, we will, hopefully, have the answers to our questions.

"Does Sara know?" Styker asked.

"No, and neither do her siblings," Mac said as he tapped his pencil on his desk.

"Two brothers have unique DNA profiles though there are still some similarities. In Sara's case, she has 12.5% of the genes of Michael Kelly, implying, inversely, that 87.5% of her genes are different. Lex's paternity test must have all fifteen markers and match 100% to confirm he is the father. If this is confirmed, then he is indeed the father of the quadruplets."

"That's a big leap, Mac," said Stryker.

"Maybe, maybe not," Mac said, setting his coffee cup on the desk, "but I'll bet my next paycheck those tests confirm that our Lex Kelly is the father."

***

The morning sun peeked through some dark clouds offering a touch of warmth as Jeri and Jacqueline sat and enjoyed their coffee and Danish on the gazebo.

"Said it before, and I'll repeat it, this Danish is awesome."

"It is," Jeri smiled, brushing crumbs off her chin and PrAnas. "I hope Mac gets some traction on who's behind the fire. With these unsolved murders, a stalker and now the fire—."

"—don't get yourself worked up. Mac will solve the murders; find the stalker, and discover who set that fire. I have faith in him. You should too."

"Is that right, big sister," Jeri said with a smirk. She sat looking off into the woods for a moment. "A question that comes to mind is who owns the Kelly property? Is it Alex, Sara, and their brothers, Uncle Lex, or the owners of that Casino? Pretty bizarre. I hope they have a good lawyer."

"I know it's awful." Jacqueline chimed in, "Then there is the question of Emma Kelly and Sara looking so much alike. I mean, what are the odds that someone looks exactly like you?"

"Plus, let's not forget the murder of Emma. There has to be a connection somewhere. "Both sisters were silent.

A slight scraping noise floated in the background, almost unnoticeable. Jacqueline briefly looked around, then turned her attention back to Jeri as her phone rang.

"Alex," Jeri answered, "Hi! What a nice surprise." Jeri listened. "That would be great! We would love to come for dinner." Jeri said, giving Jacqueline a high five. "Four-thirty will be perfect. We'll see you then." Jeri disconnected the phone call. She heard a scraping noise, stopped, and listened. Shaking her head, she turned her attention back to Jacqueline. "Alex asked us to dinner. It will be fun to see them. I like that Kelly clan."

"Are you interested in Alex, Jeri?"

"Sure, but not in the way, I think, you're thinking. Eventually, I might want to get involved with someone, but unlike you, I think I need to take it easy. Go slow."

"Unlike me?"

"Jacqueline, you have not been married since you were a teenager."

"I divorced just before my twenty-first birthday."

"But you married when you were a kid. You have no clue what a romantic commitment is, what feelings are. You jump in and out of relationships like a scared rabbit chased by its worst enemy or nightmare. Whereas, I had children, a home, a life I built with a man I loved even though it all turned lousy. When I said I needed some space to find myself, I meant it. I am not closing that door, but right at this moment, it makes more sense to enjoy my freedom and enjoy a nice guy. I don't need anything more than that now. But Jacqueline, listen to me. This Mac is a great person, and I think he has a thing for you. And I think you have a thing for him. Let it happen, Sis. WHAT?" Jeri turned around and shrieked in frustration. "What the hell is that noise?"

They both sat in silence, waiting for the noise to reoccur.

"Everything seems quiet," said Jacqueline. "Another example of our active imaginations?"

"Except, we both heard it."

They sat still for several seconds.

"Listen, Jeri. I hear what you're saying. Sounds crazy, but I know there is something, it's there, and you know? I think I'm glad it's there. It's exciting, it catches my breath, and it's this free feeling. I can't explain it. On the one hand, I would like nothing better than to walk away. I have this internal struggle, which is more of a safety mechanism to prevent emotional damage. I'm scared of getting hurt and I'm afraid of possible pain, On the other hand, I'm more afraid of letting something pass by without knowing what that road promises. Just hold my hand Sis, I think I'm ready to take a chance and fly."

"Oh, my God. Do I hear this, right?" Jeri smiled. "I'm there for you, Sis. Just remember, not all paths leading to romance are like quicksand."

"Nice analogy," Jacqueline laughed. They stood and walked back to the cabin, chatting, arm in arm.

***

Nicole quietly listened as the sisters left the gazebo.

Close call, she thought, as she stood up from her crouched position. I need to be more careful in the future. Can't blow it now. As she peeked through a hole in the gazebo sideboards to ensure the intruders departed, she thought of Tony's promise to her.

"Nicole, it all will be ours someday. They will pay for what they did to you."

She slid down the dirt tunnel wall and sat in darkness. Ignoring the stench of the tunnel, she stayed, thinking of Tony Russo and Emma Kelly.

CHAPTER 26

Nicole met Tony in 2015, working on the streets on a hot August night in Reno, Nevada. Since the day she was born, life handed her lemons. She tried to make lemonade, but it never quite tasted right, never quite worked. When she was young, she would watch women with glamorous hair and sparkling dresses walk the street in front of her foster parents' home. She envied their glamour and dreamed of the day she would become one of them.

At the age of fifteen, she dressed in the most seductive clothes she could find in her closet. A tight two-piece dress that barely covered her upper thighs. Cost, $2.85 at a local Goodwill store. She wore cheap black plastic shoes and bright red lipstick, which she hoped would make her look older. She snuck out of the house and stood with those glamorous women on the corner of Sixteenth and Browning Streets. She tried not to cry when he took her. Her eyes focused on a stain on the ceiling of the car. She felt her spirit leave her body to become one with that stain. She made $130 that night. Eventually, she made $1,200 a week.

She tried to work in a few brothels but found them to be confining. Even when Nicole wasn't on the clock, she was not allowed to leave. She returned to work independently on the streets, where she continued to learn by the hard knocks of her life, learned to feel comfortable lying to get out of trouble, and embellish the truth when it suited her. She had a cruel disregard for everyone around her and felt little concern for her safety in ruthless situations. It was in that place and time she met Tony. It was on Fourth Street, called "the track" by Reno locals.

A sleek black Cadillac Escalade slowly turned the corner and stopped. Several girls approached the car but stepped back, giving the driver the finger with words exchanged. The Escalade slowly rolled forward, where Nicole stood and stopped. The window slid down, and the driver motioned her closer. She stepped to the side of the car. He spoke a few words, she opened the door, got in, and they sped off.

She had been with Tony for four years. They had waited patiently and planned.

Slowly she removed her cell phone and punched in Tony's number. He answered on the third ring.

"What do you want, Nicole? I'm busy here."

"I'm lonely, Tony, really lonely."

"Jesus. Nicole, would you get your shit together. I am up to my ass in alligators here, and what I don't need is a call from you crying about your fucking loneliness! Is everything ok, no problems with the hostage?"

"No, everything is fine. I just love you, Tony." The words came easily, but were not heartfelt.

"I'll be there soon. Just get a grip and take care of things until I get there." He uttered before disconnecting the line.

***

Tony looked at his cell phone with disgust. He wondered, not for the first time, why he got involved with this nightmare. Nicole was becoming a whining liability.

He often paid for high-priced prostitutes. With his stature and money, he was used to getting extra service for those extra dollars. If he liked a girl and they had a great time, he would drop an extra ten grand on her. Who cares? It did not change his life. Street prostitutes were a completely different world. The law exposed you to extreme vulnerability, which is why he saw it as a challenge, a dare, and excitement. He knew the rules. Stash all valuables, be cautious of a hooker who looks too damn good, do not call attention to yourself, and get the hell out of the neighborhood. He was up to the challenge because he could do whatever he wanted, even slapping the whore around. Again, who cares? She won't go to the police, and it helped to relieve his stress.

He turned the corner that night with no specific hooker in mind. The first two were losers. He had dealt with them before. Then he saw Nicole. She was an identical twin to Emma Kelly. Damn, he thought, she could be Emma. Tall, slender, a tight skirt, faux fur vest, and knee-high boots. Red hair piled on top of her head with small waves like a nest wrapped around tilting slightly to the side, loose wisps of hair floating around her face. She was beautiful, yet a hard life had left marks of age. He knew he had found another one of Lex's daughters.

He knew this because one night, years back, a very drunk and uncommonly talkative Lex Kelly shared the secret he had held for so many years. He had raped his brother's wife.

One night, in a drunken stupor, he had stumbled into the Kelly lakefront home and found his brother's wife alone. His lust became unbearable. He dragged her screaming into the bedroom where he brutally raped her.

Afterward, frightened and beaten, she cowered in the corner of the room. Lex looked at her in disgust. "Shut up, you tramp!" he yelled as he smashed his glass above her head. "I swear I will kill you if you ever tell anyone about this."

Terrified, she swore, between moans, sobs and pain that she would never tell. Lex turned and staggered through the front door, slamming it as he exited. Silence. She was alone. She carried that secret to her grave with two exceptions.

Two months later, she discovered she was pregnant. She shared her humiliation with Dr. Strucker, her gynecologist. She was traumatized when she found she was to have multiple births.

In the next months, she was tormented and suffered deep depression. She eventually had a nervous breakdown. In her depression, she felt tumors were growing in her body, and she wanted them removed and destroyed.

Dr. Strucker knew of services that dealt with newborn babies that were passed into illegal markets. Privately, arrangements were made for Annie to give birth in one of these facilities where the quadruplets would be given up for adoption or sent to a state foster care system.

A nurse placed the first newborn infant on Annie's stomach. She folded her arms around her and would not let go.

"Annie, we discussed this. Let the nurse have the child."

"This one. This one is the daughter we always wanted," she whispered to no one but herself. "Sara."

Dr. Strucker silently watched Annie hold the child.

"All right, Annie," he said with compassion. "This is a decision only you can make."

Dr. Strucker secreted the three newborns through the facilities informing the family that only one child had survived. Funeral services for the three stillborn infants took place shortly after.

Several years later, Dr. Strucker approached Lex about the rape, the quadruplets and proceeded to blackmail him. Though the statute of limitations for rape was ten years, Strucker still had him by the gonads. In the years since Kelly had made a fortune, and if this information came out, it would ruin him, even if he no longer had the threat of jail.

Years later, Lex found one of the children and adopted her. A simple DNA test confirmed that she was indeed his child. He brought her home to give her a better life.

Second, she confessed to her son Alex on her deathbed. It was her hope that Alex would be able to protect Sara from Lex. She didn't trust him, and needed to keep her safe.

Nicole was furious with what she had found out. She told Tony she had suffered her entire life because of Lex Kelly, and she was going to get even. Tony convinced her that if they played their cards right, they could take full advantage of this knowledge, turning it into a win for both of them. Time was on their side.

Nicole's fury seemed to dissolve as her love for Tony grew. He knew no one in her life had given a damn, that he was everything to her. Tony took her to New York and set her up in an apartment. "But I want to live with you, Tony," she whined.

"It can't happen, Nicole. We need to keep you out of sight. If anyone finds out about you, our plans are all for nothing."

Three and a half weeks ago, through a conversation with a friend of Emma, Tony found that Emma had stumbled upon the duplicate deeds on the Tahoe property.

"So what, Tony. What does that have to do with us and our plans?"

"Think, Nicole, she finds out about you, Marian and Sara, it's over. Lex dies, you have three sisters; do you want our money split three ways? You want that? I don't want that. And, trust me, you don't want that. We need her to disappear?"

"What the hell do we do now?" Nicole whined. "Leave it to me," Tony answered. "I'll call you."

Two days later, Tony briefed her on the plan.

***

The following evening Tony followed Emma into her office.

"Working late?'

"Need to wrap up some things. Leaving town for a few days and didn't want to leave loose ends. What are you doing here at this time of night, Tony?"

"Same thing. I'll walk you out to your car if you're finished. It's late, and I don't want anything to happen to the boss's daughter."

"Thanks Tony, I appreciate that. Give me a few minutes, and I'll be ready to go."

Tony and Emma walked out of the UN Office building. As they chatted, Tony maneuvered her near the back of the Enterprise truck he had rented. He briefly scanned the streets for activity but saw no one.

***

Nicole watched Tony and Emma as they crossed the plaza. Her hatred for this sister bubbled to the surface, suffocating her. When they were inches away, she jumped out of the back of the truck and grabbed Emma by the hair. Tony held her while Nicole stuck cotton soaked with chloroform against her nose and mouth. She took great pleasure, smashing her hard against the truck.

"What the—?" Emma moaned as she slumped into Tony's arms.

"Quick," he whispered, "get her into the truck!"

With Tony's help, Nicole pulled Emma into the truck and slammed the door. She switched on the flashlight and quickly duct-taped Emma's hands and feet. Putting the tape over her mouth, she finished the task with a kick to the ribs. "Bitch!"

She switched off the light, jumped to the pavement, slammed and locked the truck. She then ran to the driver's side, hopped in, and started the engine.

Tony tapped on the window.

She pressed the power button. "What?" She spat in an irritated tone.

"Lighten up, damn it, I just wanted to tell you to be careful. I'll see you in Lake Tahoe in three days."

"Right," she said and stomped on the accelerator.

CHAPTER 27

It took twenty hours to get halfway across the states. Nicole pulled off into a rest area in Omaha, Nebraska, at one the following afternoon. She needed to wait until it got dark before she checked on her cargo. Watching the activity of travelers coming and going, she pulled out her revolver, set it on the floor near her feet, opened up a bottle of Absolut Vodka, and lit a cigarette. She settled back and took a deep drag waiting for the hours to crawl by.

A noise woke her. Alert, she looked around but saw nothing. It was dark. A glance at the dashboard clock showed the time to be two o'clock a.m.

"Shit, I've been asleep for what— eight hours." She grabbed her gun, slid out of the truck cab, and looked around for movement. She heard no noise; she saw nothing stirring. She walked to the back of the truck, slipped the lock, and pulled the door open, winching at the squeak the door made.

Emma was lying in the same position she had left her. Didn't look like she had moved a muscle. Nicole took the side step and pulled herself up into the truck, and nudged her sister. A groan escaped her lips, but she remained still. Nicole jumped to the ground, closed the door, and headed to the rest area facilities. Walking into the stall, she relieved herself, found a drinking fountain, bought a coke and snacks from the vending machine, and strolled toward the truck.

A twig snapped. Nicole felt a hand over her mouth. Someone grabbed her from behind, pulled her down, and threw her to the grass. Her attacker sat on her holding her down as she struggled to free herself.

"Stop the struggle." He whispered. "If you do what I say, I won't hurt you."

"What do you want?"

"Want to know what you got in that truck over there." He sneered. He pointed a gun at Nicole's chest. "Heard a groan. Like maybe someone was drunk. You been drinkin' all afternoon. Been watching you. Where's your friend?"

"I have no friend. Get the hell off of me!" She whispered as she tried to free herself.

"Not until you show me what's in that truck you're carrying, little lady."

"Okay, just get off me."

He got up, holding the gun on her.

Nicole slowly got to her feet. She did not take her eyes off the gun pointed at her.

"Go on, lead the way."

They walked over to the back of the truck. Nicole slipped the lock and opened the door, watching him closely.

He stuck his head in the door. "What the hell? What you got that girl all tied up for?"

A loud moan came from the dark shadow on the floor. The figure tempted to move closer, a desperate sob escaping taped lips.

Nicole took out her gun and whacked the stranger hard on the head. She watched him collapse and quickly checked out the rest area for any movement. A groan came from inside the truck. "Shut-up," Nicole whispered. "I swear you are a dead woman if you make another sound. You got that?"

Emma laid her head back down and remained quiet.

Nicole shut the door softly, locked it, then turned and looked at the form lying at her feet.

Now, what the hell do I do? She thought. Squatting down, she picked up his gun, struck him hard again, and shoved his weapon into the waistband of her jeans.

"That should keep you quiet for a while." She murmured.

She ruffled through his jacket and jean pockets taking his wallet and keys. Looking around, she heard, rather than saw, water running in a ravine behind the rest stop facility.

Lifting the stranger by the legs, she found him to be light, enabling her to drag the body over to the top edge of the ravine. She let go, heard the body roll down the hill, and settle with a splash at the bottom. She crouched down, feeling the sudden flow of adrenaline, and listened for any movement in the area. It was dark and still. She crept back to her vehicle, made sure the truck's rear door was secure, and got into the cab. She placed the guns on the floor along with the wallet and keys, then calmly lit a cigarette, took a long swallow of vodka from the bottle, backed up the truck, and headed for South Lake Tahoe.

The rest of the drive to Lake Tahoe was uneventful. No cops, no tickets, no flat tires. Tony flew in and met Nicole as she arrived at the Givens mansion.

"Any problems on the road?"

"Nope. Nothing I couldn't handle." Nicole jeered.

They carried Emma's limp body to the staircase closet. Tony pushed a hidden lever on the left side of the back wall just under the ceiling. The wall slowly opened, revealing an old staircase that led into a tunnel.

"Just because a wall looks solid doesn't always mean there's nothing behind it," Tony said with a caustic smile.

"How the hell did you know about this place?" Nicole asked as she heaved Emma's dead weight through the door onto the tunnel steps. She stopped to catch her breath.

"Place used to belong to Kelly's grandparents before they sold it. Lex told me about it the night he told me about his brother's wife. He found this hidden door when he was a kid. About eight-years-old, I think he said. Said he'd probably been in this old Victorian house a dozen times before he found this closet. He thought he heard someone in the old mansion one time and hid in this closet. Said, as a dumb kid, he was pretty scared. He stood on a stool to reach for a ceiling light. As he searched for the light, he lost his balance and grabbed something to break his fall. One hand found the short string pull switch, and the other hand slammed against this back wall and hit this hidden mechanism.

In a million years, no one could find this door. The door's camouflaged so that it appears to be part of the architectural structure. A damn fluke for an eight-year-old kid. Go figure."

"He didn't tell anyone?"

"Nah, kept it to himself. It was a secret," He said. "His secret. Said the tunnel was pitch black and looked old as hell. Saw these stairs and later brought a flashlight to check it out, but it scared the shit out of him. He made sure the door showed no visual signs of entry and sealed it shut. From what I understand, no one's been down here since, except you and me.

"Come on, let's get this bitch into the room."

Between them, they were able to carry Emma's limp body to a hidden room. They made sure she was bound securely and placed in the corner.

"Take good care of her," Tony said. "She's our ticket to a fortune. You need to get some food and water. She hurt bad?"

"No, I just slammed her head into the truck. She'll be alright. I'll put a friggin band-aid on it."

Tony turned to leave.

"Where in the hell do you think you're going? And what makes you think I'm going to stay down in this smelly dump and babysit?"

Tony grabbed Nicole by the neck and slammed her into the wall. "Because I said you are, and if you want to cash in on this, you just better wise up and do what you need to do. Is that fucking clear?"

"Okay, okay," Nicole mumbled as she rubbed her raw neck. "Asshole! All men are assholes!"

"Keep your damn complaints to yourself. I have to go back to New York to take care of things. I should be back in a week, but I'll keep in touch by phone. We will figure out what to do with Emma then. For now, I need to be sure our steps are covered, and we're clean."

CHAPTER 28

On day one of Emma's captivity, Nicole showed her the butcher knife. "You behave, and I never have to use this on you, capiche?"

Crying, Emma nodded her head.

In the following days, Nicole shopped at McDonald's for burgers and fries and at the local liquor store for vodka and cigarettes. She also purchased a small bottle of hydrogen peroxide and some gauze for her prisoner's head wounds.

Tony did not return in the next two weeks. Only three phone calls. Three lousy phone calls! In the beginning, Nicole tended to ingratiate herself into Emma's confidence for nothing more than some entertainment, ensuring that nothing would happen to her as long as Daddy came through with the cash. She talked Emma into sharing her early life and her years with Lex Kelly.

Nicole learned that Emma's early days were somewhat similar to hers. One foster family after another. The difference was that her father found and adopted her and gave her all the advantages that Nicole never got. Emma finished high school, went to college, and joined her father's firm.   Emma was astounded that she and Nicole looked so much alike.   She was stunned to find she had a sister.

Once a day, Nicole would allow Emma to relieve herself in a pail. Otherwise, she kept Emma taped up, sometimes forgetting to bring her food or provide water.

Though they were sisters, Nicole felt they had nothing in common other than they looked alike. Nicole was strong, understood the hard life, understood what it took to get what you wanted and needed from people. Emma was a whiner. All she did was whine and cry. She was given a good life on a platter.

What the hell did she have to whine about? Nicole could not stand weak people, and this Emma was pathetic.

She was always asking why, why, why me?

Nicole felt she had to answer the same question over and over again. "Because your Dad has money that Tony and I want and because I hate your sniveling guts." God, how she hated that feeble excuse for a woman. Nicole had to put up with Emma's constant whining for two weeks. Toward the end, she grew weary with it all. She couldn't take it anymore.

On day fourteen, she returned to the hidden room after getting some food and a booze supply. She set the bag on the floor, turned her flashlight toward the corner where Emma was bound, stopped, and drew in a deep breath. It was empty.

"Outraged, she picked up the kitchen knife, slipped silently through the door, stopped, and listened. She thought she heard something, a sound to her left. She took off at a fast pace. The noise was close to the tunnel located underneath the old cabin. Nicole heard footsteps and muffled sobs before she saw her prisoner.

"Stop!" Nicole shouted as she dove toward Emma. Her flashlight fell, casting an eerie shadow on the tunnel walls. She grabbed Emma around her legs, and both tumbled to the tunnel floor. Emma pulled chunks of Nicole's hair, scratched her arms until they bled, clawed and dug her nails into her flesh. "Leave me alone!" Emma shouted. "I won't go back to that room. You'll have to kill me first."

Amid the thrashing of arms, Nicole was able to hold onto the knife and regain her balance. From the corner of her eye, she saw Emma jump up, turn and take a step toward what she hoped was freedom. She heard her sister's blood-curdling scream as she embedded the knife in her back. Nicole viciously continued to turn the blade. She then thrust the knife again and again with an intense passion until her sister fell to her knees. Nicole stumbled and fell against the tunnel wall. Taking deep gulps of air, she stared at Emma. She stared at her agony and last moments.

"Why?" Emma moaned as the light faded from her eyes. "Why?"

"Why? Why do you keep asking why?" Nicole screamed. "Because I hate you, that's the only answer you need."

She touched the blood oozing from her scalp, where hair was missing, and brushed the blood from her arms while she tried to catch her breath. Once her heart slowed, she grabbed Emma by the hair and dragged her body toward the steps. Slowly she pulled Emma's body up the cement stairway, one step at a time. When she reached the landing, she collapsed in exhaustion.

***

Tony was pissed!

"She tried to escape, damn it. She took out chunks of my hair. My arms are raw and shredded. The bitch tried to kill me. What was I supposed to do, Tony?"

"How the hell did she get out of the duct tape?"

"I found wet tape. Emma must have used water to moisten the tape. Hell, for all I know, she spit and licked it off. Whatever, moisture loosened the damn tape."

"Where is she now?"

"I put her body in the closet in the mansion until we can figure what to do with her. No one goes there. The place is empty. No one will find her."

"You idiot," Tony shouted. "You're going to fuck up everything."

"Tony, it's not my fault. I didn't know what else to do. Tony? Tony!" Nicole shouted, and then realized she was talking into a dead phone.

***

Coming back to the present, Nicole slowly stood. Turning on her flashlight, she began to walk through the dark tunnel toward the hidden room, ignoring the light squeaks and scampering noises around her. She heard a whimper in the corner when she entered the room. She picked up the knife, turned, and walked over to her sister. "Shut up, you whore! Or, I'll slice you up! She leaned close and whispered, "Did one sister— trust me, I have no problem taking care of you the same way!"

CHAPTER 29

Outside the Kelly estate, the air grew heavy with the promise of a thunderstorm. Trees gently tossed by winds caused leaves to dance on limbs, the afternoon shadows darkened. A lake gale abruptly increased in intensity, blowing waves of water toward the shore. In the silence, a jagged streak of lightning brightened the sky, followed by a faint rumble. The gloomy skies matched the thoughts of those who sat around the dining room table.

The evening had begun on a cheerful note. Mac's heart skipped a beat when he saw Jacqueline was there, which was a pleasant surprise. He was delighted and felt she was pleased, as well. Everyone relaxed with drinks and delicious appetizers; a soft background of music created the right atmosphere. Mac listened to the light conversation, trying not to focus his full attention on Jacqueline.

"Alex, can you share some insights about yourself?" Jeri said. "I mean, with all that you and your family have accomplished, I'm just curious who you feel has been the most influential person in your life."

Alex was thoughtful for a moment. He briefly looked at Sara, Dustin, and Zed. "I would have to say my mother first, then my father. My mom, interestingly, was the disciplinarian of the family. She did this through the power of words. She allowed mistakes but never allowed us to spend recklessly, get drunk or be disrespectful. She was tough, compassionate towards her kids, and selfless. She was one-of-a-kind. On the other hand, dad was not a 'do as I say, not as I do' kind of guy. He led by example, which spoke volumes about him. With dad, business was a gift. He would work three jobs to keep the roof over our heads, and it paid off. He would do whatever it took to provide safety and keep us out of harm's way. He loved my mother, unconditionally."

"I would agree with that," Sara spoke up. "Mom had so much love in her heart for us, and Dad was our strength. We were truly blessed. What about your parents, Jeri?"

"Our father died when we were very young. I was five. Mom worked hard to keep us fed, clothed, and, like your dad, she worked hard to provide a solid roof over our heads. Jacqueline and I behaved ourselves in support of our mom and supported each other.

"I'm so sorry," Alex said.

"We had a good childhood. Our mom worked hard to ensure we did. She was strong-willed but tenderhearted and devoted to us, but we did miss our father. Mom made sure that we kept his memory alive." Jacqueline said.

"Mac, Detective Mendoza called," Sara interjected, "but I wasn't able to phone him back this morning. Do you know what his call was about? Was it about my father?"

"I'm sure it was the results of the DNA tests both you and Dustin took. He called and left a message. Said he would contact you directly if he didn't hear from me."

"Well?"

"I think you should talk with Detective Mendoza about the results."

"Mac, I have a right to know what those results are. If you know something, you have to tell me. If you need permission, you have it. You asked me to take those tests. I'm asking you, right now, to give me the results."

Mac sat silent for a few moments and stared into Sara's eyes. He threw up his hands in a sign of resignation. "Okay," he said softly. "Sara, your DNA is not a match with your father. Dustin, your DNA is a positive match." Sara was about to interrupt, but Mac held up his hand. "Stop Sara, you asked for this information, but you need to listen. When we exhumed your sisters' caskets, they were empty. We took a sample of Emma Kelly's DNA and your DNA, and they are a match. We finally were able to get a sample of DNA from Lex Kelly. Both you and Emma are matches to his DNA. Lex Kelly is the father of the quadruplets. He is your biological father, Sara."

Sara sat stone still. "And my mother?" she whispered.

"Your mother is your biological mother. I know this is difficult. These tests prove that your three sisters lived, and for reasons we are not aware of, were given up for adoption. We just don't have all the answers at this time."

Dustin looked at his sister with concern, as tears filled Sara's eyes. This new turn of events was a jolt.

"I'm in a state of disbelief," she sighed. "I'm still trying to comprehend all that has happened with these DNA results, and now—, I feel shell shocked. To find out my father is not my father, but my uncle? Oh God, my Uncle—" She buried her face in her hands, unable to fight back the tears.

"Sara, you need to take some time to think this through. Don't rush in the way you handle this. We all love you. Nothing has changed." Zed said.

"Uncle Lex wasn't even on my birth certificate," Sara choked. "So why would anything like this even cross my mind? I'm sorry, but I'm having a hard time dealing with all of this."

"Sara," Alex broke in, "just before Mom passed away, she shared what happened to her with me. Uncle Lex had raped her, and she gave birth to the quadruplets."

Stunned, everyone looked at Alex in silence.

"You knew this and never told me?" Sara said dumbfounded.

Shaking his head, Alex looked at Sara with regret. "Mom told me hoping I could protect you, and I've tried to honor her request. She loved you so much, Sara, and was afraid for your safety. She didn't trust Lex Kelly." Taking a deep breath, he continued, "She kept you, and the other three were put up for adoption or taken to foster homes. You were the first she gave birth to, and she couldn't— wouldn't, let you go. I did not want you to take the DNA tests because I did not want you to find out. Not this way. But I was wrong. You did have a right to know, and I can only say I'm sorry."

"Did Dad know?"

"No, she never told him. As far as he was concerned, you were his one surviving daughter, and he buried his other three daughters. Parents are not just people who contribute to your genetic material, Sara. Parents are the ones who take the time, energy, love, and resources that make you who you are today. And you are one amazing and beautiful person, thanks to Dad and Mom."

Sara gazed at her empty plate, deep in thought. "So, Mac, do you have any idea where my other two sisters are?"

"We believe we found one of your sisters, but she has disappeared. She could be another victim. And the other sister, as of this moment, is a possible suspect. Until we find her, we can't assume anything."

Sara leaned her head against Alex's shoulder and brushed her tears away. "Alex, this is all so crazy. Yes, I have a biological father, but he is no more than just that, 'biological', and that man is not who I called Dad. My dad is our dad, always has been and always will be. But the most important thing is that you are my brothers and I am your sister. God, I'm lucky to have you guys and so fortunate to have had such loving parents."

"So, you're okay? We're good?" Alex asked with some hesitation.

"Your heart was in the right place. I can't fault you for that." She squeezed his hand.

***

Jacqueline and Jeri did not feel that Sara was ready to be alone, so they invited her back to their cabin.

"Let's have an old-fashioned pajama party. We'll order a pizza and get toasted on some wine or beer, your choice, Sara. What do you say?"

"We just ate, and it's late."

"It's never too late for pizza. Think of it as dessert."

"I say, yes! How could I possibly say no?" She laughed.

A return to a near cheerful tone replaced the sullen mood that had previously hung over the group. The three of them walked over to the cabin. Jeri ordered pizza while Jacqueline went into the kitchen to get a bottle of wine. When she grabbed a bottle, she noted something not right. She stopped. Standing still, she looked curiously at the wine bottles. She could not quite grasp the oddity. She shrugged and went into the living room to join the others.

"Sara, that cleaning service you hired today did a great job cleaning up the porch," Jacqueline said. "You wouldn't even know there was a fire but for the dark spot on the floor and discolored ceiling and walls. Fortunately, there was minimal damage. And, the smell of smoke residue is gone."

"Glad we could get it done quickly, so you can continue to enjoy the cabin."

Twenty minutes later, their pizza arrived. Wine was poured and consumed along with pizza.

"It's been so long since I've had a pizza. It's just crazy delicious," Jeri grinned.

Everyone laughed and nodded in agreement. They talked about their lives and the events of the past two days as they watched dusk form illusions of patterns on the lake. They watched the sun slowly descend toward the western horizon. A flash of lightning caught the corner of Sara's eye. She stifled a yawn, raised her arms to the ceiling, stretched, and got up to go home.

"Oh no, you don't," Jeri said, "you're staying overnight with us. Remember? We're having a pajama party; Jacqueline and I can double up in her room. We have twin beds in there. You can have my room. We have pajamas and extra toothbrushes."

"Sorry, I forgot, I have an appointment tomorrow to see our attorney with Alex."

"Okay, we'll be sure you get up so you can make your appointment. We'll let 'Siri' know to set the alarm. You have to stay. We want you here with us."

"Say no more, I'm so tired, and you know, I just feel so lucky to have met you two and found two new friends. You have made my day. And as an aside, Jacqueline, I think Mac is infatuated with you."

Jacqueline blushed, and Jeri smiled sheepishly, looking at her sister as Sara hugged them both. "You got me, guys. Let's hit the sack."

Above the cabin, another lightning bolt split the sky in two.

***

The loud clap of thunder hid the creak as the hidden trap door opened. Nicole stepped slowly off the ladder onto the closet floor. She peered through the slats and saw her sister asleep. Earlier, she had watched her, and the other two women walk to the cabin. She heard their laughing conversation about a pajama party. *How moronic*, she thought.

Slowly opening the closet door, she quietly tiptoed to the bed and watched Sara's breathing as she slept. Sara was a picture of herself, only softer. Staring at Sara, jealousy and hurt consumed her. Her hand slid a razor blade from her pocket. She envisioned that face sliced, eliminating any beauty, leaving a ravaged scarred remembrance of what was. Throat sliced from ear to ear. How easy. She slowly slid the blade down the arm to the wrist. She could slash the wrists and watch the life ebb as precious blood flowed to the floor. God, she hated her.

Sara stirred. She began to open her eyes.

Nicole quickly reached out and pressed a large piece of cotton soaked with chloroform over Sara's face. Lightning lit up the room, reflecting a silhouette of Nicole's image, had someone been there to see it. Thunder swallowed Sara's gasp of surprise. She woke and struggled. Nicole jumped on top of her, holding the chloroform tight on her nose and mouth. Sara relaxed with a soft moan. Nicole took out a syringe. She injected 150+ milligrams of ketamine. "That will keep you quiet for a while." She watched as Sara slumped into unconsciousness.

Nicole pulled her sister off the bed onto the floor. Her body landed with a thud. Nicole held her breath as she waited to see if the loud noise had stirred those sleeping in the next room.

She heard nothing. She grasped her sister under the arms and pulled her across the floor, into the closet, then dropped the dead weight through the trap door to the tunnel floor below. Sara fell eight feet, just missing the ladder attached to the tunnel wall.

After she made sure Sara was out cold, Nicole turned and swiftly made the bed. She crept to the kitchen and grabbed a bottle of wine. The second bottle she had stolen in the last two days. Returning quickly to the bedroom, she sneaked through the closet door and stepped onto the ladder, ensuring the trap door was securely closed.

Once she reached the tunnel floor, Nicole took the flashlight from her pocket, turned it on, but nothing happened. No light. "Damn," she said, as she struck the flashlight against the tunnel wall. Light instantly flooded the area where she stood. With the wine in one hand, Nicole grabbed Sara by the foot with the other hand and slowly dragged her to the hidden room.

DAY FIVE...

Listen to her broken heart
Step lightly, least you find
Shattered fragments of anguish
False hopes of dreams forgotten

CHAPTER 30

Jeri woke to the smell of coffee and the sound of pounding rain. She walked into the kitchen and looked around.

"Sara's not up yet?"

"I checked her room. It looked like Sara made the bed." Jacqueline slipped two pieces of bread into the toaster. "I assumed she got up early and headed home."

Jeri watched her sister. "Strange, I mean, she left without even saying goodbye."

"We were asleep."

"Still," Jeri mused as she poured herself a cup of coffee.

"It's not that strange. Remember, Sara said, she and Alex had an appointment with her attorney this morning. She probably got up early to meet her brother."

Jeri heard a knock at the back door. "Who could that be?"

"Could be Sara. Maybe she forgot something," Jacqueline said as toast popped up. She grabbed the toast and a knife and began to spread the right amount of butter, which melted immediately. "Yum," Jacqueline murmured. She watched Jeri turn and head to the back door.

Alex stood in the rain.

"Alex, you're soaked! Come in and get out of the rain before you drown," Jeri laughed.

She opened the door wider to let him in.

Alex stepped into the small utility room with an apologetic grin. "Sorry for the puddle of water. Just came by to pick up Sara."

"Sara?" Jacqueline said, surprised. "She's not here. We thought she went home earlier this morning."

"No, she hasn't been home. I haven't seen her since last evening."

"When I got up this morning, I checked her room. It seemed in order, the bed made, but she was gone. Jacqueline said. An uneasiness washed over her as she turned and headed toward Jeri's bedroom. Jeri and Alex followed. They looked around the room, saw the made bed but no pajamas. She opened a small chest of drawers, which was empty, then stepped over to the closet and opened the doors. "Oh my God," she whispered. She turned around to face her sister and Alex. "Her clothes are here."

Alex looked questioningly at Jacqueline, then at Jeri. "I don't have a good feeling about this. I think we should call Mac."

***

Mac and Ricks arrived at the cabin within minutes of the 911 call. Mac did a thorough search of the cabin, but found nothing out of order. Jacqueline and Jeri's room showed beds unmade, minimal chaos prevailed, whereas Sara's room was pristine, the bed made. He returned to the dining room to join the others.

"Jacqueline, do you know if anything is missing?"

"No, I don't think so," Jacqueline said.

"Let's go over last night and this morning."

"We didn't think Sara wanted to be alone, so we invited her to come over for a pajama party," Jeri said. "We ordered a pizza, had some wine, talked, and went to bed."

"Sara did say she had to meet with her attorney and Alex. We promised to wake her up in time for that appointment. When I gave her a wake-up call, she wasn't there," Jacqueline said. "Her room was in order, so I assumed she had gotten dressed and went home. I didn't think to look in the closet for her clothes."

"It's all just so strange," Jeri spoke up. "I can't imagine she would walk out of this cabin in her pajamas and leave her clothes and shoes. It doesn't make sense."

"No, it doesn't," Mac said.

"Jesus Mac, I can't believe this is happening," Alex exhaled. Stunned and confused, he ran his fingers through his hair. "Where can she possibly be?"

"We'll find her Alex, trust me."

"Alex, can you think of any place else that Sara might have gone?"

"No," Alex answered. "We have a crucial appointment with our family attorney this morning. She would not miss that meeting!"

"But," Mac paused, "she did have a bombshell dropped on her yesterday."

"Mac, she was fine," Jeri said. "We had a relaxing evening. We had some pizza and wine. Sara was calm and grounded."

"Checked around the perimeter of the house Chief," Ricks called out as he walked into the cabin kitchen. "Nothing outside." He stomped his feet and tried, in vain, not to leave a muddy mess on the floor and continued to the living room to join the others.

"Okay, Ricks, let's put out an APB on Sara, right away."

"On it," Ricks said. He headed back to the police cruiser. The back-screen door slammed shut after him.

Mac turned to Jacqueline and Jeri. "I want you two to stay put. See if you can stay out of trouble."

"Mac," Jacqueline said, "with Sara missing, trust me, we don't want to cause any concern over us."

"I don't want anything to happen to you or your sister."

"I know, Mac. We will be okay. Just find Sara."

***

After everyone left, Jacqueline and Jeri tried to occupy themselves. They quickly mopped up the mud and water Alex and Ricks had left on the kitchen and utility room floors. They ate a light brunch, read for several hours, and pulled two rocking chairs to the picture windows to sit and relax as they gazed at thunderous clouds, which seemed to explode in a downpour over the lake. Whitecaps danced across the water.

Lost in no particular thought, Jacqueline rocked back and forth, a rhythmic creak, the only sound in the room.

She turned to Jeri. "It's already past 3:00. I am going to go crazy if I just sit here. I just can't get those sounds we heard at the gazebo out of my head."

"Me either," Jeri sighed.

"Let's go take a look."

"Are you serious? If that thunder, lightning, and torrent of rain doesn't put some sense in that head of yours, remember what Mac told us."

"Stay out of trouble," they both said in unison.

"There isn't anything that can hurt us or get us in trouble."

"You don't know that," Jeri replied.

"I know I can't relax with all that's going on. I feel like I have to do something."

"Don't expect me to join you. I'll be snuggling in my chair."

"We're just going to take a look! Maybe we will find a tunnel or two. Come on, let's go check and see if there is any rain gear around."

Jeri pulled a blanket over her legs and nestled in her rocker. "I am not your servant, Jacqueline. You have already pulled me into two of your crazy escapades. I am not going to be led down that path a third time. Someone's going to get hurt."

"I resent what you're implying. How could you even think I would put you in jeopardy?"

"How? Because you don't consider my feelings, Jacqueline. You think because you're the older sister, you can do whatever you want. That I'll follow you wherever you go."

"You can be so negative."

"Negative!" Jeri said, jumping out of her rocker. "How dare you say that to me? You can be so full of yourself! I have always supported you and do not deserve that. You never listen to me!" Jeri yelled. "I'm done." Jeri turned, went into her bedroom, and slammed the door.

***

Jacqueline felt terrible about the rift with her sister. She knocked on Jeri's bedroom door after twenty minutes of stewing over it.

"Jeri... Jeri? I'm sorry."

Jeri opened the door. "I'm sorry too," she said as she hugged her sister.

"I'll see you when I get back."

"No, I'm going too. I wouldn't feel right letting you go out on your own."

"Are you sure?"

"Come on, let's do this thing."

Jacqueline found an old poncho dotted with some rips and holes, but she felt it would keep her dry. Jeri found a slicker with a rain hat. Oversized rain boots completed their ensemble.

Jacqueline grabbed a flashlight off the kitchen counter, opened the front door, and walked out into the torrential rain. She pulled her poncho firmly around her and splashed through puddles, followed by Jeri. They turned toward the gazebo, the rain-soaked path now swollen to the size of a small river.

Jeri reached the gazebo first. She stepped onto the first riser, slipped, and fell on the gazebo's wet, rotted floorboards.

"Jeri, are you all right?" Jacqueline shouted through the downpour. She ran up the stairs, barely missed the first step, and almost fell herself.

"Yes, I'm fine."

Jacqueline could not keep the smirk off her face as she took Jeri's hand to help her up.

"How can you even grin like that? I swear Jacqueline—"

"—Sorry. Let's see if we can find something . . . anything. It's cold, and my hands are blue, so let's get this done. If there is a trap door, I'm sure it would be in a less conspicuous location. It would probably be seamless and blended into the surrounding floor. These floorboards are pretty old. Be careful."

Jacqueline got down on her hands and knees and began to check the gazebo surface. She moved her hands over the wooden planks and carefully checked for some sort of abnormality or disturbance. She suddenly stopped and looked up at Jeri. "Are you going to help?"

"No, I'll watch. This is your dog and pony show."

Jacqueline shook her head in dismay, turned her attention to the task at hand, and continued her search. "Ouch!" She cried.

"What is it?

"I have a huge splinter in my hand. Damn, it hurts. Hand me that flashlight." Jacqueline took the flashlight, turned it on, and fixed the light on her hand. "It's bleeding like crazy. Hold that flashlight for me so I can pull this sliver of wood out." Jacqueline pulled out the fragment and watched it fall through the cracks of the aged floorboards. The flashlight beam cast shadows of light onto a subflooring beneath. Jacqueline, dumbfounded, looked up at her sister. "Oh my God, is that what I think it is?"

Jacqueline and Jeri stared at what possibly could be the trap door they were looking for.

***

Rain pounded the roof of the gazebo as the day prematurely darkened. Small leaks soon soaked the area they stood on.

"This could be a way into the tunnel, Jeri."

"Maybe, but how do we pull these old wooden planks up? We need something. Maybe a crowbar."

"You're right. You stay here. I'll go back, get another flashlight and find something to lift these floorboards."

Twenty minutes later, Jacqueline was back with another flashlight, a crowbar she found in a toolbox, and a bandaged hand.

"Can you handle that crowbar with your hand hurt and bandaged?" Jeri asked

"It was just a splinter. Hold the flashlight," Jacqueline said, as she knelt, took the crowbar, and pried planks up without difficulty. The wood was old and wet. After she removed several slats, she looked up. "Jeri, it's true! Those stories about the tunnel are true!"

"Keep going," Jeri said excitedly. "Let's remove the rest of these boards. See if there is something for sure under the deck."

The sisters took turns removing the rest of the two-foot by two-foot strips of wood.

When they finally were able to lift the boards, a trap door was revealed. "Wow."

"Yeah, me too. Let's see if we can open it," Jacqueline said. She leaned over and grabbed a corroded iron ring. "This door is ancient. It doesn't look like it's been opened in years." Together, both sisters pulled on the ring, tugging with all their might. "It won't budge.

Maybe we should use that crowbar to pry it open." Jeri suggested as she brushed raindrops off her face and neck.

"Look here. There seems to be a lock in the middle of that ring. We need a key," Jacqueline murmured. She swirled a hundred and eighty degrees to examine the gazebo floor. "There!" Jacqueline shouted above the pelting rain. She pointed her finger just below a piece of splintered wood.

A single skeleton key mounted onto an old piece of ivory hung partially hidden. Jeri lifted the key off a small s-shaped hook and slowly rolled it over in her hand. She inserted the key into the center of the ring and tried to turn it.

"It doesn't seem to want to move."

"Let me try," Jacqueline said as she leaned over to help. She took the key from Jeri and reinserted the skeleton key into the keyhole. Holding their breath, both sisters twisted the key hard to the right until they heard a soft *click*.

"Success," Jacqueline murmured. "Let's try again to pull this iron ring." Together they pulled, their efforts finally rewarded by movement. With one final joint effort, the resistant trap door opened.

The sisters sat back on their heels and looked into a hole of inky blackness. Lightning lit the sky. It offered no light to the darkness below.

The thought of going into this black hole, to be swallowed up so totally as not to see your hands in front of you, momentarily immobilized Jeri in terrifying fear. A loud clap of thunder shook her to her core.

"You okay, Jeri?"

She had barely enough breath left to gasp a reply. "I'm fine. It's just—"

"—It's just what?" Jacqueline asked, watching Jeri with concern.

"I have this feeling, like a horrible bad feeling," Jeri whispered. A blanket of dread enveloped her.

CHAPTER 31

Consciousness slowly opened its door. Sara thought she heard a sound. A voice. Her heart pounded with fear. Eyes opened to pitch black. It was so dark she feared she had gone blind. *Where am I?*

Her skin crawled. Tendrils of terror balled in her stomach. Nausea and fear clogged her throat. A cold, wet dirt surface lay beneath her. *The floor is so slimy,* she thought, in disgust. *What is that repugnant smell?* Her hand touched fabric, and she realized she was still wearing pajamas. She tried to fill her lungs with air. Her ribs screamed with pain. *I can't breathe.* She panicked and attempted to move. Pain shot through her ankle. She cried in agony. Tape bound her wrists and ankles. She struggled, but the effort only caused a rush of adrenaline and additional pain. Her legs and skin felt numb, clammy, and cold. The darkness was terrifying and suffocating.

"You're awake," a voice whispered in the dark.

Sara's heart jumped through her chest. She tried to wiggle away from the voice. The movement immediately increased the pain in her ankle and head. She began to sweat profusely.

"Who . . . who are you?" Sara barely murmured.

"Marian," the voice whispered.

"Where are we?"

"In a room, but I don't know where. I'm sure it's underground, though."

"How can you be sure?"

"The dirt floor and walls. It's always dank, wet, and musty, and no fresh air. There's a crazy woman who says she's my sister."

"Your sister?" Sara moaned.

"Shhhh—I hear her coming. Be quiet. Trust me. She'll kill us both!"

"Quiet," Sara mumbled, laying her head on the floor.

There was a commotion in the darkness close by. A strong scent of alcohol filled the room, causing Sara to choke down bile and gag. It sounded like someone was trying to light a match, then something hit the floor and rolled. "Damn it!" A voice slurred. Another match lit the darkness. A hand wavered over a candle as the candle wick suddenly flickered, forming a flame that cast a small glow in the cold room. She saw a woman fall on her knees, drop a bottle, and lean over the candle. "Did it," the woman hiccuped. The person picked up the bottle, took the last swallow, and threw it across the room. The bottle shattered against the wall and fell to the dirt floor in pieces. "Fucking out of Jack Daniels." Falling on the mattress, she began to snore.

Sara stared at the figure passed out on the mattress. She tried to raise her head to get a better view, but pain hit like a hammer. She laid still for a moment, took a painful breath, and again tried to focus on the form across from her. She was both shocked and astonished at what she saw. Sara looked up at the figure next to her. Confusion and questions clouded her mind even more. While both women looked alike, there were stark differences in their appearance. The person passed out on the mattress seemed older, haggard, and wiry, whereas the person next to her was beautiful with lush red hair like her own. It was like seeing herself in a mirror. Although the woman on the mattress had black hair, the unmistakable resemblance was still there.

"You look exactly like me," Sara whispered. "And that person, over there, she looks like us. Who are you? Who is she?"

***

Marian listened, scared that she might lose her mind. Looking at Sara, she felt she saw herself, seeing the same face and hair, leaving her numb with disbelief. The past hours had drained her energy and her ability to think clearly. She was exhausted and frightened. *Think*, she thought. *Get a hold of yourself.*

"I'm just as confused as you are," she finally said. "What I do know is that we're in deep, deep trouble."

"How did you get here?"

"I was kidnapped. I went to bed early and woke up struggling with two people on top of me. They gave me something that put me out cold. I came to in the trunk of a car. When they opened the trunk, I tried to escape, but they knocked me out again. When I opened my eyes, I found myself in this awful place with that crazy person, and I do mean crazy. She calls me her sister. After seeing you, I'm—" Marian choked back tears, "—after seeing you, I don't know what to think anymore. But I do know one thing. You and I have to get out of here. That woman will kill us. I'm sure of that. What's your name?"

"Sara."

"How bad are you hurt, Sara?"

"I have a broken ankle, I think. I have some bruises, my ribs really hurt, and my head hit something hard. This pounding headache is making me nauseous and dizzy."

"Shhh," Marian whispered, "she's waking up."

***

Nicole woke, badly in need of air. Head throbbing, her mouth felt dry, and the stench in the room was suffocating. She stumbled off the mattress, grabbed a flashlight, and doused the candle flame. Still intoxicated, Nicole turned her flashlight on and staggered over to Marian and Sara to make sure both women were securely taped, then headed to the tunnel door. She stopped and wondered if she should put duct tape on their mouths. Afraid that the tape would cut off her air, she had taken the tape off Marian earlier, after getting a promise she would not make any noise. Suffocating the hostages would definitely piss Tony off.

Consequently, she didn't use the duct tape on either of them. Both seemed to be asleep. "They're fine," Nicole mumbled, sliding through the door. Once again, Nicole thought about

Marian and her wealthy father. "We're talking billions here," she said to herself, reaching the tunnel exit to the mansion.

Climbing the stairs to the closet entryway, Nicole pressed the lever on the door, patiently waited as it slid open, then headed outdoors for fresh air and a cigarette.

***

Marian opened her eyes. "Sara, Nicole left, and I'm not sure for how long. With her gone, this might be our only chance to escape."

"How?"

"I heard a bottle shatter against the wall. If I can somehow work my way over to those pieces of glass, I might be able to free my wrists and ankles from the duct tape."

"Be careful." Sara whispered, "Is there anything I can do to help?"

"No, only one of us can do this. You're hurt, and we don't know how bad your ankle is. It's better if you don't move."

With her wrists and ankles taped in front of her, Marian inched her way along the wall. The dirt floor smelled filthy and was slimy to the touch. Marian put this out of her mind and concentrated on the task. Progress was slow. Her taped wrists and ankles hindered her ability to move faster. After what seemed like an eternity, she touched a sharp object. "Ouch!" she cried as she felt a sudden pain in her lower leg.

"Marian?" Sara asked, alarmed.

"I'm okay," Marian said, "slid across some glass. Compared to everything else, this is not a problem." A few moments later, she found a piece of glass she thought she could work with. She took the fragment in her fingers and hunched over to cut the tape on her ankles one thread at a time, her breathing labored.

"Marian," Sara called out.

"It's alright. I think I've got it," Marian said as she cut through the tape. She ripped the tape off her ankles, ignoring the pain and raw, bloody skin. Ankles free, she tried to cut the tape around her wrists.

"Sara, I can't work the glass into this tape on my wrists. I need your help. You'll have to cut this tape."

They heard a terrified scream.

Marian stopped. Both she and Sara held their breath.

"That sounded like Jacqueline!" Sara whimpered as tears rolled down her cheeks. "I'm here. We're here," Sara whispered. "Marian, hurry, we've got to find Jacqueline and Jeri!"

CHAPTER 32

Lex was tired and nervous. All he had done today was sit and wait for tomorrow to come.

The Chief of Police had asked for a DNA test, which did not help his anxiety. The police would find out that Emma was his biological daughter. What sort of red flags would that raise, what questions? Why would they even want to know? Something was in the air, but he could not put his finger on it, making him even more nervous and apprehensive. In addition, the Chief asked to see him at eight o'clock tomorrow morning in his office. That could only be about Joe Carver. It was not looking good.

"Come on, Tony, let's get the hell out of here." They left and made the rounds of several casinos, ignoring the pelting rain. They stopped first at the Lakeside Inn & Casino for an early dinner. After dinner and a few drinks, they played some blackjack. After losing a few hundred, they moved on to the Montbleu Casino even as rain, thunder, and lightning tested their progress.

Some more drinks, some more blackjack, and more money lost.

"I need to get out of this place. I'm getting wasted and losing my fucking money," Tony mumbled to no one in particular.

"Good idea, Tony, let's blow this joint. One more casino and we'll call it a night."

"Okay with me," Tony said, leaning against the wall feeling the drinks.

The cab left the men off in front of Harrah's Casino. Both stumbled into the bar and ordered another drink.

"I used to own a casino in this town," Lex slurred.

"No, shit? When was that?"

"Years ago," Lex said. He checked his pocket for a pack of cigarettes.

"What happened? Why don't you have it now?" Tony asked. He popped a twenty in the bar twenty-five cent slots, punched *deal,* and won ten bucks.

"Sold it years ago. Mob screwed me big time. Set their stones in a vise, though," Lex chuckled. He took a long swallow of Jack Daniels, grabbed some matches off the bar, and lit his cigarette.

"Like you did your daughters?"

Lex slammed his glass on the bar. "What the fuck are you talking about, Tony?"

"Come on, Lex, I know all about your kids and how they got dumped into the foster system. Stellar Dad of the year," Tony smirked. He played the slot machine again. It hit another ten bucks.

Lex grew quiet. He stared into the bar mirror at his reflection, slowly took a long drag off his cigarette, and polished off his Jack.

"I don't need this kind of aggravation in my life. You are a real asshole. You do know that, right?"

"We're finished here," Tony muttered. He collected his winnings and threw a twenty on the bar. "Let's get back to the motel. I don't have time for this crap."

"Hold on, don't get your shorts in a knot. I need to talk with you."

"About what?" Tony asked. He took a cigarette, lit it, and sat back down.

"I need to get the hell out of this town. Like yesterday."

"Thought that the Chief of Police told both of us to stick around and not leave the area."

"Yeah, but I have a bad feeling about this appointment with the Chief in the morning. First, he wants a DNA test. What the hell for? To find out, my adopted daughter is my biological daughter? What's the point? As I think about it, I figure they are going to find out that Sara is also my daughter. This whole situation is not good, Tony. It could ruin me. And this meeting with the Chief of Police in the morning. It has to be about Joe.

I already told him that Joe took off on his own, but I don't think the dick believes me."

"So what? We didn't kill him."

"No, but if he finds out we were there, it could complicate things."

Tony sat in silence. "Hey boss, I think we should head back to the room and sleep on this."

"Yeah. Okay," Lex said.

***

Tony's mind raced. *The police will find out about Lex's daughters.* He could see his plans go up in flames.

Lex followed Tony outside. They walked across the street, crossing the Nevada state line into California, and stood on the corner in front of the Lake Tahoe Resort Hotel. The usually crowded street was empty.

"Where's a cab when you need one?" Tony whined, zipping his jacket to stay dry in the torrential downpour. He looked up and down the road and saw no other person around.

He turned fast and surprised Lex with a punch to the jaw. Lex grabbed Tony by the neck and slammed him into a 1956 vintage Chevy Impala parked on the street. Both men bounced off the car door to the ground.

Lex staggered to his feet.

"You prick, who the hell do you think you are!" Lex yelled as he slammed his fist into Tony's stomach. "You dead ass piece of shit. You've picked the wrong person to mess with Tony. I made you from nothing. Nothing!" Lex shouted in rage. "You repay me like this?"

Lex dug his fingers deep into Tony's neck, cutting off his lifeline. Tony grabbed at Lex's pocket as he gasped for air. Lex loosened his grip to slap Tony's hand away from his pocket, where he carried his gun. Tony rolled, sat up, and pulled a pistol from his boot. He slammed it into Lex's stomach and pulled the trigger four times. Lex fell back, his eyes wide in shock before the light dimmed and went out.

"NO! You're the stupid piece of shit!" Tony shouted. He stood up, stared down at the dead body, and kicked it in the head to make sure Lex was dead.

Tony stood and listened. He heard only the heavy rain, as lightning lit the sky, momentarily casting an eerie glow over the corpse. Thunder shook the ground beneath them. He leaned down and rifled through Lex's pockets, lifting his wallet and watch to make it look like a robbery gone wrong.

"This is good," Tony whispered. "Lex is dead, the sisters will be dead, and Nicole will inherit millions. She's my ticket!" Tony snickered. He heard voices coming his way. He kicked the body one more time, *for good measure,* and took off running.

***

Mac donned his London Fog police rain slicker, grabbed his keys, and locked his office for the day. He told the night dispatcher he was on his way out for a final run through town and left a message at the front Public Service Office to have Officer Clairborn contact him immediately if they found anything on Sara.

"Nasty night," he sighed, pulling his collar up as he ran to the cruiser. He quickly opened the door, jumped in, and shut himself in against the cloudburst. The excess rainwater off his slicker soaked the front seat. He sighed again, turned the key, and pulled out of the police parking lot.

A half-hour later, Mac was cruising down Highway 50. No other cars seemed to be on the road. His thoughts turned to Jacqueline, as they often seemed to do these past few days.

Checking the time, he thought he'd call it a night and head for the cabin to make sure Jacqueline and her sister were all right. *And staying out of trouble,* he thought with a grin.

"All units, code 10-71. Shots fired. Location of shots on the corner of Stateline and Highway 50."

"Roger that," Mac answered the dispatcher. "Code 3. Contact Styker and Ricks. Have them meet me there."

214

"10-4 Chief."

"Damn," Mac muttered, turning on his lights and siren. He made a U-turn and headed toward the state line.

By the time he arrived, several cruisers were already on the scene, lights glared. Styker and Ricks had sealed off the crime scene with yellow tape.

Mac parked next to Styker's cruiser. He got out of the car and swore again at the unrelenting rain.

"This weather sure doesn't help us with this damn crime scene," cursed Styker. "Washed every piece of evidence there might have been down the sewers of Tahoe."

"Any clues about who this is?"

"You're not going to like this," Ricks uttered.

Mac stared at the body, shrouded with a piece of plastic. "Try me,"

"Lex Kelly."

"You don't say," Mac muttered as he knelt to lift the piece of plastic. "Sure enough, that is our Mr. Kelly."

"Looks like he took several bullets in the stomach—close range. The rain hasn't washed the powder burns off," Styker said.

"Anybody see anything?"

"Couple were walking by on their way to Harrah's and found the body. Thought they heard voices but weren't sure because of the rain."

"They around?"

"Have them in the cruiser, out of the rain."

"Local?"

"Yeah, they live here in Tahoe on Birch Avenue. I see no connection other than them stumbling across the deceased."

"Be sure we have their names, address, and phone number and send them home. Let them know we will be contacting them."

"Will do."

Jobs walked over and stood behind Mac. "Just got back from Harrah's, Chief. Bartender said he saw Kelly with some guy. Description matches that of his sidekick Tony Russo. Said they got into an argument and were in no pain when they left the bar. We have them both on security cameras in and around the casino. Images faded though when they distanced themselves because of the heavy rainfall."

Mac stood up to assess the crime scene. "I don't like this! I'm worried about the safety of the Kelly family. I'm especially worried about Sara."

"No one's heard anything," Jobs said. "It's like she just vanished into thin air."

"Let's put an APB on Tony Russo. I need to find this guy sooner rather than later. Run over to that motel he's staying at. I think it's the Lazy S Lodge out on Highway 89. If you don't find anything, stop by the Kelly's. Keep an eye on their place. Let me know if you see anything suspicious. In the meantime, I need to check on Jacqueline and Jeri to make sure they're safe and not in any trouble. I'll see you over at the Kelly's once I check on them."

"Okay, Chief." Jobs said. He turned and headed to his cruiser.

Mac watched Detective Mendoza pull up and park.

"Evening, Chief." Mendoza smiled, looking up into the dark sky. "Nice night for a murder. Interrupted an evening of fun, which, by the way, was way overdue. Don't think I've ever seen this much rain." He pulled his raincoat tighter. "What do we have here?"

"Looks like a homicide, —multiple gunshot wounds in the stomach at close range.

Decedent is Lex Kelly."

"You don't say!"

"I'm headed out. Let me know when you have something."
"Will do, Chief."

CHAPTER 33

"Are we actually going down there?" Jeri asked.

"Of course," Jacqueline said as she turned on her flashlight.

"I think we should call the police. At least let Mac know. Let someone know."

"What for? I mean, yes, there were two murders, but they were in the mansion. No one even knows about this tunnel, but you and me."

"Jacqueline?"

"Okay, okay, where's my phone? Damn, I left it on the kitchen counter so I would have room for the flashlights and crowbar. Use your phone."

"My phone was dead. I left it charging in the bedroom."

"Great. Look, we just want to take a peek. We won't go far. Just do a look-see, and then we'll come back up. Easy, down and up," Jacqueline said. She turned on her flashlight and focused the light on the open trap door of the tunnel. "Look, there seems to be some narrow steps that lead down into the tunnel."

"Well, let's do this before I completely lose my nerve," Jeri whispered to herself.

The sisters slowly descended the steps and were immediately assaulted by the odor of decay. Repulsed and disgusted, they gasped in unison. They stopped their descent and stared down the stairwell into the black hole.

Dante's Inferno, Jeri thought. She had never read the book, but she imagined it to be this. A dense darkness prevailed, the sound of lead pipes dripping into muddy puddles of foul, stagnant water. Rats scattered to rid themselves of the beam that lit up their night like a hand-held torch. The stench of filth overwhelmed the senses.

"Jacqueline, I think I'm going to be sick," Jeri murmured wiping the sweat off her forehead. Her mouth felt clammy and sour. Her damp palms slid down the cold rock walls. She felt herself lurch and tumbled down the remainder of the stairs, unable to stop her fall, landing with a jolt on the chilly dirt tunnel floor.

"*JERI!*" Jacqueline screamed. Jacqueline quickly descended the steps two at a time. "Are you hurt?"

Jeri sat up and looked into her sister's eyes, highlighted by the flashlight at her feet. "I guess I'm the klutz," Jeri whimpered.

"I would say," Jacqueline smiled. "Here, let me help you up. Are you all right?"

"Only my pride is hurt, but since it's just you here, I don't have a problem. Do the flashlights still work?"

"Yes," Jacqueline said. She directed the beam of her flashlight around them. "My God, why would anyone want to come down here? The smell is suffocating. Do you want to turn back?"

"No, we've come this far, and I do feel better. I think it was just an adrenaline high. I'm fine now."

"You sure?"

"I'm sure, but let's take these boots off. They're too big and getting in the way." They removed their boots and turned from the stairs. They began to walk into the tunnel.

"Look, Jeri, footsteps! It looks like someone has been through here before."

***

Nicole walked in the rain toward the lake. She was just about to try and light her cigarette when she saw two figures in the gazebo. She quickly ducked behind a tree and watched. Nicole realized it was the two sisters who rented that cabin. "What a couple of frigging dorks," she mumbled. "What the hell are they up to now?" Standing still, she watched the sisters and suddenly realized this gave her the chance to get that last bottle of wine in their kitchen. One last glance and she headed to the cabin.

She ran up the cabin front steps, checked the door, and found it open. She noticed her rain-soaked clothes dripping on the floor but didn't care. In the kitchen, she flipped the light switch, chose a bottle of wine, then stopped. She stared at a cell phone on the counter. A plan began to formulate in her head. *Nicole, today is your lucky day.* She picked up the phone and returned to the mansion.

Once at the mansion, Nicole went directly to the kitchen, which seemed to be the only room in the whole godforsaken place that didn't smell. She grabbed an old tin cup and slumped onto the floor; lightning, thunder, and the constant sound of rain her only companions.

"Damn, no wine opener. Well! When you got nothing, you go for broke," she laughed, hit the top of the wine bottle against the counter, and poured herself a cup of wine. She didn't bother about the shredded glass on the neck of the bottle. There were other priorities.

She picked up the mobile phone and dialed the number she had memorized.

***

"Hello?" A voice weighed with a heavy burden and fear answered.

"Mr. Procini," Nicole said. She took a long drink of wine, draining the cup. She slumped over awkwardly, put the cup on the floor, and poured more wine in the cup. Spilled wine left spots on the floor that looked like drops of blood.

"Yes? Who is this?"

"Please, you know who this is," Nicole said. "God, I hate stupid people."

"Where is my daughter?" Procini asked in a stronger, louder voice. "I will do whatever you ask. I will give you whatever you want for my daughter's safe return."

Nicole smiled into the phone. "I want one million dollars. Did you get that? And I want it now."

Procini hesitated momentarily. "I don't have that kind of money in cash. You need to give me some time."

"Are you fuckin' messing with my mind? I'll kill that precious kid of yours if you don't get with the program, Dad. Listen up!"

"Yes . . . yes, I understand. Please tell me when and where I need to go."

The phone went flying through the air. It slammed into the far kitchen wall before disintegrating into pieces.

"What the hell?" Nicole screamed. The shock of the kick ran up her arm into a sudden bolt of pain into her shoulder.

"Just what the hell do you think you're doing?" Tony shouted. Red-faced, his forehead veins bulging, Tony seemed on the brink of a total meltdown. "You crazy bitch!"

"Tony? What are you doing here?" Nicole said, perplexed. "I figured we could get more money. I was looking out for our future, that's all, Tony."

Tony sank to the floor, legs crossed. He held his head in his hands. Running his fingers through his wet hair, he looked over at Nicole.

"Jesus, Nicole. What have you done? You asked Procini for a lousy million dollars, and we're looking at five hundred million with Lex and your sisters. Are you just plain crazy? Don't you realize that the FBI is all over that Procini guy? We've got his fucking daughter! They've probably already put a trace on that call!"

"No way, Tony, I talked no more than 30 seconds, a minute max."

High emotions deflated, Tony groaned.

"You know how I feel about you, Nicole, don't you?"

She knew she was his ticket. He told her that many times. He needed her on his side. He needed to keep her trust, and she did trust him. "Sure, Tony, I know you love me. You tell me all the time."

"That phone call . . . . It only takes a minute, and the FBI can find out where we are."

"I'm sorry, Tony," she whimpered, staring at the floor.

"Look, Lex is dead."

"Dead?"

"Yes, dead. Lex tried to kill me, and I had to shoot him. It was his fucking fault. With Lex out of the way, we need to get rid of your sisters. Once they're gone, you inherit your old man's company, the Tahoe house, and God knows what else he owned. But right now, the FBI is about to breathe down our necks, so we need to move fast. We need to clean this mess up and get the hell out of here without anyone knowing your involvement. Later, we can come back. The bereaved sister will come to town and collect what's hers."

"Are you with the program Nicole? We're in this together, right?" Tony asked softly. He stood and pulled Nicole to her feet.

He slowly pressed his lips to hers and kissed her long and hard.

Nicole looked into Tony's eyes. She so needed to be needed. She loved him and could never lose him.

"Okay, Tony. We'll make this right."

CHAPTER 34

Mac took a right on Lakeview Lane then headed towards the cabin.

"Unit 1."

"Unit 1, go ahead."

"I have a call from Police Chief Crawford from the Sacramento Police Department who says he has an urgent phone call. Are you available for a call live?"

"Affirmative, have him contact me on my cell."

"10-4."

A minute later, Mac's telephone rang.

"Chief Givens?"

"I'm here."

"This is Police Chief Crawford."

"What can I do for you, Crawford?"

"Chief Givens, recently a young woman was kidnapped in Sacramento. The woman's name is Marian Procini. She is the daughter of the billionaire giant Jerome Procini."

"Yes, one of my officers mentioned that earlier today. We have a mutual interest in that abduction. My office investigating two recent murders. One of the homicides is a woman who is an identical look-alike to Ms. Procini. Her name is Emma Kelly. I have a missing person who is also an identical look-alike. Her name is Sara Kelly. We are pretty sure these women are sisters. Quadruplets. We have identified three of them. We believe the fourth quad to be a suspect, but we haven't been able to pinpoint her location."

"Interesting. I think we can help each other here. We haven't heard a word from the kidnappers until a few minutes ago. That call came from a mobile phone registered to Jacqueline Renee."

"That's not possible," Mac said, stunned.

"We located that phone call at the address of 32 Lakeview Lane. My information is that this call is within your jurisdiction, and the caller's location is from your property."

Mac pulled his cruiser to the side of the road and braked to an abrupt stop.

"Jesus, what the hell is going on?" Mac mumbled to himself. "Did Jacqueline lose her phone?   And if she did lose it, who could have it now?"

"Chief Givens . . . Chief Givens, are you there?"

Mac briefly hesitated. "Yes, I'm here. I appreciate the information. We will handle it from here, and I will be sure to keep you informed."

Mac immediately contacted his dispatcher. "Unit 1."

"Go ahead, Unit 1."

"Got a Code 207 Kidnap and Hostage situation. Need a call live?"

"Affirmative."

Moments later, a call came in from the dispatcher on Mac's cell phone. "Contact all units and direct them to 32 Lakeview Lane."

"Hey Chief, that's your old house!"

"Affirmative. Convey to all units that they are not, I repeat, they are not to use sirens or lights. I want floodlights placed on the west and north sides of the residence. Officers need to surround the house and wait to hear from me. Call out the SO SWAT team. Urgent request to 32 Lakeview Lane."

"Got it, Chief. It's already done."

Mac slammed his cruiser into drive and took off in a swirl of spewing mud and rocks as he headed to Jacqueline and Jeri's, his mind uneasy.

He parked the cruiser, cut the engine, and turned off the headlights. He glanced to his left and saw Jacqueline's car silhouetted through the downpour. Mac also spotted the cruiser assigned to the cabin. He walked over and tapped on the window. The officer rolled down the window.

"Evening, Chief."

"See anything?"

"Nope. Everything is quiet."

The lights on in the cabin gave Mac a sense of relief that the girls were home and safe.

Still, something didn't feel right.

Mac tapped the butt of his Glock 22.40 caliber service weapon. A quick assessment of the area confirmed there was no movement, and all was indeed quiet. He jogged to the cabin back porch taking the three stairs all at once, trying in vain to get out of the rain and not get soaked. He knocked, waited, but heard nothing. He stamped the excess water off his boots while looking through the door window.

After waiting a moment, he knocked a second time. Again, he got no response.

He tried the door and found it locked. Squinting to look through the window, it didn't seem like anyone was home!

"Strange," he said softly, looking back at Jacqueline's car.

He drew his Glock.

Mac turned, stepped down the stairs, and cautiously headed to the front of the house. He found the door unlocked, held his gun up, and opened the door. Weapon poised and ready, he guardedly stepped into the glassed-in porch. Hearing no sounds, Mac carefully opened the door, which led into the cabin dining room.

"Jacqueline? Jeri?" Mac called as he looked around. The sound of silence was his answer.

Puddles of water and clumps of dirt made a path to the kitchen, where it abruptly stopped. Mac looked around the cabin, waited, and listened.

He carefully followed the path of dirt into the kitchen, crouched down on his heels, and checked a wet footprint, careful not to contaminate or disturb the print. Leaning down, he took a closer look. He was surprised to see that the footprint resembled the footprint found by the tree and the print found the night before by the lake. If he was right, all three prints found belonged to the same person. The muddy footmarks moved back into the dining room and exited the front door of the cabin. Nothing seemed out of place, only the footprints on the floor. *Where were Jacqueline and Jeri?* A cold chill crawled up his spine.

Mac holstered his firearm, took his cell phone from his right breast pocket, and dialed Jacqueline's number. After four rings, her voice mail answered.

"Hi, this is Jacqueline. Leave your name and number. I'll get back to you as soon as I can. Thanks, and have a great day." Mac stood and stared at the phone.

***

"It's hard to believe that Mamie and Uncle Geoffrey could even think about sex in this place," Jeri said, her nose wrinkled in disgust.

"According to folklore, this tunnel has been here since the 1800s," Jacqueline answered. "Back then, the earth was fresh, smelled musty at most. I think it might even have been a bit cozy down here."

"Your definition of cozy and mine are unquestionably different," Jeri chuckled.

As they walked, the tunnel made a sharp turn to the left. Both Jeri and Jacqueline stopped short. Their flashlights exposed stairs that lead up into the darkness.

"Stairs. Where do you think they lead too?"

"Stay here, Jeri. I'll take a look." Jacqueline made her way up the stone stairs until she came to a wall. Moving her flashlight and hand along the wall, she checked for a door or some sort of exit. Finding none, she turned around and followed the stairs back to the tunnel floor. "Nothing, just a wall. Why would someone construct stairs to nowhere?" Jacqueline asked.

"Winchester Mystery House comes to mind," said Jeri.

"Winchester Mystery House?"

"Remember? Sarah Winchester, heiress to the Winchester family fortune. Her husband's family manufactured the first repeating rifle. After her husband died, she bought a house in San Jose, California. She had stairs and walls constructed all over the house that went nowhere."

"What's your point?"

"The world's full of people who do crazy things that don't make sense."

They continued forward and found themselves in an open space. The tunnel ceiling was much higher, which gave the impression of a small room. The walls and ceiling seemed to diminish in size on the far end of the room that led back into the narrow tunnel. They crossed the room, reentered the tunnel, and walked until they came to the end, where they stopped short. Jeri and Jacqueline stared at a ladder bolted to the rock wall.

"A ladder? What is a ladder doing here in this tunnel?"

"More to the point, where does it lead?" Jacqueline shined her flashlight toward the ceiling above the ladder. "That looks like a trap door or something up there."

"Here, hold my flashlight. I'll go up and check it out."

"Are you sure you don't want me to do this?" Jacqueline asked.

"Why? You think I'll fall on my butt," Jeri said, feigning indignation. "Just hold that flashlight, so I can see where I'm going."

"No problem," Jacqueline grinned as she pointed both flashlights toward the ladder. Jeri began the climb.

"Shine it above me so I can see where I'm going."

"This better?"

"Much," Jeri answered as she reached the tunnel ceiling. "You're right! There is a trap door up here."

"Can you see where it goes?" Jacqueline called.

"There seems to be a latch of some sort," Jeri answered. She pulled hard on the latch.

The latch released, and the trap door popped open with a thump. "It's open! I'll check out where this goes," Jeri called back.

"Okay, but be careful."

***

Mac began a search of the cabin. After he checked both bedrooms, he slowly walked back to the kitchen.

The girls were not here. He holstered his gun and headed for his cruiser. THUMP!

Mac stopped in his tracks. THUMP!

Mac cocked his head to the side and listened intently. The sound was coming from the back of the cabin. He again drew his gun, slowly inching his way toward the bedrooms, then stopped and listened. He heard a movement and turned to the left. Someone was in the bedroom.

***

Jeri climbed the last rungs of the ladder. She heaved herself up through the opening and stepped onto a floor.

She looked through slats in a door. "No way," she hissed, stepping softly into a room. "My God! This is my room. I cannot believe this."

Suddenly a bolt of lightning lit the room. Thunder shook the cabin. Jeri heard the rain pounding the cabin roof.

A sound from the hallway caught her attention. She turned and warily moved toward the bedroom door. Another bolt of lightning lit the room. A shadow loomed in the doorway.

"Don't move!"

Jeri screamed in terror. A sheet of lightning instantly turned night into day. Jeri saw a shadow in the doorway with a gun pointed directly at her.

***

Shaken, Mac turned on the bedroom light while immediately holstering his gun. Sweat beaded his forehead. "Jesus, Jeri, I could have killed you."

Jeri threw herself into Mac's arms sobbing. "I'm sorry, I'm sorry, I'm so scared," she cried.

"Jeri, what the hell is going on here? Where's Jacqueline?"

"She's down in the tunnel!"

"What tunnel? You're not making any sense!"

Jeri grabbed Mac's arm and pulled him toward the closet. "In here, Mac. There's a trap door that leads into a tunnel. Jacqueline's down there."

"Jacqueline!" Jeri yelled…

Jeri and Mac looked through the trap door. No flashlights shone—only blackness and silence.

"Jacqueline!" Jeri screamed. "Mac, she was there! Where is she?"

Mac held onto Jeri as she fell into his arms, heart hammering. He realized that this was the first time in many years that dread and terror grabbed him. It would not let go.

CHAPTER 35

Oscar was one of Mac Givens best officers and a cousin through marriage. During the past ten years on the force, he had quickly been promoted to Lieutenant. They had always had a tight bond throughout their childhood and into their adult lives. Mac was the godfather to his only son. His Aunt Edna and Grace had recently confided that Mac had an interest in some woman renting the Kelly cabin. *About time.*

He pulled into the driveway, stopped, and watched the garage door open with sleepy eyes. Once open, Oscar put the car in gear and drove into the only vacant spot in the three-car garage. *This garage is definitely on the top of my priority list of projects.* Oscar thought, not for the first time. He opened the car door, trying to miss the boat, and stumbled on a skateboard left in the wrong spot.

"Damn," he swore, catching the car door handle to stop his fall, then putting the skateboard in the boat.

Yawning again, he stepped into the kitchen, placed his 7TS holster and weapon in the upper cupboard, and immediately felt the warmth of his life.

"Hi, Daddy," Liam shouted. He threw down his pencil, ran to his father, and leaped into his arms.

"Hey Champ," Oscar grabbed his eight-year-old son and started to wrestle, kneeling on the kitchen floor.

Liam jumped up, stepped to his father's side to initiate his newly learned wrestling penetration step, and grabbed his father's leg as Oscar rolled over on his back. Liam jumped on top to pin his father's shoulders to the floor and counted two seconds.

"Give up! Give up, Dad? That's a single leg takedown. How'd I do?"

"Can't believe you pinned me, Dude. Sweet job."

"Awesome!"

"Finish your homework, Dude," Mindy said, walking into the kitchen to stir the pot of minestrone simmering on the stove.

Oscar got up, ruffled his son's hair, walked over to his wife, and nuzzled her neck. God, how he loved this woman. She made him feel valued, cherished, and affirmed.

"I missed you today."

Mindy turned around and snuggled into his arms. "You're silly. Twelve hours on a shift, and you're all gooey?"

"Gooey? What is that? I thought I was romantic with the woman I love."

She pecked him on the cheek. "You hungry?"

"What I am is beat. Caught a bite to eat on duty. I'm going to bed to get some sleep. Care to join me?"

Mindy smiled, a twinkle in her eyes. "Not if you're going to sleep. I need to help Liam with his homework anyway, and he also needs to eat, so, later, tough guy."

Faking insult, Oscar headed for the bedroom. Tall, lean, and according to his wife, awesomely cute, he was the type of guy you want to hug because you know he's safe. Oscar never was the kind of guy to break fragile hearts because of his kind, caring, and considerate nature. He worked out every day for at least an hour to maintain body and mind. The department encouraged all officers and personnel to take advantage of the onsite exercise facilities. It was an asset to his job. He stripped off his uniform, took a quick shower, and threw on a t-shirt and boxer shorts. When his head hit the pillow, he was out.

He was back in California, soaking up the rays on the Santa Monica beach when the shaking began. *Earthquake*, he thought. He needed to jump up, but he was so tired he just wanted to enjoy the sun and get some z's. He felt hands on his arm and shoulder, the shaking becoming more intense. He suddenly realized the ground wasn't shaking. Someone was shaking him.

"Oscar, your cell phone's ringing. Wake up. Here take the phone."

He opened his eyes as the California sun faded away. Sitting up, he took the phone and answered. "Allan."

"Commander Allan, we have a kidnap and hostage situation. SWAT team to report to the department immediately."

"On my way." Oscar jumped out of bed, dressed, and headed for his car.

"Oscar?"

"Have a call out for the SWAT team."

"Take care, baby."

"Always!" Oscar blew his wife a quick kiss and headed to the South Lake Tahoe Police Station.

Oscar had always wanted to become a police officer, but his real dream was to make it on the SWAT team. Few reached that goal, but Oscar was one of those who did. The nature of the team required a high level of cohesion, expertise, and precision. For that reason, Oscar spent a great deal of his time training and honing his skills to be ready to respond at a moment's notice.

Arriving at the police station, Oscar immediately designated one of his men to go directly to the scene and inform him of the situation. He then did a quick briefing with the rest of his team.

"Okay, let's move!" Tensions running high, the team picked up their gear, black duffle bags, climbed into the military-grade armored car, and headed to the scene.

CHAPTER 36

Nicole followed Tony. She knew she had more than enough liquor. She stumbled in the kitchen, tripped on the rug in the living room, and bounced off the closet wall beneath the stairs.

"Goddamn it, Nicole, you left the damn closet door open again." Anger overwhelmed him. His face an inch from hers, he raised his right arm and jammed his finger hard toward her forehead.

"For God's sake!" Tony shouted. "You just don't use that fucking head of yours." His face turned alarmingly red, and sweat rolled down his brow to his neck. He grabbed her and threw her against the closet wall. "You're a train wreck! You know that! You fucking know that?"

"Tony, stop! What difference does it make? It's just the closet door," Nicole shrieked in pain.

Tony pressed her against the wall with his body. Breathing hard, his breath hot, he whispered, "Nicole, you need to listen to me. Someone could walk in here, nose around, and find the hidden door in the closet to the tunnel.

"Tony, you're frightening me," Nicole cried, trying to pull away. "Besides, if no one has found that stupid door in all these years, what makes you think they'll find it now?"

He pressed her harder against the wall. "You need to do exactly as I say from now on."

"Tony, I —"

"— Are you listening to me, you crazy bitch? And no booze Nicole, I mean it. NONE. Do we understand each other here?"

Nicole met Tony's hostile eyes. Numbly she shook her head.

"Yes, Tony," she murmured. She started to cry. "Tony, don't be mad. I love you."

***

He watched in disgust as she used her hand to wipe the snot that dripped from her nose and the tears from her eyes. He walked into the closet, engaged the lock device embedded in the back-closet wall, and waited as the panel door slowly slid open. He grabbed and pushed her toward the tunnel stairs.

"Get down the stairs."

Tony snapped on a flashlight. Nicole took a step, lost her footing several times, but managed to avoid falling in each instance. Once on the tunnel floor, she continued to stagger after Tony. They made their way to the room where they held the hostages.

Just as Tony was about to open the door, Nicole tugged at his sleeve and pointed down the tunnel. A light was moving their way.

"What the hell," Tony whispered. "Who the hell is that?"

"I bet it's one of those sisters."

"What sisters?" Tony asked, confused.

"The sisters that are staying in the old cabin. I saw the two of them over by the gazebo earlier nosing around. They must have found that trap door in the cabin."

"And you're just telling me this now? Go back to the stairs and wait for me."

"Okay, Tony," Nicole whispered.

Tony turned off his flashlight and slowly moved farther into the tunnel toward the light.

"Who's there?" A woman asked.

"It's okay. I'm a police officer," said Tony.

"Thank God. I'm Jacqueline Renee. I know Mac. Have I met you—?"

Before she could finish the sentence, Tony lifted his flashlight and brought it down hard. He turned his flashlight on and checked the woman who laid at his feet. She was out cold. He dragged her through the tunnel toward the hostage room.

Tony taped Jacqueline's ankles and wrists, left her slumped next to the other two women, then retreated into the tunnel to rejoin Nicole on the steps.

"This is crazy," Tony said in frustration. He sat next to Nicole. "We need to figure out a plan. What are we going to do with three bodies? We do not want anyone to know about this tunnel. We might need it again." Tony lit a cigarette, took a long drag, and blew the smoke in slow curls.

"I got a great idea, Tony," Nicole said enthusiastically. "We kill the three of them, now. Once they're dead, we entomb the bodies in this room. We use brick and cement to seal the door. No one knows about the tunnel, and no one will ever find them."

"If no one ever finds your sisters, Nicole, how the hell do we collect the inheritance?"

"Easy, Tony. We wait for seven-years and then have them officially declared dead. Once they're declared dead, we reap the rewards," Nicole beamed.

Tony thought for a moment. "Nah, this seven-year stuff doesn't work for me. I mean, seven years. Are you out of your mind? Use your head, Nicole. It's an implausible solution to our problem." Tony snuffed out his cigarette with the heel of his shoe on the tunnel floor, and then lit another.

"Here is what we do, Sugar. Like you said, kill the three of them now. We roll the corpses in plastic tarps, duct tape them, and leave the bodies here in the room. No one will find them.

We wait for a while until things blow over." "How much is a while, Tony?"

"I figure two, maybe three months. Then we come back, get the bodies, and toss them in the woods. Somewhere remote, like the Mokelumne Wilderness, where hikers will find them. The bodies will have decayed by that time. There are no clues, they're pronounced dead, and you inherit Lex's estate. In two or three months, we're fucking rich beyond our dreams."

"I like it, Tony. I like it a lot."

He grabbed her hand and pulled her up. "Let's check the shed," he said. Together they ascended the stairs.

***

Mac felt Jeri's sobs slowly subside. She took deep breaths to get control of her hiccups. "Jeri, I need to go down that ladder and look for Jacqueline."

"Yes, we need to do that, Mac," Jeri answered firmly.

"No, Jeri, just me. It's too dangerous for you to come. I need you to sit in my cruiser with the doors locked for your protection. I'll call Officer Jobs. He's assigned to watch the Kelly place. I'll have him come over and stay with you until we know what's going on here."

"I'll stay here in the cabin."

"No, it's not safe," Mac said. He led her toward the backdoor of the cabin. He hit the two way on his shoulder radio to contact Jobs.

"Unit 8."

"Unit 8, Unit 1, go ahead."

"Move to a call live."

"10-4."

Moments later, Mac's cell phone rang.

"Chief, it's all quiet at the Kelly house. I'm about to head out to join the troops at the mansion."

"Cancel that. I want you to get over to the cabin and secure the area. A cruiser has already been assigned to watch the area. The cabin leads into a tunnel. I need to make sure no one enters or leaves that tunnel located in the cabin."

"I'm on my way."

"Listen, Jeb. I cannot find Jacqueline. I have to look for her, but I need Jeri to be protected until I get back. I can't have her stay in the cabin, so I'm going to have her wait in my cruiser. Keep a watch on her as well."

"10-4, Chief."

Mac led Jeri through the cabin into the kitchen. "What's all that dirt on the floor, Mac?"

"Careful, don't step in it. Just keep going." Mac opened the kitchen door to a torrent of rain and pulled Jeri along to the cruiser.

"Stay put, Jeri," Mac shouted above the rain as he steered Jeri into the passenger seat and closed the door. He opened the driver's door and slid in.

"You ok?"

"I suppose."

Mac picked up his cell and punched a number.

"Dispatch."

"It's Mac. I need three officers relocated to the gazebo at 32 Lakeview Lane. I have two officers covering the cabin at 30 Lakeview Lane. There is a tunnel that leads from the cabin to the gazebo and possibly to the mansion as well. I believe the hostages are being held in the tunnel but have no exact location at this time. Have all officers stand-down until they hear from me."

"10-4."

Mac watched as Job's parked his cruiser a short distance away. Before opening his door, he turned to Jeri.

"Remember. Stay put. Officer Jobs is right over there. You don't have anything to worry about." He slipped out of the patrol car, shut the door, and headed back to the cabin to begin his search for Jacqueline. As he entered the bedroom where Jeri said she last saw Jacqueline, his cell phone came to life.

"Mac."

"Chief, the SWAT team is on the way. ETA thirty minutes. Commander Allan wants to know if there are any updates."

"We have another possible kidnapping. I'm going into the tunnel. We have a backup to cover the gazebo and cabin tunnel entrances. When the team arrives, surround the mansion and contact me when they're set."

"10-4."

Mac stood in the closet. He noticed that the trap door had fallen shut. He leaned down and opened the door. He took his gun out of his holster, turned on his flashlight, and cautiously stepped on the first rung of the ladder. When he reached the tunnel floor, he turned his flashlight and looked around.

"Well, I'll be damned," he said to no one. "There is a tunnel, after all."

***

Jeri started to cry. Tears flowed down swollen cheeks as she watched Mac run back to the cabin and disappear.

"If I could get to the gazebo and go down the tunnel from that direction while Mac goes through the cabin, one of us is certain to find Jacqueline," Jeri murmured. She looked down at the door and realized that Mac had not locked her in. She saw Jeb's cruiser parked close by, waited for a flash of lightning, then opened the door a crack, and slid out of the car into mud and rain. Softly shutting the door, Jeri squatted down and ran to the side of the cabin. She hugged the cabin wall, then cautiously peeked around the corner to see if Officer Jobs had followed. She saw Jobs open Mac's cruiser door and look around.

Jeri took off toward the gazebo.

CHAPTER 37

Ricks had relocated his vehicle near the gazebo. He and fellow officers had surrounded the mansion without lights and sirens as requested, no questions asked. The sky was tar-black, the rain strumming against the roof of his vehicle. He sat wondering, not for the first time, what the hell was going on. Why the silent surveillance, the stand down, the hold until they heard further instructions? It wasn't like Mac to leave them in the dark, and it made him uneasy. The unrelenting rain sounded like the buzzing of angry bees. A glance to the left briefly caught a shadow as it streaked across a group of trees and disappeared.

"What the . . . ?"

Grabbing a flashlight, Ricks opened the cruiser door, slid silently into the rain, and ran toward the shadow and the trees. Lightning lit the skies, silhouetting a figure running toward the gazebo. The outline of the gazebo through the rain emitted a look of gloom. A blanket of never-ending dreariness seemed to flood the structure and the surrounding grounds. Ricks stood still, held his breath, and listened.

Droplets of moisture dripped off the leaves above. The mournful cry of a lonely fox echoed through the night with a huffing wind suspiring through the air. If someone were close by, they would know his location. The flashlight was not an option. Heavy rain pelted the gazebo roof, the sound not like soft, saturated, swollen drops of spring rain, but rather ball-bearings hitting with force.

Ricks took several steps before sinking into a spongy waterlogged grass mud hole and falling backward hitting the ground with a thud with his gun drawn,

Ricks swore, working one foot through the muck to get free. "This shit sucks," he grumbled, getting to his feet. With gun drawn he moved cautiously toward the gazebo steps, stopped, and again listened.

A sound like the echoing of footsteps came from the gazebo. Ricks stood still trying to get bearings on the noise, the rain blurring his attempts.

Walking forward, he took two steps up to the gazebo floor, tripped on some unseen wood pieces, fell, and disappeared through the gazebo's trap door, hitting hard on cement stairs, which stopped his fall.

"What the—?" Lying still for a moment, he tried to sit up. "Who puts a hole in the middle of a damn floor?" He poked his head through the open hole before pulling himself back onto the gazebo floor.

He moaned, blood oozing from a cut on his forehead, mixed with rain.

Footsteps could be heard in the hole far below.

Where the hell is my gun and flashlight? They have to be at the bottom of this hole. I must have lost them when I tripped and fell.

The rain washed the blood off Ricks' forehead. Taking a deep breath, he moved back through the hole and stepped down the stairs into total darkness.

The dirt floor was damp from the rain that dripped through the opening above, the smell suffocating. Ricks took some matches from his pocket and lit one that produced a sudden burst of light. The small bit of light revealed no flashlight or gun, but oddly two pairs of boots.

Ricks quickly shook his hand to put out the flame before it burned his fingers, lit another match, and slowly made his way into the dark tunnel.

***

Jacqueline woke with a headache. She saw nothing but black. It was cold, and the earth slimy. Panic set in. Fearing she had been buried alive, she became immobilized with terror. The blackness suffocated her. *Is that Sara's voice?* She gradually became more aware and realized that someone was holding her. Her mind backed from the edge of chaos and oblivion.

"Jacqueline."

"Sara . . . Sara, is that you?" She whimpered.

"Yes, thank God you're ok, Jacqueline. When they first brought you here, we thought you were dead," Sara stifled a sob. "Be still, Jacqueline, we have to cut the tape on your ankles and wrists with a piece of glass, and we don't want to cut you."

"Why do I have tape? Who are 'we'? Where are we?"

"In a room, in a tunnel."

"I remember the tunnel now," Jacqueline said. "Who's the other person?

"I'm Marian. Nicole and that guy haven't been back for a while. We're fortunate that they didn't check the tape on Sara and me when they brought you here," Marian said as she cut the last piece of tape. "I think if we're going to try and get out of here, this is our only chance. I'm at a disadvantage because I know little to nothing about these tunnels. I woke up in this room."

"I think we need to turn right once we leave this room," Jacqueline said. "Jeri and I entered the tunnel at the gazebo and walked, at least twenty minutes before we hit a dead-end under the cabin. My gut tells me that we should go right. I know the gazebo trap door is open."

"Sara, do you think you can make it?" Marian asked.

"I think I can, with some help. How about you, Jacqueline?"

"What's wrong with you, Sara?"

"I took a nasty fall. I think I broke some ribs, and I'm not sure about my ankle. It's either sprained or broken," Sara said, with raw panic in her voice.

"I'm in the dark here. I'll have to follow your lead," Jacqueline whispered, feeling a lump the size of an egg on her forehead. I thought someone had buried me. I've never been this frightened in my life," she choked, dread twisting her gut.

"Jacqueline, we're going to be okay, but I'm going to need help. I can't walk on this ankle."

"Lean on me."

"I'll try," Sara said. With a sense of dread, she felt Jacqueline's cold and clammy hands under her arms as she tried to get up.

Marian took the lead, her terror mounting with every step.

***

When they reached the top of the stairs, Tony was about to open the hidden door to the closet but stopped short. He grabbed Nicole's arm, pressing both of them against the wall. "Be quiet," he whispered, hearing movement below. It sounded like someone was in the tunnel. A light floated past the bottom of the stairs and disappeared into the tunnel toward the hidden room.

"What the hell?" murmured Tony.

They waited a few minutes to be sure that whoever it was, was farther down the tunnel.

Tony took a step down the stairs when another set of footsteps passed by the bottom of the stairs going in the same direction as the previous intruder. They waited a few more minutes to make sure there was no one else.

"Sit tight, Nicole. I'm going to check this out."

Pulling a gun from his pocket, Tony slowly descended the stairs and stepped to the tunnel floor. He walked toward the flicker of light.

***

Marian silently felt her way to the door in the dark. Even without sight, she knew where that door was.

She heard Jacqueline help Sara to her feet. Sara moaned after one step.

"Jacqueline, I think it's broken."

"Just let me hold you. Don't use that foot. Try and let me be your anchor."

"Marian," Jacqueline whispered louder, "say something. I need some direction."

"Here . . . I'm over here."

Marian could hear Jacqueline move in the direction of her voice. She became impatient, knowing that danger could return at any moment. She heard Sara groan again, but this time the sound seemed closer to the door. Once she felt Jacqueline's hand, she breathed a sigh of relief. She stepped outside the door, stopped, and listened for any movement or noise.

"Stay close," Marian whispered. They turned right and hugged the dirt walls. Progress was slow but steady bringing them closer to the gazebo and freedom.

A slight touch of light seemed to float in the air somewhere far ahead. Marian halted. "I think there's someone up there," she whispered.

"Be quiet and don't move." They held their breath.

Marion watched the pinch of light grow. Someone was walking toward them.

She got ready to jump on the intruder as the light grew closer. The light hit Jacqueline's face first.

"Jacqueline?"

"Jeri? Jeri!" Jacqueline whispered, frantically grabbing Jeri's flashlight and turning it off.

"What are you doing? Give me that flashlight!"

"Jacqueline, who is this?"

"It's alright, Marian, it's my sister, Jeri." "How did you get here?" Jacqueline asked.

"Through the gazebo trap door," Jeri said. "I was so scared when Mac and I returned to the closet, and you weren't there. Give me the damn flashlight."

Jacqueline grabbed Jeri and hugged her with all her might.

"I'm so glad to see you. Of all people, you are the last person I thought I would see in this tunnel."

"Sorry," Marian whispered. "Right now, we need to find a way out of here before crazy Nicole kills us."

"Right," Jacqueline whispered as she tried to take hold of Jeri's hand. "Is that a gun?"

"I found it with the flashlight at the bottom of the gazebo stairs. It sounded like someone fell and then dropped the gun and flashlight. I grabbed them both and ran."

"Jeri," Jacqueline whispered desperately, "do you know who it was? Are you being followed?"

"No, I don't think so."

"Yes, I think so," said a masculine voice.

Marian and the others turned and stood motionless in the darkness. A match flared illuminating their faces, temporarily blinding them. They could only make out the outline of a figure.

"Who are you?" Jacqueline asked.

"I'm a police officer."

"Right," Jacqueline said as she slammed her foot toward the voice, neatly connecting to his soft spot. "I fell for that once, you moran, but I'll be damned if I'll fall for that a second time."

***

Waves of pain hit Ricks. All his air seemed to be sucked into space. He crumbled to the tunnel floor in a defenseless fetal position. He didn't see the butt of the gun that Jeri coldcocked him with.

CHAPTER 38

Wearing ATN-NVG7 night vision goggles, Tony walked quickly toward the sounds and easily overtook the women. He stood back and counted four. *Four? What the hell? Where did another bitch come from*, he wondered angrily.

Inching forward, he pointed his gun directly at Jacqueline's head. Jacqueline shrieked in utter terror. Frightened and unnerved, she stood still in the darkness feeling something hard against the back of her head.

"You all go back to the room. NOW! Or this pretty lady here is going to die."

Marian turned on her flashlight and fixed the light on Tony, glaring at him with a hatred she was sure could destroy him while grabbing Jeri and holding her behind her back. Sara screeched with fright and moaned in pain as she leaned against the cold dirt wall.

"You must be the guy with that Nicole," Jacqueline said. "That gun must make you feel like a real man, huh?"

"Don't, Jacqueline. We'll go back." Marian said.

"Good advice bitch. You would do well to listen to your friend."

Tony saw a woman holding a gun step out from behind Marian just as she pulled the trigger. The bullet ricocheted off the tunnel wall behind him. He swung his gun around and shot her. Just as quickly turning his weapon back towards Jacqueline as Jeri fell to the tunnel floor.

"Jeri!" Jacqueline screamed and lurched toward Jeri. "You shot my sister!" Jacqueline began to sob.

Tony grabbed Jacqueline and held her tight, pressing his revolver harder into her temple. "You should be careful what you say, you stupid bitch. I'll kill the rest of you now if you don't shut the fuck up and do what I tell you."

Jacqueline sobbed in her attempt to struggle to her feet while Marian helped Sara.

Marian put her arms around Jacqueline's shoulders and tried to console her.

"Idiots," Tony murmured. He picked up the gun off the floor and followed the three women back to the room. *Like leading lambs to the slaughter*, Tony thought. He failed to see Ricks' unconscious body curled up in the darkened tunnel.

Once in the room, Sara was unable to go farther. She cried out in pain as Jacqueline gently laid her down. Both women watched Tony throw his goggles on the mattress, and Nicole light a candle.

"For God's sake, why did you have to shoot my sister?" Jacqueline asked in a whisper.

"What? Tony, you finally off'd one of them," Nicole chuckled, blowing out the match. "Well done, baby."

"It was you! You're the one that's been stalking my sister and me. Why? Why are you doing this?"

Nicole walked over, jabbing her fingers toward Jacqueline's chest, stopping two inches from her.

"Because you poked your nose into my business one too many times," she screeched, spitting in her face.

Wiping the drool, Jacqueline fell to her knees. "My sister," she wept, "you shot my sister." Marian kneeled and wrapped her arms around Jacqueline.

"Enough of this shit. Tape them, Nicole, and make sure you do a decent job this time."

***

The tunnel was narrow, hot, and dark. Making his way through the blackness, Mac heard the sound of a fired gun echo through dirt walls and movement in the distance. Voices up ahead confirmed this conjecture. However, these same voices faded into the darkness. Mac stood still; silence prevailed in dead air. He pulled his gun and moved forward, one step at a time, straining to hear anything. Wiping the sweat off his brow, he thought he heard a sound up ahead. *Was that a moan?* He moved forward with caution and snapped on the flashlight. The beam fell on a single figure.

"Jesus," Mac whispered.

Blood covered Jeri's head. He ran over and knelt beside her, checked her pulse and her injury. A superficial gunshot wound. A bleeder for sure, but not life-threatening.

"Jeri, can you hear me," Mac said softly.

Jeri moaned as she opened her eyes. She put her hand on her forehead and felt the blood. "Mac?"

"Yeah, it's me. You're going to have a hell of a headache, but you'll be ok. Can you sit up?"

"I think so."

"What are you doing here, Jeri? I told you to stay in my patrol car. Can you stand up?"

"Yes," she said, slowly getting to her feet.

"Come on, let's get you out of here."

They headed toward the gazebo. A few feet further, Mac's light fell on an unconscious Ricks curled up on the side of the tunnel floor.

Mac quickly looked for signs of a gunshot wound, seeing only a small amount of blood where some kind of object hit him. Not wanting to inflict further injury to Ricks' head or neck, Mac employed a sternal rub.

"Ricks, Ricks," Mac murmured. The uncomfortable pressure brought his lifeless body around.

Ricks gripped his head as he cried out in pain.

"Take it easy," Mac said as he helped him to sit up.

"Are you alright?"

"I feel like a sledgehammer hit me in the head, and my balls were tortured in a vise just before I was struck by lightning."

Mac hesitated, then slowly smiled, "That's good. I thought you might be hurt."

Ricks looked up and saw Jeri standing next to Mac. "You stole my gun and my flashlight. I should throw your ass in jail and throw away the goddamn key. I'll tell you what, Mac, if you're even thinking of getting hitched to this woman's sister, I suggest you see a shrink. She kicked me in the balls. I'm sitting here questioning my manhood. And that one," Ricks said, pointing to Jeri, "knocked me out with my damn gun. Those women are trouble with a capital T."

***

Mac and Ricks stood in silence and listened to Jeri. Ricks was still pissed. He felt the knot on his head and jerked with pain.

"Mac, I came into the tunnel through the gazebo," Jeri said, pointing her finger towards that direction. Okay, I see you're frustrated," Jeri rushed on, holding her hands up. "I know. I know. I was supposed to stay in the police car, but I needed to find Jacqueline. I figured if you went through the cabin and I went through the gazebo, we would find her. When I got to the bottom of the stairs, I heard some noises come from the gazebo, so I tried to hide.

I heard a thump like someone fell, and then a gun and a flashlight landed at my feet. I picked the gun and flashlight up and ran. I came across Jacqueline in the tunnel; she was with Sara and some other woman. Said her name was Marian. Mac, she was a carbon copy of Sara."

"She's Sara's sister. What happened to them?"

"Some guy followed them and put a gun to Jacqueline's head and said if we didn't follow him back to some room, he would shoot Jacqueline. I still had the gun. I aimed but missed, and he shot me instead."

"And, you're damn lucky!"

"I know," Jeri whispered. "We need to find them, Mac, that guy, he's crazy. He will kill them unless we find them first."

"Do you have any idea where he took them?"

"I didn't see, but Jacqueline, Sara, and Marian came from there," Jeri said, pointing her finger, "and so did that crazy guy. He did say he wanted them to go back to a room. If they came from that direction, I'm sure the room is that way."

"I would say that's pretty much on target," Mac uttered as he looked down the tunnel. Mac's cell vibrated.

"Givens."

"Chief, Commander Allan. My team has moved into position. Ready to take the lead up here."

"Thanks, I'm sending someone out through the gazebo. Let me know when you have her, and she's safe. She's sustained a superficial GSW to the head. Have one of your men take a look. I'll let you know as soon as I have located the hostages."

"10-4."

He shut off his cell and turned to Jeri. "You have to go back to the gazebo."

"Mac, I won't. I need to help find Jacqueline."

"Listen to me, Jeri. I cannot go after Jacqueline and the others and worry about you as well."

Jeri started to speak, but Mac held up his hand and stopped her.

"We both want your sister back. The SWAT team has surrounded the mansion. I want you to go back the way you came and ask for Commander Allan. He's a good guy, knows you're coming out. Knows I'm here, and he knows the hostages are somewhere in this tunnel."

"Okay, I'll go, but promise you will bring Jacqueline back alive. Promise me, Mac!"

"Jeri, Jacqueline means everything. I promise I will bring her back alive and well."

Jeri, touched Mac's cheek with one finger then turned to go. "Here, take this," he tossed her the flashlight. "You'll need it."

CHAPTER 39

They say trees never bend with the rainfall, only with the wind. This night was no exception. Trees stood still as swollen drops fell straight down upon the SWAT tactical unit.

The SWAT response team was stationed around the perimeter of the house, cabin, and gazebo. They were well equipped to resolve this high-risk situation and rescue the hostages.

Their equipment included support detectors to determine hostages or hostage-takers positions and a commercial van for use as a command post and to house equipment. Each SWAT team member wore protective body armor, ballistic shields, night vision devices, and carried specialized firearms, tear gas, and stun grenades. They also had flashbangs, which create a massive explosion that will disorient the perpetrator but not kill them. Set in place, they watched and waited.

***

Jeri hurried quickly through the tunnel to the gazebo entrance. She looked up and saw that the trap door was still open and rushed up the steps. Once she reached the trap door, she began to lift herself through the exit but stopped and listened. The night was silent but for the sound of rain. *Where are the SWAT guys Mac was talking about?* She asked herself, perplexed. She got to her knees and stood up.

Suddenly flood lights flickered on, one after another. The intense light and the rain together formed the image of an alien landscape. Jeri squinted and tried to see, but crystal rain droplets obscured her vision.

"Get down! Now! And do not move."

"What? Who are you?"

"I said, get down now!"

Jeri saw not one gun but five submachine guns aimed at her. She slowly slid to the ground and laid on the alien landscape. Rain splattered her face causing tracks of salt to blend with fresh tears. The rain seemed to lose any warmth while freezing Jeri's pale skin on contact.

"You don't understand. Police Chief Givens told me to come here and ask for Commander Allan. Mac has found the hostages and the people holding them. I need to speak with the Commander." Jeri pleaded as she began to tremble in stark terror.

"Don't move," said a rough male voice.

Jeri heard him walk away and did as she was told. She did not move a muscle.

After what seemed a long time, she heard footsteps march through the pools of mud and rain. She saw boots stop in front of her. Uncontrollably shaking, Jeri tried hard not to move.

A man crouched down and took Jeri's arm. He helped her to her feet. "I'm Commander Allan. I'm sorry; these men did not get the word in time to provide for your safety. Your name is?"

"Jeri, Jeri Winters. Chief Givens told me to ask for you. You have to help them in the tunnel. My sister Jacqueline, Sara, and a woman by the name of Marian are being held by two people who will kill them. Those two are crazy."

"Lower your weapons, men."

"Johnson, take two more of your men and secure this gazebo entrance. Do not enter the tunnel until given the order. Brown, take two more of your men and help secure the cabin tunnel entrance."

"Access is in the bedroom closet," Jeri told him.

"Okay, men, you have your orders."

Allan turned to Jeri. "Chief Givens told me you have a head wound. We have a medic. Let's have him take a look at that injury. Miss Winters, please come with me."

***

Mac and Ricks headed down the dark tunnel with their flashlights off, Mac with gun in hand. They went slow and listened for any sound that might come from the direction they were moving toward.

They had advanced approximately 100 feet when Mac stopped and lit a match. Looking at Ricks, he put his finger to his lips then pointed his finger down the tunnel.

"Voices," he whispered.

"Yeah, not too far. Should we wait to hear from Allan? Make sure Jeri is out of the tunnel and safe?"

"No, we don't have time to wait. This Tony and Nicole are going to kill those hostages. We've got to move now," Mac said. He blew the match out. "Let's move."

Mac turned and led the way farther through the dark tunnel. He couldn't pinpoint the origin of the voices ahead of them, but it seemed as though they were on the left side of the tunnel. *Behind a possible door?* Mac asked himself.

Slowing his pace, he stood and listened. The sound was to the left of him and close. Mac turned to Ricks.

"There must be a door," Mac whispered. "Feel the walls for any crevices."

They ran their hands along the tunnel walls. As they moved forward, the muffled voices grew louder.

"Ricks," Mac whispered, "I think I've found a door, but there's no knob. Stand back. I'm going to kick it in."

Suddenly, the voices stopped. Mac stood still, placed his ear against the door, and listened. He grunted as a lead door smashed him against the tunnel wall, where he collapsed, his gun landing further down the tunnel.

***

Ricks stared at the gun, pointed directly at his head from the open door.

"Hand over your weapons, or you're one dead cop."

"Don't have a weapon. Lost it back there in the tunnel."

"Bullshit! Nicole, check both of these guys."

255

Nicole did as she was told. "No weapons on either one of them."

"Pull your friend into the room."

Ricks sighed in disgust, turned and heaved Mac under his arms, dragging him through the door into a dark room lit only by a few candles.

"Haul him and yourself over there."

"Mac," cried Jacqueline.

"Shut up!" Tony shouted.

"Bring him over here, Ricks," said Jacqueline, ignoring Tony's outburst.

Ricks noticed the lit candles added minimal light to the room. In the corner were Jacqueline, Sara, and another woman. He assumed this was the missing Marian Porcini. The three women were bound with tape on their ankles and wrists.

"Look, I don't know who you are," Ricks said, "but I can tell you right now, you are done. Police and a SWAT team are all over this place. There is no way out. If you give yourselves up, it will go easier on you."

"Shut up!" Tony yelled. "Just shut the fuck up!"

"Tony, what are we going to do?" Nicole began to whine as she danced around.

"We're changing our plans. That's what we're going to do. We use our hostages as just that, hostages. We're going to use them to get some transportation out of here. And for Christ's sake, stop jumping around."

"How, Tony? How do we get out of here?"

Tony was silent, thinking hard on his plan. He threw Nicole a roll of duct tape. "Take the handcuffs off those two cops and tape them together. That whore with the broken foot is useless to us and will only slow us down. Take the tape off the other two and handcuff those two bitches together. Then hand me the keys."

Ricks watched as she got up and followed directions. She seemed to take great satisfaction in Marian and Jacqueline's painful cries and discomfort when she pulled off the tape along with some skin. Pulling the manacles out of Mac's pocket, Nicole handcuffed Marian and Jacqueline together.

Realizing that Tony and Nicole would leave Sara, Ricks, and himself taped up but unharmed, Mac grasped with sudden anguish and understanding that Jacqueline and Marian would be going with them. Neither of them might survive to see the morning.

CHAPTER 40

Once Sara, Mac, and Ricks were secured with tape, Tony and Nicole herded Marian and Jacqueline out the door, slamming it shut. Heading down the tunnel to the house, Tony could not shut Nicole up.

"Kill them, Tony," Nicole shouted, following with a gun pointed at Marian's back. "We need to kill them now and get out of here."

Tony kept moving toward the mansion access, trying to ignore Nicole's outbursts while he pulled his hostages toward the steps.

"You left Sara back there, do you realize that? She needs to be dead! Who cares if she has a broken foot! Tony, are you listening to me? The two of them cannot survive. I came here to get rid of my sisters, and I plan on doing just that. Tony, I have to kill them. This has to be done now!"

"Shut up and help me get these two up the stairs into the mansion."

"What are you going to do, Tony?"

"These two are my ticket outta here."

"Our ticket Tony!"

"Move it."

Tony walked up the stairs with Nicole pulling up the rear. Jacqueline and Marian staggered up the stairs between the two. Once reaching the top of the stairs, Tony opened the hidden door, and they entered the mansion through the small closet. Bright lights seemed to envelop the rooms making daylight of a rainy night.

"Shit." Tony moaned. "Those cops were right on. The police and SWAT are everywhere."

Tony grabbed Jacqueline by the throat, pulling both Jacqueline and Marian to the front door.

"Open it," Tony shouted, slamming Jacqueline and Marian into the door. Bright lights met them, flooding the front lawn. A voice enriched by a megaphone boomed.

"Lay down your arms, and let the hostages go. You are surrounded. It's over. Throw down your arms."

"No fuckin' way," Tony shouted. "You will get me transportation out of here, or these two will be dead."

"That is impossible."

"Oh yeah?" Tony shouted. He turned and shot Marian in the leg.

Marian screamed and fell on Jacqueline as both collapsed onto the porch. Tony's gun rested directly on Jacqueline's skull.

"We are listening to your demands. Do not shoot the hostages. I repeat, do not shoot the hostages."

"Good, I like it when people listen to me," he yelled. "I want a car to the airport and a plane. You better have it within 15 minutes, or they die here and now. He pulled Marian and Jacqueline back through the door and slammed it shut with his foot.

Jacqueline, with much difficulty, pulled Marian onto the carpet and laid her down. She tore a piece of her blouse to make a tourniquet with her un-cuffed hand. She wrapped it around Marian's thigh to stop the heavy flow of blood as best she could.

"It's ok, Marian, I'm stopping the bleeding. It's going to be okay."

A faint smile was all Marian could muster, "I know Jacqueline," she said as her eyes closed from exhaustion and pain.

Nicole stomped through rooms mumbling to herself. "Kill them, Tony, kill them, kill them, we need to kill them!"

Tony stood still as he watched Nicole losing it. Running over to Nicole, he grabbed her arm, and with a sudden jerk, twisted her around.

"Shut up, you crazy bitch!"

While Tony and Nicole argued, Jacqueline and Marian looked for an opportunity to escape.

***

Oscar turned to his second in command, Chuck Conrad. "I'm not getting through to Chief Givens, and dispatch is unable to make contact with him either. I'm feeling very uneasy. Haven't heard from Ricks either, and he is supposed to be with Givens. We need to step up our game here and move. Have we got any further information about this hostage-taker and this woman who is with him?"

"Talked with the person we picked up, Jeri Winters. She said this guy is crazy. Officer Jobs said this guy's name is Tony Russo. The police are pretty sure this guy Russo is the one who shot Kelly earlier tonight. The woman is Nicole Platt. It seems she is the sister of two of the hostages and is bent on killing them. My take is that she is one very outraged, unstable, and dangerous person who will take everyone with her given half the chance."

"Who do we have for a clean shot?"

"Jim Savage, he's our best sniper, sir,"

"Good, I want him up high." He pointed to one of the trees behind them. "Once he's in place, I want him to zero in on our two kidnappers. The minute those assholes show any visibility; he is to take his best shot. I want all hostages alive. Shoot to kill if they are threatened. Are we clear, Conrad?"

"Yes sir! Consider it done."

***

Savage and his spotter positioned themselves on two large thick branches of a tree. Savage decided this was his best vantage point for a clear shot as it also offered him the best field of fire. They were less than 100 meters from their target. His spotter, located just to Savage's left and only slightly behind him, carried a unique scope to help Savage observe objectives. Savage knew he could pull the trigger and hit his target in the crosshairs. His handheld anemometer ensured his ability to calculate wind speed more accurately as well as eliminate spindrift. Because of the rain, the bullet could move slower, therefore dropping faster in dense air. Savage made adjustments to accommodate the weather. Verifying that their position was well camouflaged, they ranged the target, read the wind, adjusted angles, and checked for final variables that could affect the sniper's shot. Savage noted activity in the two windows on either side of the mansion's front door. They settled in.

He switched on his two-way radio. "Able Charlie, this is Bald Eagle. Ready and standing by."

"Roger that Bald Eagle."

Savage waited for his target to appear.

CHAPTER 41

When Mac came to, his shoulder felt like a hotbed of coals. He took a deep breath, surveyed his predicament, and tried to put the searing pain out of his mind. Sara was awake but seemed out of touch. She stared at the wall, not saying a word. Mac was sure she was in a state of shock. Ricks, taped wrist to wrist with him, labored unsuccessfully to get out of the tape, binding them together. Mac looked at Sara.

"Sara," he said.

Sara continued to stare at the wall with no response.

"Sara, you have to listen to me." He raised his voice and tried again. "Sara, listen to me."

"It's no use, Mac. I've tried to talk to her," said Ricks. "She's in shock and can't help us."

Mac tried again. "Listen to me, Sara. I have a pocket knife here in my right pocket. We can't reach it, but you can. I know it will hurt you to move over this way, but Sara, you are our only hope of getting out of here. Sara!" Mac said louder.

Sara sluggishly turned her eyes to Ricks and then to Mac. "Mac?"

"Sara, you've got to help us. You're the only one who can."

"Knife." Sara's eyes cleared; the fog lifted. "Where's the knife?"

"Here, in my slacks. We can take it slow and try to move over towards each other. Can you do that, Sara?"

"Yes, I think so." She moved at a snail's pace toward Mac. She whimpered with each attempt as she dragged her broken foot.

"That's good, Sara. I know it hurts, but you're doing a great job," Mac said, as he and Ricks shuffled closer to her. "Another foot, and we're there."

In another few minutes, Sara was able to get next to Mac. She put her back to him so that her bound hands could get access to the knife.

"Here, in my right front pocket."

The tape restricted Sara's hands, not allowing her hand to grab Mac's switchblade. She tried to inch her fingers into his tight pants.

"Mac, I can't do it."

"Yes you can, keep trying. Take it slow."

Sara tried again. She inched her fingers between the material until she felt a small piece of metal.

"I think I found it."

"Careful, Sara," Ricks said softly.

Sara tried to put her fingers around the knife, but it slipped away. "I lost it!" She reached to get a stronger hold and pulled it out.

"Mac, I've got it! But I can't open it. I can't move," she began to weep. "My ankle, the pain is so bad. I'm sorry, Mac,"

"Ricks, we need to shift ourselves closer, so I can get that knife."

Together they repositioned themselves within inches of Sara. Once they moved, Mac was able to take the knife and open it. He slipped the knife back to Sara. He and Ricks changed positions again so that their taped hands were next to Sara's hand with the knife.

"Okay, Sara, now try and cut the tape on my wrist."

"I'll try."

Sara was able to insert the knife between the tape binding Mac and Ricks' wrists. Within minutes Mac felt the give as the tape began to split.

"A little more, and I think you've got it," Mac mumbled. After several moments the tape was cut. Turning around, he took the knife from Sara.

"Sara, you did a great job," he said. He worked on both Ricks and Sara to free them. Once released, he left the cut tape stuck around their ankles and wrists.

"Sara, you stay here while we find Marian and Jacqueline."

"Mac, I can't," Sara wept. She fought a rising panic.

"Sara, you have to. You can't walk with that ankle."

Fear of being left alone tormented her.

"I'm so scared," she whispered.

"We'll be back soon, I promise. Here, take one of these flashlights."

Sara took the flashlight but left it off.

Mac leaned over and kissed Sara on the cheek. "I'm here with you, Sara. I promise I won't let anything happen to you."

"Go, Mac. Hurry."

Mac and Ricks headed for the door. Mac slipped through first, then turned his flashlight to search the tunnel floor for his gun.

"Found it," he said. "At least something is in our favor."

Ricks looked back. "Will she make it, Mac?"

"She has to. We have no options here."

***

Sara watched Mac and Ricks reach the door and disappear with the light. She laid in the dark, her mind thick with fear. After a moment, she heard something scurry past and felt a rat brush her leg. Her heart leapt to her throat. She quickly turned the flashlight on; her body weighed down by dread.

***

Jacqueline sat on the carpeted floor with Marian's head in her lap. She stroked Marian's damp hair while she watched Tony and Nicole lose control of the situation.

Nicole continued to walk from room to room, mumbling to herself. "Kill them, shoot them, kill them!"

Jacqueline watched Tony run his hands through his greasy black hair and pace back and forth in front of the mansion's door, stopping short of the windows. *He's like a wounded caged animal,* she thought—*a dangerous one.*

She looked down at Marian. There was no way she would be able to help them escape in her present state. If they were to get out of this mess, Jacqueline would need to take the lead.

She had to get to that front door without Tony stopping her. It was their only chance. But how?

***

Tony watched Nicole, convinced she had finally lost any sense of reality. This whole thing was turning out bad. Very bad. His head, like this scheme, was about to explode.

"It's almost fifteen fucking minutes," he shouted, pointing his gun at the front door. "Where the hell are they?"

He turned and stared at Nicole, mumbling to herself. He watched her pace from room to room. He had been close to losing control with Nicole over the last day but managed to hold it together by focusing on the prize. Lex's death stoked the fire, and with the money now lost, an inferno erupted. Tony snapped.

He ran over, grabbed her arm, and with a sudden jerk, twisted it behind her back. Stunned, Nicole let out a scream of pain as Tony pushed her arm further up her back, dislocating her shoulder. Tony shoved his foot directly onto Nicole's back and, with the strength of an enraged man out of control, sent her flying into the wall corner edge. Nicole's head hit hard, cracking her skull. She collapsed to the floor, breath rattling in her throat. She died as she lived. Alone.

Tony turned to Jacqueline and Marian. "Do not move!"

"You monster!" Jacqueline screamed.

"See, that's the difference between you and me. I'm a survivor. I leave the weight behind."

"You're a loser and a murderer!" Jacqueline yelled.

Marian moaned with pain at the sudden movement of Jacqueline's outburst.

"It's okay, Marian. I'm sorry," she whispered. She tried to calm Marian as well as herself.

CHAPTER 42

Savage waited patiently for his target to show himself in one of the windows. He noted activity occurring sporadically with no clear shot presenting itself.

He thought he saw a scuffle and someone slammed against a wall. He waited for the perfect chance to take these SOBs out.

***

Commander Allan had asked Officer Conrad to find a place outside the yellow taped area where Jeri would be safe.

Jeri wanted to be with her sister, in their pajamas, sipping a hot cup of tea and discussing the day's events as they watched the lake. Instead, she was sitting in a police car. Alex had found her, his presence a comfort. She turned and offered a weak smile and squeezed his hand.

Her body shook in terror. Anxious for Jacqueline's safety and the others, she shivered as she watched the scene in front of her unfold.

***

Mac and Ricks raced through the tunnel, looking for an exit. They found steps that led up, took them two at a time, and stopped when they reached the top. Hearing voices, Mac quickly snapped off his flashlight. Darkness enveloped them.

"What?" Ricks whispered.

"Voices. I think I hear Jacqueline," Mac whispered. "We need to get into the house."

"How? I don't see a door here,"

"There's got to be a hidden door. Something in this wall. Look for some sort of lock device," Mac said as he ran his fingers along the floor, working his way up to the ceiling. "Bingo," he whispered as his fingers touched an object. The wall slowly slid open. Mac stepped down to the tunnel floor and called Allan. "I'm in the mansion."

"Exactly where?"

"Closet. It's an entrance to the tunnel."

"Have a sniper ready to take out the perp. Located outside the front door."

"That's good. I can see Tony from my vantage point. I'm going to try and get closer."

"Okay, but watch it, Mac. This guy is a time bomb."

Mac went back up the stone stairs and cautiously crept through the closet door with his gun drawn. Ricks followed. They tiptoed to a wall that gave them both cover. Motioning to Ricks to stay where he was, Mac crept forward and snuck a quick look around the wall to the hall by the front door. He looked right and saw a woman on the floor on the far wall. She was definitely dead. To the left, Mac saw Jacqueline and Marian. Tony had a gun pointed at the back of Jacqueline's head.

"Get up, bitch."

***

Jacqueline felt the gun pointed at her head. Tony had lost all self-control, and she was terrified for her and Marian's safety. He was a bundle of energy with no concept of reality. Slamming Nicole against the far wall seemed to have taken him over the edge. She was alarmed that Marian's strength seemed to be declining, her pallor pasty white, and her pulse weak. In and out of consciousness, Jacqueline tried to keep her awake. Marian had lost a lot of blood and was quickly losing awareness. Jacqueline tried to think of a way to get them free before they ran out of time. But, maybe, it was already too late.

"Unlock the cuffs," Tony said, throwing the keys into Jacqueline's lap. Tony pressed his gun hard into the side of her neck.

Jacqueline did as she was told. Marian whimpered with the movement of her wrist and hand. Jacqueline tried to be gentle, but Marian's swollen wrist made her efforts to remove the restraints difficult. She finally was able to unlock and detach the handcuffs.

"Get up and move to the door, or your next breath will be your last."

Jacqueline laid Marian down and ignored the pain in her side as she stood, afraid any sudden movement would cause the gun to accidentally fire.

Tony's face was bright red with rage.

He dragged Jacqueline to the front door. "Open the fucking door!" He screamed.

Jacqueline tried to open the door, but her hands were shaking badly. Sweat caused her to lose her grip on the door handle several times before she was finally able to open it.

She swung the door open and narrowed her eyes to the bright floodlights.

"Okay, you assholes," Tony screamed, pushing Jacqueline through the door. "It's been fifteen minutes, and I haven't heard any positive results here."

"We're working on the plane," came a voice on a bullhorn. "We need some more time to make this happen."

"Sorry, you don't have any more time. I said if you didn't get me my transportation, these hostages were dead. You're just fucking with me, and no one fucks with Tony Russo!" he shrieked, his voice breaking in a frenzied fury.

***

A strong hand pushed Jacqueline down as she sunk to her knees, weeping. She felt she was experiencing a terrifying nightmare. Soon, she would wake up, and this horrendous sense of terror and panic would end.

Blinded by floodlights, she felt the cold hard steel of the gun's barrel against her neck.

"Please, please," Jacqueline sobbed. "Someone, please help us."

The color drained from her face as she lowered her eyes and stared at her shaking hands. Her thoughts were a jumble of pain and sorrow. She thought she heard her sister scream, but that was not possible. Jeri was dead. Unrelenting remorse washed over her. The death of her sister was Jacqueline's fault, and the burden of that fact weighed heavily on her. She heard Tony's crazed voice shouting as his spittle hit the back of her neck. When she opened her mouth to speak, no words formed on her lips as violent, uncontrollable tremors shook her body.

"You didn't listen to me." He screamed. His shaking hand held the cold metal revolver against Jacqueline's head. "Are you listening to me now? She's a dead woman!" He shouted. His grip on the gun stiffened. His finger ready to squeeze the trigger.

***

"Here we go," Savage said, alert as he zeroed in on his target and the one hostage. They stood in the open doorway, the target with a gun directed toward the back of his hostage's skull.

***

Jeri felt the breath go out of her when she saw her sister and the kidnapper come through the front door. She reached for the door handle and yanked open the patrol car door.

"Hey, where do you think you're going? Stop Jeri, what the hell are you doing?" Alex yelled. He tried to grab her arm and pull her back.

She pulled her arm from his grasp, ripping her jacket. "Don't you shoot my sister!" She screamed. She flew across the space between them. She saw Tony briefly turn towards her.

***

Thunder boomed as the earth seemed to shudder to its core. A gunshot traveling a speed of 3200 feet per second divided Tony's hand from his gun. A second bullet sliced through Tony's skull between the soft tissue of the parietal and occipital lobes. Tony, for a mini second, seemed surprised. The bullet ripped through the back of his skull. It exited through his frontal lobe, the projectile spewing a misty crimson cloud like a gossamer, the delicate filmy cobweb floating in the air along with brain matter scattered from the initial exit wound. Tony abruptly died where he stood. His body fell forward, striking the cement porch with a dull thud as Jacqueline wept. Blood trickled and leaked from the wound where Tony dropped, a ribbon of red flowing to the edge of the porch.

***

Jacqueline heard a voice shouting, "Hold your fire, I'm a police officer, don't shoot," Warm arms encircled her. A soft voice whispered in her ear. "You're okay."

Jacqueline looked up into Mac's face. "Hold on to me, Jacqueline. I'm here." She held on with her entire being.

***

Jeri ran to Jacqueline and Mac. Tears of joy consumed her as she wrapped her arms around them both.

"You're alive," Jacqueline whispered.

"Yes, I am alive."

"How? I saw Tony shoot you."

"The shot nicked my head. Other than a headache, I'm fine."

Jacqueline touched Jeri's wound then took her in her arms. "You and Mac. You saved my life. I love you, Sis!"

Horrified, Alex ran up and dropped to his knees. "Jeri, you scared the hell out of me. You all scared the hell out of me." He put his arms around Jeri. "Are you alright?"

"I'm fine now, Alex."

Ricks came up from behind. "Nice shooting, Chief. Messy but effective."

Commander Allan and Officer Savage walked up the stairs. "So, Mac, you were the one who fired that shot," Savage said in admiration. "Great shot. Right on target. You ever want a job with the SWAT team, you got one." Savage hesitated, shaking his head. "My shot would not have saved the hostage. A shot in the head would not have prevented the reflex on the trigger from my vantage point. He turned to Jacqueline. Your sister screaming and distracting this guy saved your life." Savage did a quick salute to Jeri and Mac. "You both saved her life."

Mac looked over at Allan and Alex. They did a fist bump. "Good job, Chief." Allan nodded.

Mac directed his attention to Jacqueline. He heard the ambulance sirens getting louder and closer.

"I need to help Marian and Sara. Jeri and Alex are here. I'll be back."

Jacqueline squeezed Mac's arm. "Go."

Mac moved over to Marian. She had lost a lot of blood and was extremely pale. He checked the tourniquet and found it had, at least, stopped the bleeding.

"Marian."

Marian opened her eyes. She had difficulty focusing.

"Marian, I'm a police officer. You're going to be okay. Hang tight. An ambulance is on its way."

She smiled weakly.

The front rooms were filling with law enforcement.

Emergency responders arrived and immediately took charge of the wounded.

Mac moved over to Allan. "You need to come with me. I have another hostage who is hurt in the tunnel. We need to hurry."

Allan, along with several emergency medical team members, followed Mac through the house, closet, and into the tunnel. With the help of a flashlight, they located the hidden room where they found Sara.

Mac knelt, leaned over, and shook her gently.

"Sara."

Trembling, Sara forced her eyes open. "Mac."

She wrapped her arms around Mac's neck, held him tight and wept.

"Marian and Jacqueline?" she whispered through her tears.

"They're okay, Sara. We're all okay," he said, embracing her. "Come on, let's get you out of here."

Allan looked around, then turned. "Jesus, Mac! What is this place?"

***

For the rest of the night and far into the next two days, the PD did a thorough search of the tunnel and passages connecting the cabin, gazebo, and mansion.

DAY SIX...

The pages of the broken are closed
Life's chapters concluded too early
So many words unspoken
Too soon for life's stages to end

***

Soft winds begin to blow, the sun shines
The rivers flow once again with peace
Laughter once again fills the air
As love replaces all the despair

CHAPTER 43

Mac and Oscar walked into the hospital room with four fresh bouquets. The room looked more like a dorm with four single beds, two on each side of the room, with one patient occupying each bed. A light atmosphere prevailed.

Sara was in one of the beds on the left side of the room, enjoying her breakfast. Aside from the cast on her ankle, the dark circles under her eyes and faded bruises were the last signs of her nightmare.

Marian sat in the bed next to Sara's. The bullet wound to her leg had been wrapped with a clean dressing. Two units of blood, along with antibiotics and IV fluids, put color back in her cheeks. Her swollen wrist, wrapped in bandages, hindered her progress with her breakfast tray, but her spirits were high. She and Sara chatted and laughed like old friends.

***

Jerome Porcini sat next to his daughter's bed, mesmerized by the two sisters. If not for the bruises on Sara's face and the different lengths of their hair, he would not be able to tell the two apart. *Amazing*, he thought, as his heart warmed with love for his daughter and her newfound sister. He watched a police officer approach his daughter's bed. The officer introduced himself, leaned over, and gave her cheek a peck.

"Wanted to meet my missing cousin," Oscar smiled warmly. "Welcome to the family." He handed her his bouquet, then turned to Sara. "And these are for my other crazy cousin," he chuckled as he hugged her.

***

On the other side of the room, Jacqueline complained that she wasn't hurt and didn't need to be in bed, let alone a hospital. But when she saw Mac walk in, she put her head back on her pillow with a warm smile. He had become her rock, her savior, the love of her life. When he was around, she was safe and secure. She never wanted to be without him again. She briefly thought about her trip back home in two days. A pang of regret struck her heart. She turned her face into her pillow so Mac would not see the teardrop. She quickly brushed it away.

Mac took her hand. "Are you okay?" he asked, concerned.

"She is now that you're here," Jeri crooned, lying in bed next to Jacqueline. She scratched the bandage wrapped around her head. "Damn, I can't wait until they take this giant Band-Aid off. Itches like crazy. Did I tell you I talked with the kids? Told them not to come to Tahoe. I would see them in a few days when I get home. They're coming to Denver for a few days."

"So see? There is an upside to getting shot. You get to see Ally and James!" Jacqueline laughed.

Mac helped Jacqueline sit up. He turned to assist the nurse with the breakfast tray. While she and Jeri settled in to eat, Alex, Zed, and Dustin came into the room. The guys embraced Mac, who introduced them to Marian's father. Alex walked over to Jeri and gave her a warm hug before he sat down.

Dustin strolled over to a refrigerator stored with snacks and a minibar.

"Are you kidding me? I never heard of such a thing in a hospital room," he laughed. "This is frigging great," he said as he previewed the stock of juices, wines, and beer. He took one bottled water.

Ricks strolled in carrying a one-pound box of See's truffle candy to be shared by all.

Jacqueline couldn't help but laugh. "Ricks, you are the best. Bring that box over here." Taking a piece, she almost fainted with delight. "Guys, you've got to have one of these."

"Well, I know a party when I see one," Edna said, entering the hospital room, followed by her sister.

Jeri looked up from her search for that perfect piece of chocolate. "Edna! Gracie! What a nice surprise."

"Aunt Edna." Mac smiled warmly at his aunt as he gave Edna and Gracie affectionate hugs. "Is that one of your special blueberry pies?"

"It is, and it's for the girls," Edna said, swatting Mac's hand away affectionately.

"Aunt Edna, do I get some of that?"

Edna and Gracie stepped over to Sara and Marian. "Oh my, this is our Annie's daughter, Gracie whispered as tears stung her eyes. "Just look at the two of you. So much alike."

"Marian, this is your Aunt Edna and Aunt Gracie. They make the best blueberry pie on the planet."

Marian turned and gave Edna and Gracie a warm hug. "This is my dad."

"Oh, my dear, don't feel bad. None of this was your fault."

"Not bad, Gracie, this is her dad, her father for heaven sake! Shaking her head, she looked at Marian. "When the Lord was handing out brains, Gracie thought God said trains. She passed on the good Lord's offer because she doesn't like to travel." She patted Marian's hand. "You'll get used to her. I've had to."

Mac looked over at Oscar. "We did a good job."

"We did an awesome job."

Alex spoke up, "so after two days, has law enforcement put a picture together on this whole thing?"

***

"I think we've pieced together a pretty clear picture," Mac said, settling back into a chair next to Jacqueline's bed.

"We were able to interview the doctor who delivered the quadruplets. Dr. Strucker is now ninety-five. We found him in a senior citizen facility. Still has a good memory, not too remorseful for his part with the quadruplets. He was Mrs. Kelly's doctor for many years and delivered Alex, there, and Zed and Dustin. The Kellys wanted one additional child, hoping for a girl. It's seriously unfortunate that Lex Kelly raped her one night when her husband was not at home, and she became pregnant.

"Some women are prone to producing more than one egg during ovulation, and Mrs. Kelly was a candidate. She was over 35, she already had several children, and her mother was a fraternal triplet, which, according to our Dr. Strucker, is a prerequisite for multiple births. Also, according to the doc, the odds of a natural quadruplet birth are 1 in 729,000. But, here's the kicker. The chances of having a set of identical quadruplets is one in eleven million. It has happened before, the last time in 2007. I mean, think about those odds!"

"It's so hard to comprehend. I mean how awful it all must have been," Marian said.

"And the odds on quadruplets, it's mind-boggling," Sara added.

"Your mom had a nervous breakdown during her pregnancy. She did not want any of the babies, but she bonded with the firstborn when she gave birth. That was you, Sara. The other three were pronounced dead and empty caskets were buried. Arrangements were made for the other three to be sent to an adoption agency.

Neither Annie nor the doc ever revealed their secret. At least, that's what your mother thought. It turns out, Dr. Strucker approached Kelly about the quadruplets. Strucker told Lex his brother's wife got pregnant; they were his children, she kept one, and the others were given up for adoption. Dr. Strucker blackmailed him for many years. The first ten were to keep the rape a secret and Kelly out of jail; the remaining years, because Kelly had created a financial empire, and if anyone found out, it would ruin him.

"Lex had seen pictures of Sara on the family website, so when he found Emma, he immediately knew that Emma was his daughter. He had a DNA test done to confirm her legitimacy. As for Mrs. Kelly, she felt she would have lost her husband and family had she said anything.

"Pretty harsh in my book." Mac paused thoughtfully. "But it's not my job to judge, just to find out the facts."

Sara was quiet.

"She told one other person, me," Alex said. "She told me because she was afraid for Sara's safety. She didn't trust Lex Kelly. It never occurred to her that the concern would be one of the sisters."

"I need you all to know my mother was a wonderful person," Sara said softly, as she silently began to weep. "She was always loving, compassionate, and supportive in every way. Marian, you need to know that. She was devoted to her family and my best friend. Knowing her as I did, it must have been so horrible to carry that burden for so many years. It's even more tragic, given the dreadful, heartbreaking childhoods both Emma and Nicole experienced. You and I were the lucky ones, Marian. In some ways, maybe Emma was too. I mean, at least she found help with her father. But poor Nicole. I'm not condoning what she did, but how can you not have compassion for what she went through? It all just breaks my heart." Sara continued to weep.

Mac watched Sara in silence before continuing.

"It was unfortunate for those two. Both wound up in the foster care system, and neither did well. Like you said, Sara, Emma's father, did somehow find her and took her in. She was also the first murder victim.

"Nicole was a bad apple from the beginning. She never caught a break. Each foster parent was worse than the last. She got lost in the system, which unfortunately happens. Once she turned of age, this same system dropped her on the streets, which regrettably also happens when foster kids age out. The road led her to prostitution and eventually to Reno, Nevada. That is apparently where she and this Tony Russo hooked up. From what we've gathered from interviews, she bonded with this guy big time. Fell in love and followed him to New York, where he worked in the Daniel Corporation, which just happened to be owned by Kelly.

"The day before the night Emma Kelly disappeared, we know that Tony Russo rented an Enterprise truck. He'd found out that Lex's daughter was heading to California through a friend, and he was afraid she would crush his plans with Nicole. Next thing we know, Emma Kelly is found dead in South Lake Tahoe, and Nicole is spotted in the same area.

"We do know that Nicole shot Joe Carver. However, I believe she meant to shoot Lex Kelly. We know, Tony Russo shot Lex Kelly. We also found the knife that Nicole used to kill Emma. Her ultimate intent was to kill both Sara and Marian as well, and inherit your father's estate."

"He's not my father," Sara said bitterly.

"She came pretty close," Marian murmured. "I mean, to killing us."

Sara sighed. "I still feel sorry for her. I mean, her fate wasn't her fault. She was a victim all her life. It's horrible what she has done, but I can't help thinking, if she had caught a break, all this would not have happened." Lowering her eyes, she was silent for a moment. "I'm also sorry we were not able to meet Emma."

I'm sorry too," Marian said. "But I'm glad we found each other. I've found my sister, and it's for life."

Jacqueline and Jeri knew exactly how Marian felt. Sisters are a lifetime of happiness.

DAY NINE...

Though it's been days of few
It is time to say goodbye
No mountains, hills nor valleys
Can separate hearts who are now of one

CHAPTER 44

Jacqueline and Jeri were all packed and ready to leave in the morning.

The celebration was winding down. Everyone was sitting around the cabin dining room table, where it all started nine days ago. Good Chinese food, ice-cold beer, and excellent wine left everyone satiated and mellow.

Jacqueline, stifling a yawn with her hand, looked around the table. "One more question before everyone leaves. We have the answers to the murders, but there's still the issue of your property, Sara."

"I saw our lawyer yesterday," Alex said. "Turns out, they were able to confirm the falsification of the documents that Uncle Lex had forged. They were also able to find and arrest the notary who was responsible for falsifying the documents."

Sara jumped in. "Our understanding is that Uncle Lex, back in 1975, needed a lot of money to get out of town. He was stealing from the Mafia. His partners, who he owned a Casino with, found out. To pay off a portion of the debt, he first quitclaimed a deed for the Tahoe property one hundred percent to this guy named Manny and his partners. Uncle Lex forged my father's name. Manny filed that claim before he died. My uncle then signed a quitclaim deed to our father for his share of the property, for which my father paid cash. I guess my uncle figured he would be long gone before anyone caught the two deeds. My father filed his claim three days later. When Manny died, his partners did not have a clue about the first deed until some guy was looking for property and found the deed. Since the first deed was fraudulent, the deed my dad filed became valid."

"So, what happens now?" Marian asked.

"Well, Marian," Alex answered, "you and Sara are the only descendants of Uncle Lex's estate, so you two will inherit any assets he had. My guess is his company is worth a considerable sum. The lawyers feel there are other properties and possessions. Assessments on the valuation of all assets will have to occur before further steps are taken. As for our home, Sara, I have spoken with Dustin and Zed, and we all agree that you still own an equal portion of this house and property. Also, you will continue to be a partner in the family corporation. Nothing for us has changed.

"I love you guys. We have plenty of time to sort this all out." Sara said as she looked for her crutches and rose from her place at the table. "I'm exhausted and need to head for home." Turning to Jacqueline and Jeri, she smiled warmly. "I can't begin to tell you both how much I'm going to miss you. But we live so close. We will never be strangers."

"That's a promise," Jeri beamed.

"Absolutely," Jacqueline said as she hugged Sara.

Sara turned to Marian and her father. "Please come and spend the night with us. We have plenty of room, and I'm not ready to say goodbye to you yet, Marian."

"I think that's a good idea," Marian's father said warmly. "You two need time to rest and catch up. Spend some quality time together. I, however, must return to Sacramento. Marian, you stay as long as you wish. I'll have a car sent to you when you are ready."

"Thanks, Dad."

Marian put her arm around Sara, and together with Zed and Dustin, they headed home.

Alex leaned over and took Jeri in his arms. "I'm coming to Colorado. So that you know, you can't keep me away."

"I wouldn't even think of it," Jeri laughed.

Mac grabbed Jacqueline's arm. "Come on," he winked, "follow me."

***

With her hand in his, they stood gazing at the lake. Bright stars replaced rain clouds.

The moon-glow seemed to be skipping across the surface of the lake like tiny ripples of diamonds. Mac's hand felt strong and solid. Warm to the touch.

"It's so beautiful here. Honestly, I hate the thought of going home. But vacations are just that, vacations. This vacation has been one wild and crazy couple of days. Sad that two sisters died but amazing that Sara and Marian have found a new start in their relationship."

"Sometimes, when you meet someone new, the intensity of feelings can hit you hard," Mac said, turning to Jacqueline. "I felt an instant connection when we met."

Looking into his eyes, she experienced an energy of excitement. "I felt something, too," she whispered.

"But we have time," Mac said as he brushed a strand of hair over her ear. "I believe we have something extraordinary here. I know we are still strangers. I don't know if you even know how to cook, and you don't know if I can mow a lawn, but I want to spend the rest of my life learning everything about you. How you breathe when you sleep, how you brush your teeth, how you boil water." He smiled as he looked deep into her eyes.

"Now that I've found you, I'm just not sure how I let you go." He whispered. Before she could respond, his arms pulled her softly to him. She felt the tenderness of his touch that sent shivers through her. He leaned down and touched her lips, intensifying the warmth leaving her breathless. The kiss was deep, with a driving hunger. She could feel his heartbeat and moaned with a passion so intense it frightened her.

"Jacqueline," Jeri called.

"No," Jacqueline sighed.

"Jacqueline, you out there?"

Mac slowly pushed her away, a smile crossing his lips. "So beautiful," he whispered as he touched her cheek.

"I'm sorry."

"Why," he murmured, "some things are worth waiting for. I have these feelings, and they are not going anywhere."

They turned and strolled hand in hand toward the cabin. Jacqueline looked up at Mac and smiled, her cheeks flushed. She stepped on the first porch step, then the second. She reached for the doorknob.

"Don't go."

Jacqueline stopped and turned.

"Stay here with me. We're so right together. Don't go, Jacqueline."

THE END

Acknowledgements

Sheridan Wray Brett (sheridanwraybrett.com)

I want to thank Carol Gaskin, Dee Beardsley, Randy Peyer, and Daniel Roth for their editorial support. Their efforts on the author's behalf were as helpful to our self-assurance as their perceptive comments were to our manuscript. They helped to make this a better novel. Many thanks are owed to readers, Susan Sheehan, Nancy Camp, Kitty and Dave Ziegler, Lynn Williams, and Dee Beardsley, whose invaluable input and helpful comments of our characters and story plot suggestions improved our ability to make them work better. Much credit and thanks to Andrew Peek, Deputy Sheriff, El Dorado Sheriff's Office, Julie Redmond, Deputy Sheriff, Lyon County, and Bart Owens, retired South Lake Tahoe Chief of Police, for their input on law enforcement protocols. The authors only hope we got it right and did not make too many mistakes in our story. A special thank you to Brian Schwartz for his tremendous work in getting this book published. Most of all, I would like to thank David, my partner, for his constant support throughout this manuscript's writing.

H.M. Brett

Thanks to Jim, who stood by me and supported me during the process of writing this book.

.